1

Tollesbury Time Forever

(FRUGALITY – Book 1)

by

Stuart Ayris

Paperback Edition
Copyright 2012 by Stuart Ayris
Cover art copyright by Rebecca Ayris
Edited by Kath Middleton

PART ONE

Most of what I say is meaningless....

Prologue

In September 2008 I accompanied the police as they entered a house in Tollesbury. I was a psychiatric nurse at the time. The owner of the house was one of my patients. He had not been seen for two weeks - neither had his son nor his wife.

What I saw that evening will stay with me forever. On the walls of the lounge, in tiny, neat black writing were thousands and thousands of words. The torch beams picked them out as if they were groups of well-ordered flies. The words continued up the stairway, onto the landing walls and into the main bedroom. I had been in the house before and had seen some of the writing upstairs. Still I was mesmerised.

What you are about to read are the words that I saw on those walls. I have ordered them into chapters and taken the liberty of providing chapter headings. I have inserted two documents midway through which I trust will make sense when you come to them.

I have since resigned my post as a community mental health nurse and no longer work in psychiatry. The patient of whom I speak is called Simon Anthony. I have met him just once - yet he is, and will always remain, my hero.

1. Whiskydrunk

My name is Simon Anthony. I like the simple things in life: a good meal, a winter sun and the sound of the waves upon the shore.

I pursue a peaceful existence in a little cottage in Tollesbury, Essex. I have lived here for most of my adult life. Although I was not born in Tollesbury, I feel I am meant to be here, a seed sown perhaps by a careless hand in a wayward moment. There is a main road into the village, and a back road out. The booming dual carriageway that carries people from London to the coast is but a few miles to the north. In Tollesbury it has no meaning. For my village is entirely of its own time.

As you approach Tollesbury on the long and winding road from the neighbouring village of Tolleshunt D'arcy, you can feel the change in the air. The sky seems that bit bolder and everything opens out before you. A small wooden boat on the side of the road sprouting beautiful purple and white flowers merely confirms that you are indeed entering no ordinary place. One day, I will find out what kind of flowers they are and where that boat came from. There is still so much I long to know, so much I long to do.

My house is a small semi-detached property a third of the way down East Street complete with wooden floors, black beams and an open fire. It is old and it is dusty. The doors creak when I open and close them. They are the only voices that my house hears other than my own. I rely upon lamps and candles for lighting and upon the radio for company. The young girl next door shouts at her boyfriend most evenings and I am perpetually startled by the slamming of their front door when one or the other has had enough. They make me feel old, which I am beginning to think is no bad thing. I have an armchair in which I sit most days. The large window at the end of my front room serves as a giant TV screen, ever tuned to channel Tollesbury. It is a view of which I cannot imagine I will ever tire.

I awoke on Saturday 5th July 2008 to the gentle popping of summer rain upon my bedroom window. I am a light sleeper, perhaps largely due to the fact that I often have difficulty breathing when I lie down. I don't like to use a pillow so will often awake with a stiffness in my neck that takes time to subside. I stretched and rolled out of bed, clicking my elbows as I did so (a rare talent!) and stepped out onto my very own magic carpet of half read books and yesterday's clothes.

I pulled on my old blue jeans and my favourite baggy jumper before going downstairs. I made myself a black coffee and sat at the dining room table. It was about 5am and the sky was white with cloud. The weather had been fine in recent days, too fine perhaps for my delicate disposition. I am six feet tall and fourteen stone with a straggly beard and a knitted woollen hat constantly upon my head. I like my hat and never leave the house unless I am wearing it. It somehow completes me. I should have known then, as I studied the heat rings on my wooden table, that I wasn't really meant for this world at all.

I needed a walk to re-acquaint myself with life outside my own mind, to feel at least vaguely normal at the start of this fine summer morning. So lacing up my battered old boots, I headed out into the day.

The early Tollesbury air filled my being as I breathed deeply. The light rain continued to drift down from the baptismal summer sky and I felt each drop upon me with a sense of growing delight.

I walked slowly and deliberately as ever I have done. I have always detested haste – another reason why I love this village. As I ambled up East Street, towards the village square, I noticed nothing new, nothing surprising. All was serenity and peace. I stopped at The King's Head Pub on the corner and then crossed the narrow High Street and thereby entered Station Road. I continued on. I acknowledged the sweet sound of a milk float in the background, wobbling and clinking its

7

way down towards the harbour but I paid it little heed; for it was the salt marshes that were calling me on.

I soon left the houses behind and my boots touched the sodden earth. The trees that lined the track upon which I walked gave way to neat fields on the left but held up on the right. My pace slowed further as I sought the patterns between the branches and listened for the voices of the birds. I studied the spaces between all things for I have come to believe that is where the truth lies.

In time, the salt marshes were there before me in all their timeless splendour.

The tide was halfway to going out so I was treated to my favourite view. Despite all the years of living in Tollesbury, I had still not fully understood the movements of the sea. Some days I would go to the salt marshes and all you could see was water – other days, it was like one vast desert of mud. But on that day, back in July 2008, it was a perfect melding of the two. The sun lit the mist-filled sky and the rain eased off a little. And I sat on the bank of the sea wall to behold my heaven.

Dark water shone beneath the cracked trees that broke through it, trees bereft of foliage, pale and brittle and stark as if each and every one had been blown apart by lightning. Clumps of bright green shoots floated island-like upon the dank surface, connected beneath by myriad paths of silt and sand. It was a truly nebulous environment, moving and growing with the flow of the tide. There was a grimy, sparse majesty to it all that left me breathless. I sat there and allowed myself to drift away from the world of fallen man. Time meandered on directionless, dragging me with it. Tollesbury Time.

My musings were disturbed as a bouncy golden retriever barked a welcome and its striding owner nodded a greeting. It was Old Jed and his dog, Jake. They followed the line of the sea wall as if it was a railway track and they were but carriages of the same train. And I watched, enthralled, as man and dog merged into the indeterminate horizon, slipping over the edge of this earth - just slip sliding away only ever to remain, like all things, in my consciousness.

Having done my time, I returned home and sat in my armchair waiting for the finest pub in the land to open up its doors to me.

The King's Head spans the corner of Church Street and High Street, its front entrance facing onto the village square. I have an old sepia photograph at home that shows it used to have two adjacent doors; one leading into the public bar and one to the saloon bar. If you look closely you can still see the recess where the left-hand door once was. It has since been filled in with bricks and a window. The building itself is old and white, held together with sprawling ashen beams. A garish sign depicting the bust of Henry the Eighth hangs from a pole outside and the roof is slated and uneven. Lorries heading to and from the industrial area by the harbour occasionally nudge into the jutting wall from which Henry's face glowers. The landlord bears these mishaps stoically and can regularly be seen out back fashioning himself a roll-up whilst considering the fate of us all, and perhaps lorry drivers in particular.

On the opposite side of the square, nestled into the corner of the wall that surrounds St Mary's Church, is a six foot by three foot wooden box - a real perpendicular coffin of sorrow. It was the place where years ago, so it is said, the drunkard of the village was left to sleep off his or her excesses. There is a small aperture towards the top with bars across it. It is known as the village 'lock-up' and has been there for as long as anyone can remember.

Tollesbury is so much more than a village and The King's Head is so much more than just a place where people get drunk - which they do fairly often. I feel proud to be living within the bounds of its pulsating penumbra.

As I entered the pub, at just after midday, I felt the pang of belonging, the comfort of familiarity. There was no particular smell, not since the smoking ban, and there was no music playing. But there was the upright piano that remained forever unused and the candles and the prints of yachts upon the wall. There was the small bookcase and the faded curtains and the huge Basset Hound that drooled and sprawled just wherever you put your weary feet. There were the mirrors

9

behind the bar and there was the dull carpet embroidered with all our desperate drunken dreams. You can keep your Albert Hall and your Windsor Castle and your Harrods. Give me this place any time. Any time at all. All you got to do is call and I'll be there.

There are two reading lamps at the bar of a beautiful emerald green giving light to the wonderfully curious names of the various ales: Oscar Wilde Mild, Old Growler, Puck's Folly and A Drop of Nelson's Blood, to name but a few. Or imagine asking the Landlord for a pint of Mad Old John. Does it get any better than that? There are pubs you walk into carrying a knife. There are bars you drink at with a gun in your jacket. In the King's Head, you bring a book, a grin, or the world on your shoulders. Just have a drink and get away from your life for a while.

I sat at the bar and sipped my Aspall cider. My financial situation had led me to the point where my choice of drink was dependant upon the result of that old drunkard's equation – money in pocket multiplied by percentage of alcohol per pint - with taste being the deciding factor if things were close. For me, Aspall won every time. It's about clearing the mind, obscuring the present and negating the future - not about getting drunk. Inebriation is just a side-effect of the whole process.

The barmaid turned on one of the reading lamps and I sat at the bar reading my Jack Kerouac. As I fell in love with Tristessa all over again, the Tollesbury locals added colour to my paltry pencil sketch, ensuring I remained in the physical realm only just as much as I needed to. People drifted about like ghosts, entering and leaving as if rehearsing a forlorn play that nobody will ever see. The hushed smattering of conversations rose and fell upon a tide of weariness and resignation; yet there is a hope in such places, an intangible feeling that some good will one day come of all this melancholy. There will come a time when the audience will grant a standing ovation to such courageous persistence.

And in walks Ray. He has a paper bag face that is just one breath away from being fully inflated. It crumples when he

10

mumbles into his beer. There is nothing fey about Ray; but if you think he is strong, you are King Kong wrong. He sits at a corner table and listens to all the talk, though for most of the time he hears nothing. I have long wanted to tear his face to make him smile, just to make him do something. Jesus. A puffing painted woman blows into his ears and the frown leaves his face as it expands. Putting a hand to either side of his head, he squeezes...

Bang!

So long Ray...

"Ray's gone again," came a voice from behind me.

Two men were sitting at one of the tables by the window, shrouded from the sun by a yellowed net curtain.

"Lasted well today," said the other man. "Almost made it 'til three."

"How are the kids, Jim?" asked the balder of the two. He wore a sleeveless black t-shirt and blue jeans that were just a little too tight. The few remaining hairs that he had were falling off the back of his head; and his eyes twinkled with mischief...

"They're fine, Bill. Younger boy is a bit of a bugger, but the wife keeps him in check. Up to all sorts I don't doubt when we can't see him, over by the bus stop and round the Rec. My young 'uns can do what they like, but when they're with me I have their language clean and their hands where I can see 'em! I've always said that, Bill, haven't I? "

"True enough mate," replied Bill. "You have always said that. More or less every time I see you."

It was early afternoon and not time yet for Jim to bite on the maggots of sarcasm that Bill dangled for him.

"You know what you need to do with your boy?" tried Bill again, sipping his pint, looking up at his old friend as he did so, knowing that Jim would not be able to resist answering the question that had been thrown up so expertly. It was like an itch that just had to be scratched.

"Go on."

"Child-kill him," said Bill plainly. "Simple as that. Child-kill him."

11

Jim was savouring his pint when he received this advice from his friend. He didn't spit it out like some may have. He merely used the dusky ale to delay his response, to enable him to gather his thoughts before answering. And when he did so, he asked the questions that surely anyone would have asked.

"What do you mean, you old bastard? Are you mad?"

Bill leaned back on his chair and drained a good half a pint of his Guinness.

"Jim, Jim, my boy. You can't be talking like that. Think of the ladies."

At this point I was tempted to peer over my shoulder. Blind Lemon Jefferson wailed from the jukebox that sat regal and unforgiving from the other side of the pub. A pool cue that was leaning against the side of the immaculate pool table slid to the floor with a clack as the brutal blues beat took hold. The bells of St Mary's church chimed thrice and a man I had never seen before put his money in the payphone by the bar and began explaining to a woman at the other end of the line that he was stuck in traffic and may be some time.

"So, what do you mean, Bill? Bloody child-killing." Jim tutted. "This had better be good."

Bill waited for a moment for dramatic effect, surely aware that I was listening in on the conversation. The barmaid too was leaning over now, slowly drying a glass. The clock behind the bar ticked onto three o'clock. It was always a little slow. Or maybe it was just the way time worked in The King's Head, following its own unique course, letting things happen as they may. Some people say the whole of Tollesbury is like that - dragging behind; entirely of its own order; entirely of its own time.

"You mean you haven't heard of the Child-killer? Without him, my lads would have been well out of hand. Look at them now. Good honest boys. All at work. Not a conviction between them. Two married and one at university. You can't ask for more than that. And all straight, mind, straight as you like."

Jim sat back and waited for Bill to continue his story, relaxing a little. The sun was in the sky, the beer was in the

12

keg and the day yawned ahead like the best of half-terms. I could sense Jim's feeling of well-being even from where I sat, hunched alone at the bar. And I envied him, murderously.

"About a hundred and fifty years ago, give or take," began Bill, "Tollesbury was much the same as it is now. A few less houses, a few more farms and obviously not so many people. And those people that were there all knew each other. None of this coming down from London business to live in the country. In them days you were born in Tollesbury, you lived in Tollesbury and you were buried in Tollesbury. Just the way it was. You didn't get too many strangers round here in them times."

Bill glanced over at the payphone before continuing, but the man had gone.

"Well, the story goes that the children in the village started to rebel against their parents; they became badly behaved and disrespectful. Some even talked of leaving Tollesbury when they grew up, to go to Tiptree or even Colchester. Not D'arcy though - never D'arcy. At that time, the whole village depended upon manpower to make sure the crops were harvested and the fleets were able to bring in the fish and oysters from up the river. The elders of the village began to foresee a time when perhaps the whole fabric of their economy would fall apart. The Lord only knows what they would have made of the old Crab and Winkle railway line! These were frightening times, my old friend, frightening times for sure. But they were about to get just a bit more frightening."

"Another two beers here please, Carrie; Bill's paying," called Jim to the barmaid who was by now unashamedly taking in Bill's every word. Interesting stuff, thought Jim, but a man can't sit with an empty pint - not in The King's Head.

"So then, one night, so they say," continued Bill, "a stranger came into the village. No-one knew where he came from, he just appeared. And then, ten days later, one of the Tollesbury boys was found dead in his bed. He was only about a year old. Battered to death with a piece of wood. Poor lad. And the stranger was never seen again. Some say he was found

13

hanging down by the marshes, others that he made his way to London and carried on killing. One thing is for sure, those children started to behave right there and then, no more tantrums and no more fancy thoughts of working up in bloody Colchester and the like. The crops were harvested and the oysters were landed. And everything went back to normal."

Bill picked up his fresh pint and sipped it as if it were wine.

"And?" said Jim.

"And what?" said Bill.

"What has that got to do with anything?"

Bill smiled.

"When I was younger," he said, "I was always told that if I didn't behave, then that stranger would come and get me. The Child-Killer. Scared the life out of me. That's how you sort your lad out, Jim. Simple as that. Child-kill him. What worked back in my day still works now, mark my words."

Jim nodded solemnly.

The cider was poured and the cider was drunk. People came and went and I stayed. The day grew into evening and the evening succumbed to the blackness of night. And the cider turned into whisky. I let it burn right into me. It set me on fire inside and then numbed me as it always did.

When the final bell went, I was the last to leave. I lurched, stumbling and clattering into the village square, like a coin that had been ejected from a machine, and was left to whirl in circles before coming to a halt face down on the floor. That was me, the man that nobody cared about or dared to understand. But it had not always been thus. That was where the pain was - in the fact that it had not always been thus.

I staggered whisky drunk under the moon, falling, sprawling, tumbling and crumbling. Every now and then I stopped, just paused on all fours, hands and knees in the dirty ground, possibly grinning. And I waited like that for a moment or two as the night sky righted itself, looking for all the world as if I were about to take part in some improbable race for inebriates. Then I fell sideways and lay on my back facing the blackness and the stars.

To drink, or not to drink: there is no question:
Surely 'tis a sickness of the mind that suffers
The stinging contempt of the gorgeous blue moon.
So just let the King's Head forgive us our trespasses
And by drinking forget them. To die: to sleep;
No more...

And there I was again, where I had started my day; gazing into the profundity of the Tollesbury salt marshes. I was drunk and desperate and could think of nothing to make me leave. Old Jed and Jake walked solemnly by again. Jed nodded to me and I nodded back in return. The marshes were there before me; my life was behind me. I had no choice. Alcohol had given me no choice. Diagnosis and medication had given me no choice.

It had come to this. Fifty years old. Fifty. A decent batting average, but still not a part of the team. I had ever been lacking some identifiable quality that would give meaning to the whole. My life had been inflicted upon me and this is where it ended. I felt, at last, a feeling of peace. Nobody would miss me. It was time to go.

So I stood as best I could to my full height and let myself fall forwards into the gloom of the dark marsh water. I remember the feeling of the cold, dirty sludge consuming me and I remember saying goodbye to my life. All over in a splash.

Except it wasn't all over. For I awoke; how many hours later, I couldn't say. I was dirty, dry and alive and huddled on the urine stained floor of what seemed to be a wooden cell. It smelled of hops and vomit. The only light came through a barred window no larger than the size of a paperback book, high up in the door before me. I stood up and peered through the aperture. My fearful eyes squinted against the light that assailed them and I flopped back down again, still no nearer to discovering my whereabouts.

Before I could truly get my bearings, there was a loud crack that shook me instantly. I covered my ears as the noise continued. Someone was banging on the wooden door. I stood once more, tremulous.

"Out, drunk!"

The door opened and I fell out of the village lock-up and into Tollesbury village square. I was kneeling in filth and straw. There were cattle wandering in front of the King's Head and several people strolling purposefully about all dressed in dull, loose clothes. A smell of dung plunged into my lungs and I could do nothing but try to cough it out. A small boy walked towards me and leaned over my confused frame. I was on all fours, more akin to the cattle than the people.

"What's happening?" I asked the boy. A graveyard grin cracked his grimy little face in half.

"Away lad!" shouted a large man who now stood before me. He held a wooden baton in one hand. It must have been he who had rapped upon the door of the lock-up and yanked me out. The blue of the sky framed his oafish face.

"What's happening?" I repeated.

The man breathed deep, irritated. "What's happening? What's happening? Well, you ain't be getting drunk in Tollesbury no more stranger. Not now you've slept it off. This village don't be for the likes of you. This is 1836, not the bloody middle ages. You go back to London or wherever you came from. You not be wanted here."

I looked up at the Tollesbury sky. It had begun to darken. The bells of St Mary's church tolled. And a huge sense of foreboding filled my very soul.

2. Rage On To Me

England.

1836.

William IV was on the throne, though he was to die in April of the following year. The Viscount Melbourne was twelve months into his second term as Prime Minister (or more correctly, First Lord of the Treasury and Leader of the House of Lords) and Darwin was about to return on the Beagle to work on his theories of evolution. 1836 also saw the first running of the Grand National at Aintree as well as the monthly serialisation of Charles Dickens' first novel, The Pickwick Papers.

And what of me? Well, I remained on my knees for some moments, my head bowed, and my hands upon the ground. For what else was I to do? If I could have curled up tight on my side and snuggled up in the straw and the mud, then surely I would have; for I needed the comfort and safety only a womb can bestow. In time, the scene around me edged its way into my senses - the smells, the sounds and the sights. So I sat back slowly upon my haunches, aching unaccountably, and imbibed of all before me.

What I first noticed was the clarity of it all. I could smell the sweetness of apples, the gentle scent of newly baked bread and the charred potency of potato skins crackling over a fire. The air was a tangible construct, consisting of the fragrances around me, fragrances that pulsated within me as I breathed them in. I could taste peaches bursting, hear the crunch of lettuce and feel the smouldering smoke from a roasting lamb. It was at once dense yet pure, like nothing I had ever experienced before. Had I closed my eyes at that moment in order to further intensify the experience, I swear I would never have opened them again.

Finally, I stood, leaned back against the closed door of the village lock-up for support and stared up at the Tollesbury sky. I then gained the courage to lower my gaze, breathed deeply once more and looked straight ahead, realizing in an instant that my previous, albeit brief, view of the square had not deceived me. Grass and cattle and ragged children. Belief did not come into it. I saw what I saw, I smelled what I smelled and I felt what I felt. You can't take that away from me, not with medication, not with clever words - for it was real, absolutely real.

There were some cows being led through the square from the Recreation Ground to the direction of the High Street and a group of small children dressed in grubby smocks and knee length trousers was running in front, turning now and then to circle the bemused creatures. A large, heavy man urged the cattle on from the side with a long, bowed stick and scowled at the laughing boys and girls. But behind the scowl was a recognition of the inevitable and, perhaps, a distant memory of having once been one of those errant scamps.

Wooden barrows filled the square, people calling out their wares in such a coarse accent I could barely make out the words. I was wearing my own clothes and, perhaps a testament to my lack of sophistication, did not look too much out of place. I lifted my hand to my face. It was definitely me and I was definitely in Tollesbury. It was becoming too much to think about, somewhere between truth and doubt - too much to think about. I had no idea how all this had come to be. But come to be it had.

There were no cars and there were no street lamps. The brick bus stop where all the Tollesbury teenagers hang around in order to practice flirting, pester the man in the chip van and try in vain to get mobile phone signals; that was gone too. And there was dirt and grass where there should have been concrete, a wonderful green area that looked so fine as to render the covering of it with sand and cement nothing less than an atrocity.

But the King's Head was still there, looking more or less the same as when I had last left it. I felt the same relief as you would feel encountering a friend by chance in a distant city. For me, a pub is a sign of normality, confirmation that at least part of the world is as it should be. I have always believed I could walk into any pub in England and feel a sense of familiarity, that I would never be totally alone. I thought then also that I was probably not the first man to have staggered out of the village lock-up before going straight over to The King's Head. I needed to sit down with a pint and get things in perspective - if that were at all possible. This was all just a little too strange, even for my precarious mind.

I stood before the wooden door that led into the public bar, the sound of children running and playing cascading through the air behind me. I heard a man coughing and the hooves of horses thudding away down the High Street. All these sounds were familiar to me, yet foreign. They just didn't belong together - not here, not now; or perhaps it was I who did not belong. I leaned into the door to push it open. It remained steadfast. I was about to push harder when a woman's voice shouted down at me.

"What do you think you're playing at stranger? We don't open for three hours yet; not that you'd be welcome back, with your made up money and all!"

I stepped back and looked up to see the face of a young woman, perhaps in her late twenties, leaning out of an upstairs window. She had brown hair tied back beneath a cream coloured headscarf, which gave prominence to a round, kindly face. Despite her harsh words, there was a playfulness in her expression that I found beguiling. She sensed my puzzlement and smiled such a broad smile it looked as if her few remaining teeth would seize the moment to leap out and join their long lost brethren.

"Catch!"

The woman dropped several small gold coins out of the window, before closing the wooden shutters and retiring from view. I bent down and picked up the money - nine pound coins, 2006 vintage. No good to her it seemed; and therefore no good to me.

Well, how about that then? The pub was shut. My money was worthless. And I was a stranger in my own village. Now if this were all a dream, it surely wasn't me who was doing the dreaming!

Standing there outside the King's Head, I started to pick out those things I found familiar. There was the lock-up of course, lurking in the corner against the wall surrounding St Mary's Church. The low flat cottages adjacent to it were almost as they are now; though the car parts and the broken boat in the yard were absent, as was that dog that barks viciously whenever you walk by. Did it bark because it was tied up and scared or did it bark to ensure it remained tied up? Though that dog had always worried me I had at times felt an affinity with it.

I walked across to the cottage known then and now as Roebuck Cottage, and turned right at the corner onto East Street with the intention of seeing what condition my house was in. And what lay before me was magical. The dirt track with which I was confronted was so wide with no parked cars to constrict it. Where the Congregational Church should have stood, on the left, there was just a large patch of unkempt grass. There were one or two cottages beside it but on the right hand side as I walked in wonder, there was just the low wall that lined the graveyard of St Mary's Church. And where my house should have been, there were two horses tied to a rickety wooden bar.

I just stared at these lovely animals as they stood serene and swaying, sweating a little, moving their sturdy jaws around and around, blinking with their huge perfect eye lids. They were peaceful and silent, just standing where my little front room should have been. I felt if I stretched out my arm, I would have disturbed this wonderful mirage. So I stood there and sighed, breathed deep and exhaled in peaceful perfection.

As I stared into the void, I felt a tug upon the baggy sleeve of my jumper. I looked around and there stood the dirty looking boy with the crooked teeth whom I had seen earlier outside the village lock-up. He looked up at me, no longer grinning but frowning, as if he were concentrating intently. He

20

had a sharp looking stick in his hand. I was not sure out of the two of us who was the more perplexed.

"Hello," I ventured.

The boy just stared at me, one hand now on his hips, defiant, the other holding aloft the stick. It did indeed look very sharp.

I smiled. The boy did not. He traced a circle in the air with the stick and then drew an imaginary cross through it. Finally, he poked the stick through the circle and winked at me, smiling conspiratorially as he did so.

"Upper Outer Quadrant," I heard him whisper. "Upper Outer Quadrant."

Now I had never heard of the Upper Outer Quadrant. I knew Tollesbury well but unless this Quadrant had existed until the modern day, I knew I would be of little help to this boy. As I was about to inform him that he would have to seek another for directions, he ran around behind me. Suddenly I felt a searing pain at the top of my thigh as he jabbed at me with the pointed stick before running down the hill towards the harbour. It was an unsettling moment, to say the least. His intensity had seemed so real, more real than the earth beneath my feet or the sky above; more real even than the heart that now beat that bit faster within me. And then he was gone.

Stability required I headed for the place where I had been the previous day, if previous day it was. I walked slowly, as if on a leash, to that part of the village I was sure had always been there, unchanged, forever - the Tollesbury salt marshes.

Station Road was wide, tree-lined and empty, bereft of houses and pavements. There were no street lamps or manholes or wheelie bins or vehicles - or a station for that matter. It was the space and the openness of it all that really hit me. I always thought Tollesbury to be small and remote, a village cut off from the modern world; but this was truly rural and uplifting, broad and majestic. Yet, as I walked, I experienced a throbbing longing for that which once was, though it be all around me.

Indeed, what was about me now was a stillness and a peace that I had rarely known before. The marshes stretched to the horizon torn, gleaming and intricate, leading down to the dark depths of the Blackwater Estuary. Elegant birds flew high above, all silence and grace. White, powdery clouds formed in the sky doing their best to conceal a darkness that peeked out from behind them, ready to pounce upon the glorious light that consumed this early Tollesbury evening.

So intent was I on the grand display before me, I failed at first to notice the hunched outline of a figure some twenty yards to the right of where I stood. It was sitting cross-legged, gazing down into the dank water. I felt as if I were being watched. This was not paranoia, doctor. This was more real even than that.

I breathed slowly, apprehensive yet compelled. For these were my marshes. I felt more at home there than in my own house; though clearly that land upon which my house stood was, at that moment, being grazed upon by a couple of sturdy mares. As I approached, the figure didn't move at all. When I was but five yards away, though, it spoke in a gruff, growl of a voice that could have been the rumble of a tractor engine, the clatter of falling rocks or the creaking coming to life of an awoken conscience. I doubted even then that a mere man could speak like that.

"Sit," he said.

So I did, just where I was; a little in front and to the left of him. His head remained bowed. I was at once his to command.

That's when I got a really good look at him. I will start with his clothes, for that was all I could see to begin with. Despite the warmth of the evening, he was bundled up as if for a cold winter's night. Atop his head was a cloth hat some ten inches high, widening to a drooping brim as it rested just above the line of his eyes. I wasn't sure how it managed to keep its form, so flimsy did it look. And as I peered closer, I saw there was a tighter hat beneath, made of what could have been wool, clinging to his skull; were it to be removed, I believed his entire head may have crumbled into fragments.

There was a dirty grey piece of material wrapped about the man's neck. It could have been sketched in charcoal and nailed to his throat. Its ends were torn and ragged, as if someone had ripped an old scarf in half.

A dark brown, heavy coat enshrined his body. It looked like some kind of tarpaulin draped over him, a cocoon from which he had once grown, maybe, screaming into this world. The coat was fastened at the front by two buttons and gaped open from the stomach downwards, revealing a grimy undershirt whose colour I just could not determine - it was maybe a combination of sweat and filth, whatever colour you would like to imagine that to be! The sleeves were too long, entirely obscuring his hands. Were he to have been equipped with paws, I would not have been surprised; though I would of course have been terrified. But at least that would have been an immediate type of terror that would have enabled me to flee, rather than this growing, deepening horror that fixed me where I sat.

Covering his crossed legs were black trousers that seemed too wide and too short. His feet were bare and clean and so at odds with the rest of his grubbiness; perhaps he had been bathing them in the salty water of the marshes. Clean feet indeed, though there were hairs upon them where perhaps there should not have been hairs.

It was as I was studying his feet that the man turned to look at me. His face was surely carved from the very earth itself; that mixture of dirt and debris, sand, silt, clay and stone that had congealed and hardened over the centuries to form the crust of our world. His mouth was straight and stern, with barely a top lip. His lower lip protruded slightly but was all the more prominent for the lack of a companion. His nose was flat and broad, with nostrils that were but holes in his face and no more. The upper part of his countenance was shaded by the crooked brim of his hat, but that didn't stop the most sad and chilling eyes I had ever seen from pouring into me. Sad and chilling though they were, more than anything they were lifeless - and for lifeless, read deathly. There was no glint, no shimmer, no sign at all that a living, breathing human being existed beyond them.

23

So there we were upon the ground. He looked down again and I could not help but stare at him.

And then he spoke once more, turning his large head quickly to me as he did so.

"When did you come?" he asked plainly.

"What do you mean?"

"When did you come?" he repeated, slower this time, emphasizing every word with a rasp of his tongue, spittle forming on his hanging bottom lip.

"Where?"

"Here! When did you come here?"

"Erm, today; last night. I'm not sure."

He paused, considering my answer.

"As I thought," he murmured, nodding. "Heard the splash."

This made no sense to me at all until I realised where he was sitting. In an instant, I saw myself as I was the previous evening, drunk and forlorn and trying in vain to kill myself. The man had been staring all this time into the exact same marshy pool into which I had allowed myself to fall. And I shuddered at the coincidence, if coincidence it be.

There was nothing I could do but to sit and to wait. I could not tell you how many minutes went by, though I can tell you that every second seemed crucial as if there was a pattern to be followed, a script that was being directed by people unseen. All I know is that as I was about to speak, the man swivelled round in one frenetic, lithe, movement, his legs still crossed. And there I was, face to face with him. I breathed deep, gulping air as if it were cider.

As I looked across into his face, I sensed it slacken a little. Was it tiredness? Or maybe disappointment?

Though I had been about to speak, I honestly had nothing to say. In such a moment, anything I could have said would have been entirely meaningless anyway. There was a depth to this moment far greater than any words of mine could have filled. So I just left it to him.

"You are here because you are meant to be here. I am here because it is the only place I can be. I have waited here for you for some time, lain dormant, you might say. Now don't you be letting me down, boy. You don't want to go letting me down. Not again."

He continued in that flat, atonal voice of his, slow and dull. And it made me listen all the more.

"You will learn from me boy."

He took a pipe from his pocket, filled it slowly with tobacco, lit it and sat and puffed.

"What will you learn?" he continued, leaning towards me now until I could smell his tobacco breath oozing through the freshness of the air between us like fetid oil upon the purest of streams.

"Well, you will learn to love me and you will learn to need me; that is what you will learn. And I will lead you to a place where you will learn life, life itself, mind. Then, when the time comes, you will know of death so plain and you will give yourself up to this world. Then may we never see each other again. For the good of both our souls."

A breeze eased through me like a thousand tiny daggers. I shivered though the day be warm.

"Have you nothing to say, boy?" he asked eventually.

I sat in stillness looking down because I did not want to return his gaze. Though I could not see his eyes I could feel them. It felt as if they were seeping into me, injecting some kind of blackness into my blood. A statue, I clearly was not but, all the same, I was unable to move. My senses had left me. There was a buzzing in my head as if my mind and my brain were struggling with one another, neurotransmitters wielding dopamine and flying out from the trenches of my frontal and temporal lobes, a see-saw battle of such brutal force that I had to just let it happen. That was me, the impotent war correspondent cowering in his ramshackle hotel room, unable to comprehend the fighting even though his own head be the battlefield.

Rage on, this crazy feeling. I know it's got me reeling. Rage on to me…

"Nothing to say, boy?"

It took all my strength to shake my head. I was drained beyond belief.

"Good. Then may it all begin."

I did indeed feel as if I were on the verge of a beginning rather than an ending. Where things were going to lead, I knew not, nor did I care at that point. To have a direction, a purpose, is fundamental to human existence. Without it, we flounder in an ocean of self-doubt and ennui. And within moments of the man lapsing once more into silence, I felt I belonged here.

The brightness of the day faded into the orange of the evening. Then darkness came. The stars pricked white holes in the black cardboard sky and the marshes slowly filled with the salty water of the sea. The gentle waves reminded me of the sound my dog used to make as it licked itself clean with its clumsy pink tongue. I cherished the memory and closed my eyes briefly. I think I must have slept for a while as I failed to notice that my shoes and the ends of my trousers had become sodden as the marshes had filled.

How long had passed since that man had pronounced the beginning of who knows what, I did not know. I should have been hungry, but I wasn't. I should have been afraid, but I wasn't. I was, however, very tired so I reluctantly dragged myself to my feet to find a dry place to rest. The old man was nowhere to be seen. He had been claimed by the night. And how appropriate that was. Perhaps the night was not complete until he was a part of it. Learn to love him? I doubted that very much as I walked back to the village square, stumbling along as if pulled by a chain of my own devising.

I slept that first night beneath the 19th century firmament huddled against the inside of the low wall surrounding St Mary's Church, the shadows of the gravestones under the round moon being my only companions. The bells tolled on the hour though they were mere tings on a triangle to me; for my sleep was deep and untroubled. There were no three o'clock in the morning fears of what bills were to come through my door and no worries of telephone calls threatening me with all sorts if I did not make payment on the many loans

I had. There were no car doors slamming, no buzzing radiators and no next door neighbours trying to out-scream one another. And there was no nurse coming round to inject me once a fortnight.

Thus I slept in the sparsely populated, neatly kept graveyard of an old church in the summer of 1836 entirely unaware of what was to become of me.

3. Let It Be

The ribald yelling of a cockerel woke me with a start. Having overcome the initial shock, I stretched languorously, the joints of my arms and legs clicking with relief. The sun was just above the roof of The King's Head so I guessed it was about five or six in the morning. Birds hovered high in the air like headlines in a blue newspaper sky. I stood slowly, turning to look over the low church wall. A sigh broke from deep within me as I met the day. I folded my arms and leaned forward, resting on the perfectly irregular stone. Leaning against an old stone wall and gazing into the distance has since become one of the pleasures of my life. It is a truly profound experience when you think of the picks that quarried the stone, the arms that carried it and the hands that formed it.

There comes a time in every man's life when he must stop and consider what he has achieved. This moment is not the normal pondering of how things are or the mulling over of certain recent events. It is not a 'life-flashing-before-your-eyes' moment. It is a definitive moment where a man considers his worth, his presence in this world. You may think mine would have been the instant before I allowed myself to fall to my supposed demise in the salt marshes, but no, that was merely the pathetic folly of a drunk. My moment of self-scrutiny came that morning as the sun rose and the birds chattered. It was then that I began to fully consider the life that I had led.

I was born in Dagenham, East London in the summer of 1958. Dagenham back then, and to a large extent now, was a massive grid of similar looking streets that spoke of struggle and spirit and pride. My dad and my uncle worked alternate shifts at the huge Ford's manufacturing plant just off the old A13 road and my mum took in washing from neighbours for what she called 'pin money.' I remember the claxon that used to blast out of the factory at midday and then again an hour later. It signalled the beginning and the end of the lunch break for the workers and always used to startle me, even though I knew it was coming.

When I first began school, some of the children used to tease me, telling me that inside Ford's there was a huge monster and that the siren went off to warn the workers the monster was awake. I used to come home desperate to see my dad, hoping he hadn't been caught and devoured. It used to affect my sleep too, these worries about the monster across the road. I guess it didn't help when my dad used to try and comfort me, saying for as long as we lived in Dagenham we would never be alone. For if you closed your eyes and listened, you could here the Ford's manufacturing plant breathing, a living, puffing organism that brought only fear to my young heart.

I wouldn't say I have fond memories of Dagenham. They are tainted with loneliness and fear. People in general irk me. Angry people scare me. Sad people enhance the natural feeling of sadness within me. Dagenham, as I recall through these fading years, was a place for the lonely, the fearful, the angry and the sad. I have never been back. Even though I understand the Ford's plant has now closed down, I have no doubt that the monster is just hibernating. I have no desire to be around when it decides to waken - for creatures such as that merely sleep; they do not die.

We moved to Tollesbury just after Christmas in 1963. My grandmother, whom I had never met, had died and left us her house in this little village none of us had ever heard of. I remember my parents discussing whether or not Tollesbury was even in England. It was a big move for all of us. We didn't have a car so my dad had to stop working at Ford's. This pleased me greatly as I felt that at least we would be safe from the monster. It had felt as if we were going on holiday, a holiday from which we just never returned.

So from being lonely in Dagenham, I became lonely in Tollesbury. My parents found work at the jam factory in Tiptree and I started at Tollesbury School, just down East Street, almost opposite where we lived and where I still live to this day. The school was built in 1896 and is intimate and neat.

29

Back then though, as a shy East London boy, I found it daunting indeed. The other children all knew each other. They spoke funny. They were polite to me but, all the same, I felt excluded. Looking back, maybe it was just a village thing. I have been drinking in the King's Head for more or less my whole adult life yet I believe it has only been in the last couple of years that I have been considered a regular.

So my little five year old self had needed a friend. Fortunately for him, he found four of them - The Beatles. Even at that early age, or maybe because of it, I knew instantly that they were wonderful.

I never had a favourite; they were just The Beatles to me. To be honest, I wasn't one for all the Paul or John stuff back then. Their songs to me were the aural equivalent of seeing a brand new colour. They brought a sense to me of the vibrancy of the world. It was everything - their voices, their music and their smiles. In later years, I read and re-read the lyrics, searching for some deep poetry within them, something that would give me a clue as to their allure. But it was like trying to touch a cloud. Beauty is as beauty is. It is no more complicated than that. The moment you try to understand some things is the moment you break the spell.

So as my mind was beginning to be wonderfully overwhelmed by the sights and smells of the countryside and the sounds of the Beatles, my parents began to go their separate ways. Apparently my dad took to drink and my mum cried a lot. To my shame, I didn't really notice either until the end. When I was eight, my dad left us. He more or less just fell out of the door with a bin bag of possessions in his hand. I don't know whether my mum threw him out or whether he just decided he'd had enough. Nobody ever explained it to me. I never saw him again. And my mum was never the same. Even The Beatles changed.

And, yes, I admit it, I did cry on 31st December 1970 when Paul announced to the world that the band was splitting up. I spent day after day in my bedroom playing the early albums over and over again. I had all their records of course, but Sergeant Pepper onwards brought just confusion to me. It seemed as my life was becoming more complicated so the Beatles added to that complication rather than resolved it. By the age of thirteen, despite my desperate attempts to cling on to hope amidst a troubled childhood, I had become a maudlin, cynical youth who dragged his feet physically and metaphorically. I was at odds with the world and didn't care who knew it.

The Fab Four had once bestowed upon me a belief that life was there to be enjoyed, that anything was possible - and then when they discovered it was more complicated than that they just left me. They had made me feel people were perfect and that love was tangible. They had pretended to me that the world was a place of innocence and joy, when in reality it was just full of bullying and arguing and sadness.

In retrospect, I knew I should have gone back and listened to those later albums, but it would have broken my heart then as it would now. I have forgiven John and George and Ringo, but Paul, he didn't seem to suffer. John got shot, George got cancer and Ringo got drunk; but Paul managed to get on with his life. It was if it was all just music to him. That, to me, poor suffering adolescent as I was, seemed wholly unforgivable.

The Seventies, my formative period I suppose you could call it, was a blur of misery and anger. I truly believe I was in my mid-twenties before I could hold an adult conversation. Life was gradually opening up as my mind started to make sense of what it was truly like to be an adult. Yet throughout this transformation from caterpillar to butterfly the intensity of my feelings was matched only by my inability to express them.

I was saved by The Clash. There were perhaps other contributory elements to my salvation, but Mick Jones and Joe Strummer truly brought me into adulthood. They were angry and rebellious, just as I believed myself to be. Yet there was a humour and a sophistication in their songs that made me realise one fundamental fact – to be miserable is to capitulate. London was burning and so was I. They ignited within me a will to fight back. Just as Bob Dylan taught me how to keep on keeping on and Bruce Springsteen taught me how to run.

31

I was twenty two years old when I met my wife. Yes, I once was married and I suppose technically I still am. Her name is Julia. When I was twenty four, we had a son. His name is Robbie. He has Down's syndrome. He will be twenty-six in September this year. I haven't seen him since he was four. It may as well have been a thousand years ago for all the impact I have had on his life. Yet I miss him still.

Life comes and it goes. And it can change - just like that.

The sounds of Tollesbury waking permeated my consciousness. The smells of a country life entered my nostrils and the clarity of a country air filled my lungs. I left the shadows of the graveyard and stepped upon the dewy moisture of the village green.

Timelessness overwhelmed me. My only decision was whether to go right across the green or left towards The Recreation Ground. This was almost becoming a ZX Spectrum game from the early eighties. I would not have been at all surprised if I had seen Thorin Oakenshield cross-legged on the ground, singing about gold.

I looked languidly over my shoulder in the direction of the Recreation Ground and was enthralled to see at the end of a fifty yard dirt track, a large field surrounded by trees. It was a perfect ellipse. There were no houses guarding it, no Parish Rooms, no stone wall and no cars. There it was before me, wide and open and lush. I smiled as I breathed – such a perfect combination of muscles and nerves that can only occur in the most gorgeous of moments; and when it does, your soul is truly at one with your heart and your mind.

So I walked unencumbered to the centre of the grass ellipse. I just stood there, surveying the field like an opening batsman who has just walked out at Lord's Cricket Ground for the first time, taking in the fielding positions and the boundary line, the colours in the crowd and the possible impact of the cloud cover. I am in love with the game of cricket; and for that, unlike so many other things in my life, I feel not the need to explain myself.

Oh for a fine bat in my hand and for an umpire to signal the first ball of the day. I sigh now, even as I write these lines on my bedroom wall...

And do you know what I did? I laid myself down where the wicket would have been and I slept for hours. Call it a long held ambition; call it a kind of alternate reality jet-lag. Call it what you like. I slept because I wanted to. There was a simplicity in such an act that marked the moment as profound. My body was upon the earth as the world turned. The sky looked down upon me with, I sensed, approval.

So what do you do after a long day in the field? You have a pint. It was worth a try. I raised myself to my feet and headed optimistically for The King's Head. I pushed against one of the weather-beaten doors of the pub and it opened smoothly, not a creak in sight. Amazingly, the interior was little different than it is today; at first glance that is. The bar was in the same place and withered beams held up the ceiling. A fire place gaped in the far wall, full of roughly hewn logs. A smiling young barmaid was ready for action and a couple of old men stood huddled and wary in a shadowy corner.

On closer inspection, however, my eye was drawn to the differences, the imperfections, if I can even call them that. Between the ceiling beams was a substance that seemed to be a mixture of dried mud and straw and the floor, basically, was just trodden-in dirt. Lamps, lit by what I presumed to be oil, cast more gloom than illumination and the whole pub smelled like a farmyard. If I had lit a cigarette in there, it would have been like dabbing the most wondrous scent onto the grubbiest of necks.

"Hello, darling. What can I get you?" asked the girl behind the bar. She looked to be about thirteen years old, though I have always been poor at assessing age. I, myself, can range from anything between nineteen and a hundred during the course of a single day.

I had no money, none that I thought she would take, but then I have been in that situation before. As I was thinking of a way of willing her to give me some alcohol, I heard a voice that brought me back to reality. Yes, reality. I recognized it instantly, for how could I forget it? It was the man from the salt marshes.

"He will have ale."

So I sat down at the old man's wooden table by the window, a table whose grain and distress I could have stared at for eternity. I wondered whether it had been made from the same great tree that had provided the beams for the ceiling and, if it had, how sad that they should be so parted, destined just to gaze at each other forever, never to touch. The pale light from the candle in the centre of the table wavered and glowed as if acknowledging my musings. So incandescent and uncertain was that flame, it could have been my own soul at that moment.

The girl brought my drink to me in a stained metal tankard and set it on the table. For a moment I felt like I had an ally - the alcohol, not the girl. I tasted it - the alcohol, not the girl. At first, I almost gagged. The liquid slid down my throat, warm and weak. This surely couldn't be alcohol. The taste was indescribable. There could have been anything in it - vegetables, wood, leaves - anything at all. Then I realised, it wasn't about the taste. It was in the sitting down in peace that you got your relief in this place; the antidote to toiling in the fields, hammering at the anvil, dredging the Blackwater for clams and oysters. The ale itself was not the sustenance; the relief came in the act of imbibing, the feel of the tankard against your lips, the subsiding of your thoughts and the way your bones just melded with the earth on the floor and the wood at your elbows.

When this became apparent in my mind, the ale entered my body as would the water of bliss. It clouded my thoughts briefly before seeming to settle them down, slowing them almost. This feeling did not last. For the bark of the old man's voice dispersed it as a flung stone doth scatter a flock of pigeons.

"Where did you sleep last night?" he asked.

"What is your name?" I countered. My voice sounded weary but fearless.

To my surprise, the old man leaned back in his chair and looked at me, a smile breaking across his leathery face.

"I am Zachariah Leonard," he said, as if I should have already been aware.

Slightly disconcerted, I supped some more ale.

"Zachariah Leonard?"

He nodded slowly.

"So, last night. Where did you sleep?" he repeated.

"I slept in the churchyard, by the wall."

"A good choice."

He appeared to be wearing exactly the same clothes as the previous day. The wayward candlelight, afforded me glimpses of just how dishevelled he really was.

"Yesterday evening," I said warily, "you seemed as if you had been waiting for me, as if you knew I would turn up. And you were sitting in a place where I always used to sit."

Zachariah leaned forward and put his elbows on the table, clasping his huge dirty hands together. He peered up at me from under the dark brim of his crooked hat.

"Oh no," he said. "It is you who has been waiting for me. You have been waiting for me your whole life. That's the truth, boy."

It was oh so quiet in there, so quiet.

"But how can that be?" I asked.

"It be, and that is all," he said in almost a growl.

Zachariah drank a huge glug of ale and noisily banged his tankard back on the table, as if having made a decisive point. He stared across at me and nodded towards my tankard. I was to drink up. I closed my eyes and downed the remainder of the ale, feeling almost immediately as if I had been anaesthetised. Perhaps I had been. He rose and I followed him out into the evening air as if we were chained together. The girl winked at me from behind the bar as I passed her. I looked back over my shoulder and saw she was writing something down on a board. She seemed very pleased with herself indeed.

We walked together back towards the marshes, Zachariah in front and I behind, his crab like gait propelling

35

him like some devious clockwork toy. And after some time, we arrived at a wooden structure, hidden away amongst some trees and bushes. I hesitate to call it a house. It was literally just four walls, a roof and a door. It looked like it had been plucked from a low budget horror film and placed in the foliage by some mischievous hand. It was close to where we had sat the previous evening though I had not noticed it. So at least he actually lived somewhere. In my eyes, that fact alone made him slightly less ghoulish but no less appalling.

And as I followed Zachariah Leonard into his shack, I felt that my life was about to change forever.

It be, indeed.

Let it be.

My eyes adjusted to the gloom; though it took my nose a little longer. There were no windows, though a ragged hole in the roof seemed to serve as a chimney of sorts. Zachariah Leonard lit a small fire in a dirty grate against the back wall and a make-shift flue directed the emerging smoke into the darkening sky. I soon found myself feeling warm and light-headed.

My host, if I may call him that, sat on the floor and leaned against the wall to the left of the fire. I could not tell if his eyes were open or closed, whether he was awake or asleep. Had I not seen him walk in and slump down, I would have assumed he was nothing but a pile of rotten clothes; a pile of clothes, as I saw now, puffing upon a pipe.

I could hear the sound of my own breathing as my lungs became accustomed to the density of the atmosphere; tobacco, sweat and dirt merging with the all-consuming gloom. This was where the working man was born. This was where he first came kicking and screaming to life, obdurate, burning and at odds with the world. It was as raw a place as I had ever experienced and it both shook and thrilled me in turns.

I slid my back down the coarse wooden wall by the door and stretched my legs out before me, crossing my feet. If only I had a cowboy hat to push down slightly upon my brow and a good old cigar to light. Thus, we sat opposite one another, the length of the shack between us. I put my hands on the floor

36

and felt what seemed to be dirt, or perhaps it was sand. The light from the fire edged into the darkness, lighting the inside of the shack like a stage; for surely, that is what it was.

"Now, listen, boy," said Zachariah, eventually. His voice was a low, menacing simmer. "It starts here. This is where it starts and this is how it starts."

He took a drag of his pipe, blurted out the smoke and coughed. No smoke-rings here, I thought; and definitely no singing about gold.

"These is hard times, boy," he continued, "hard times for every man, woman and child in this land. Gone are the days when you reaped what you sowed. There are people we will never meet who dictate our every move. They say they speak for us but they will never speak to us. Them that fought the French now fight their own masters and they will never win, for you cannot fight what you cannot see, boy and that's a fact, a damnable fact. You cannot fight what you cannot see. A man is guaranteed nothing, not comfort or friendship or money or love. The harder he works for these things, the farther away they be. That is the sadness of it all."

He spoke slowly and with an underlying anger that seemed only to be quelled by my presence. Had I not been there to listen to him, I fear he would have destroyed everything before him. Zachariah Leonard was undoubtedly a violent man. I was glad I was by the door and I glanced briefly over my left shoulder just to remind myself of that fact. It brought some measure of relief, but if truth be told, not a great deal.

"Comfort; friendship; money and love." He spoke these words with intense gravity, pausing between each one, being sure I heard them. "You know of these things, these taunts, these abominations?"

I nodded, though I am not sure whether he could see my response through the darkness. But he continued anyway.

"Let us take first, 'comfort'. Look around you. I felt your disgust when you entered here, I saw you draw breath and I saw you grimace. Yet this is my home. This is my comfort. I have straw for a bed and a roof to protect me from the rain.

37

There is little light as I am sure you have noticed. But for what reason should I want light? Why should I want to see? I am safe here. I am comfortable. It belongs to me and no other. It is in the feeling, you understand? Any fool can see. A dolt has eyes the same as a wise man. It takes a deeper man to feel."

I wasn't sure where this was going, so I just listened. I felt that one word from me, however innocent, may have led to an eruption of anger from the man who smouldered across the other side of the shack, an eruption from which I surely would not survive. It was the sheer eloquence of this almost bestial being that perhaps scared me the most. He was like no-one I had ever met before.

"Then, 'friendship'," he went on. "Friendship." He said this word with such contempt it would not have been at all surprising had it hit me full in the face. He spat into the fire. His phlegm sizzled in the heat of the flames like the cracking of a whip. "Friendship," he said once more.

"No man can be a friend with another until he is a friend to himself. He who suffers self-hatred will hate others ten-fold. Take it from me, boy. Hatred is the most natural emotion of the lonely. It is not sadness. When man is alone, he may pity himself for a time, but that pity will soon turn to hatred, a hatred of those that have what he has not – a foot in the door of the world. And from hatred comes violence and from violence comes murder. That is a man alone, I tell you. When the only way a man can deal with another man is to kill him, then that man will be a friend to no-one for as long as he lives, except perhaps the devil himself. The need for friendship and the hatred of mankind is the great debate that goes on in the head of the lonely man."

I sat rapt and attentive, acutely aware that he may have been talking about me as opposed to himself.

"And so we come to money – the greatest killer of them all. It grabs you and sucks the life out of you. It breaks you in half and destroys every feeling you ever had. It makes beautiful women ugly and puts a knife in the hand of a man of peace. It will take back twice what it has given you and it will put you in the ground without your soul. If it takes hold of you, it will break you. Listen not to what they say about money for it will corrupt your sleep and burden you with irons from which you will never escape. It is a creation of the rich man, the tool with which the Sir and the Lord will taunt the peasant and the serf. Be not seduced by it boy and be not taunted by it. They say it is easier for a camel to pass through the eye of a needle than it is for a rich man to enter the kingdom of heaven. Do not listen to that claptrap. There is no heaven save what is around us, no heaven save what is within us. Mark me boy and mark me well. The love of money is not the root of all evil; it is money itself that is evil."

I held my breath. I listened for life outside. There was not a sound.

No Heaven.

Zachariah Leonard sucked upon his pipe, as if he were drawing energy from it in order to continue. I was becoming lost in the flames of the fire, intoxicated by his voice. It was as if I were being addressed not by a man but by a mountain.

"And lastly, we have love," he said, such sadness now breaking over him. "It is your turn, boy, for I cannot speak of it."

He bowed his head. His talking had taken a lot out of him it seemed. Maybe he wasn't one used to discussion. For all I knew, he had never spoken to anyone but me before; except perhaps to order ale.

I tried to swallow, but my mouth and throat had been parched by the smoke that wafted around the shack like a dark whisper. The only discernible noise was the crackling of the fire. The door to the shack may well have been bolted shut with a thousand bolts, so trapped did I feel at that moment. My only means of ending this hiatus, this purgatory, was to speak of that notion about which I too knew so little; love.

I was that instant saved by a tune that entered my head, notes that bounded through me, illuminating me from within. Such was the clarity of the music, I thought momentarily it was coming from outside my head, but Zachariah Leonard seemed not to hear it at all. If he did, he showed no acknowledgement.

"I know," I started, falteringly; "I know that money can't buy me love."

Zachariah Leonard nodded slowly, seemingly impressed by the wisdom of my words. I got the distinct feeling, however, that he wanted more.

"That's why I don't care too much for money," I continued, "because money can't buy me love."

I waited for a moment, allowing him to digest what I had just said

"Some people say that all you need is love, that love is all you need," I added, but as I spoke the words, they sounded so hollow in so deep a moment.

At this, Zachariah made as if to rise and my heart battered my chest. He was merely adjusting his position. I still couldn't see his face. And that troubled me more than I can say. He was waiting for me to tell him what love was and, it was clear, he would wait for as long as it took.

I looked down at my hands though I knew not why. I turned them over and gazed at my filthy palms and my eyes were drawn to the pale skin that circled the base of the third finger of my left hand. I had been married and I had a son, yet when asked about love, all I could do was repeat lines that others had sung. Julia had always told me she loved me to the point where it used to irritate me. What I wouldn't have given then to have heard those words from her pretty red mouth, to have had her whisper 'I love you' to me, her soft lips resting gently upon my ear as she spoke.

This was too much, too much. I chewed the inside of my bottom lip as my eyes stung, not with the smoke but with the tears that were lining up so impatiently behind them, like the exhausted Ford workers who having heard the claxon, were now queuing up for their lunch. I let the tears tumble out upon my face and I felt lighter for it. I was thus baptized by the water of my own condemnation.

What had Zachariah thought of my breaking? To this day, I like to think he was maybe crying too.

Time passed. The flames in the fire were receding and the dense, putrid air was clearing just a little.

"I will ask you again, boy. What is love?"

Words came to my mouth from some source unknown to me.

"Love is what stops you from killing yourself," I said plainly.

For that is all I truly knew love to be. My dad had been kind to me and my mum had been sad and quiet. Julia had cared for me and I'm not sure if Robbie even knew me. I guess if you were to have asked them all, except perhaps for Robbie, they would all have said that they loved me. But that was not enough for me. I wanted to love, I wanted it so much.

"It is not about being loved. It is about loving – that's what I need." It made sense to me then, more and more as I spoke each word. Zachariah Leonard need not have been there at all. "Yes I am lonely, as you said. But I do not hate. I hate nobody and I hate no thing. But that is not the same as loving. I need to love."

"What do you see when you look at me?" whispered Zachariah. His voice was above me now. I opened my weary eyes and stared up at the ragged figure that loomed darkly. I hadn't even heard him move, let alone seen him approaching.

"I don't see anything," I said eventually. "I feel vulnerable and I feel as if I know nothing. I feel so many things. And I am scared. I guess I just don't know how to be in this world."

He smiled. I could see it even through the gloom. I say smile, but it was more a crack opening up in his face.

"Then you have hope," he said. "You have hope. Hope is a start."

And for the first time since I had met Zachariah Leonard, gazing at him as I was, his grinning, leathery face clouded in smoke and sweat, I felt akin to him. He placed a heavy hand upon my head before shuffling noisily back to where he had previously sat, the complete antithesis of the silent grace with which he had come towards me. Approach like a boat upon the ocean and leave like a steam engine. That seemed to be his way. I watched as he gathered some straw together before laying himself upon it. He brought his knees up to his chest

41

and wrapped his broad arms about them. And he spoke no more.

I had lost all track of time. No light penetrated the shack. The last of the smoke waltzed lazily around the room, twisting and hovering, gyrating on this emptying dance-floor for desperate thoughts. It was enticing me to sleep, leading me on to the dark lair of my dreams. I was powerless to its seduction and it took me with gusto. I laid myself down and I was asleep within moments.

What is sleep, but the wilful act of allowing your body to shut down? You lie there waiting for it to smother you with its mischievous blanket, be it the thick, heavy one that knocks you out cold or the colourful, patchwork quilt of half remembered moments and tangential connections that plays tricks on your body and your mind; whilst all the time creating the illusion that you are in truth at rest. Thus I was regaled with forms and images that tempted and taunted me in turn.

The sea is upon me and I am but a dot in the greenish, black blue of it all. I am at one moment above and eyes to the wide sky and the next subsumed into the depths of this earth. There is no sound, never a sound. All colours flash and the firmament cracks open. A massive factory bursts from the sea bed and pursues me until I lie breathless upon an old beam, the waves crashing into me until I can hold on no longer.

Two large clouds merge into the faces of my mum and my dad and rainy tears gush forth, pelting me like bullets and swelling the ocean that now tosses me with murderous ferocity. And then the sun bursts into the sky and blinds me as I slip beneath the surface of the pearl white sea. A yellow submarine drifts by but leaves me lonesome.

In my dream, as I am sinking to my doom, a hand clutches at my sodden sleeve, a plump hand covered in chocolate. I am pulled to safety and lie on my back on the cricket pitch at The Recreation Ground. The deepest eyes I have ever seen peer down upon me. They are the eyes of the sea and of the land, of the sun and of the firmament. They are the eyes of my son, Robbie. He is gazing down at me, pleading with me, admiring me, hating me, loving me, before disappearing across the grass and into the trees, waddling backwards, waving at me as best he can, trying to smile, behaving as if he would one day see me again.

And I awoke, hours later, dazed, but somehow refreshed. For a moment, things seemed clearer to me, but when I opened my eyes there was Zachariah Leonard. His face was but inches from mine and he held a bloody, crooked knife in his hand. He was breathing heavily and looking right through me.

How long he had been there, I knew not.

4. The Immensity of This World

Boiled Rabbit:
Ingredients:
2 dirty rabbits (blunt and rugged, ears dry and tough)
1 big pot of water

Cut rabbit with frighteningly sharp knife and hurl the insides indiscriminately over your left shoulder. Wash what is left in cold, salty marsh water in order to give the impression of cleanliness. Soak in warm water until said water turns a pinkish colour. This confirms that the rabbit is well and truly dead. Bring the head round to the side and fasten it there by means of a metal spike run through the head and the body, mumbling obscenities all the while. Put the rabbit into enough hot water to cover it and boil until tender. The length of time this takes will be dependent upon the size of the pot in which you are cooking it, the ferocity of the flames over which the pot precariously hangs and how many times the rabbit is jabbed by rough, grubby fingers. The intensity and frequency of the aforementioned obscenities may also have a bearing. When ready, serve on a battered wooden board and eat with unspeakable primeval abandon.

And thus was my breakfast cooked and prepared by Mr Zachariah Leonard. I hadn't eaten for some time, so you may well imagine that I devoured the rabbit with, if not unspeakable ferocity or even primeval abandon, then certainly great vigour. Please believe me however, when I say it was more fuel than food. My body needed it and that was all. A culinary delight it was not. To the desperately hungry, the physical act of eating is as pleasurable as any taste could aspire to. Such are the mechanics of man.

The Tollesbury sun rose into the sky and the marshlands blinked at me. A sultry breeze ruffled the leaves on the trees causing a momentary rush that led in turn to a sedentary silence of which the finest monk would have been proud. The air was of salt and of grass and of sea and of earth. I will live here forever for there is surely no more wondrous place than this.

"Did you sleep well enough, boy?" asked Zachariah, loading up his pipe as he leaned against the doorframe of the shack. It was a wonder the whole thing didn't collapse. He looked so destructive and the structure so flimsy - an absolute wrecking ball of a man.

I nodded. The aftertaste of the rabbit was popping into my throat every now and then as if some mischievous little tyke were sitting in my stomach.

"A good sleep and a good breakfast are what every man needs." Zachariah went on.

He seemed less sinister to me somehow now. I wouldn't say 'friendly', but I was certainly beginning to feel just a little more comfortable in his presence. Zachariah lit his pipe and puffed, surveying the marshes and the Blackwater estuary beyond, the very picture of a Lord overlooking his kingdom. It was indeed majestic and the feeling of pride that shone from his coal black eyes was one of which I was in full accord. The coastline of Britain is a forgotten wonder, such perfect imperfection as no human hand could sculpt or paint; for it is forged by the seas and the oceans at the behest of Albion's moon. And you cannot fault what you see, for if you do, with what are you comparing it? From high above or from just inches away, the coastline of my country is unparalleled. The Tollesbury salt marshes were to my eyes, and evidently to the eyes of the strange man with whom I had just shared a meal, a product of time itself; Tollesbury Time.

"Come and sit with me boy - over on that mound."

He indicated a patch of grass about fifteen yards to the left of the shack and I followed him. We sat together, a little too close for my liking though I did not protest.

"You see those green rubber stems?" He asked. "They will have great yellow heads by time autumn comes. You look close, you can see them turning before your eyes. Look like they should be in the sea, don't they boy?"

I smiled. It was as if I were listening to a child.

"They are Golden Samphire," I said. "Or Inula crithmoides. They flower once a year, as you say, towards the end of the summer. They can grow up to about two feet tall."

"Golden Sapphires, you say?" Zachariah turned to me.

"Yes, golden just in colour. And not sapphires, no. Samphires"

"Two feet. What do you mean two feet?"

I put my arm out and indicated what I thought was about two feet from the ground.

"And what was them other words you said boy? Foreign sounding."

"That was the Latin name," I replied, a little embarrassed. "Inula crithmoides."

"Why does it have two names, boy?"

"I don't know. It's just the way they do it?"

"The way who does it?"

"I don't know."

I could smell the salt in the air and I could hear the slapping of the water against the coastline of my country.

"Golden Samphires," Zachariah murmured, almost as if he were addressing the plants themselves, introducing himself perhaps.

"And what else do you know, boy?

I thought for a moment before replying.

"I know that the geese around here are called Brent geese."

"Brent geese," he said, as if practicing the words. "Why is that?"

"I think they used to be called Brant geese. Something to do with coming over from America. But then they changed the name to Brent."

"They again?"

"Sorry?"

"They again. Them that give the plants over there two names, the Golden Sapphires; and now change the names of geese?"

What was I getting myself into?

46

We sat for some hours gazing into the marshland and the sea. Sometimes Zachariah would ask me questions and I would answer as best I could. Other times it seemed that he drifted off to sleep. I must confess I felt safer when he was awake. I found myself completely captivated by him when he slept, agonising over the moment when he awoke, unsure as to whether he would just hurl himself at me with a rage unbridled or whether he would merely sigh and behold once more his ragged realm. At least if he went for me whilst he was awake, I would have some warning, though little good it probably would have done me.

The morning drifted into afternoon and the salty air nudged me into sleep. It was one of those breaks from being awake, as opposed to true sleep, a nap if you will, but not one that left me refreshed. On waking, Zachariah was standing beside me.

"I am off now, boy," he said, lifting a heavy looking sack over his shoulder. From where he had got it or what it contained, I did not know, nor did I, at that moment care to find out. For my thoughts then were only of myself. What would I do here alone? Tollesbury suddenly seemed large and portentous.

"Oh. Ok."

It was just like when I had left Julia.

"You may use this place for whatever you need. I will be back the day after tomorrow."

Zachariah Leonard walked slowly away from me up the hill. And as his image began to merge with the haze of the morning, he stopped and called back to me.

"There are some clothes in my cabin, over at the back. You should wear them boy. You look ridiculous."

And at that, he walked off purposefully in the direction of Tolleshunt D'arcy, the village some two miles east of Tollesbury. I watched him recede into the curve of the horizon, a shambling figure, literally disappearing from view. For all I knew, he had merely stepped off the low budget film set of my low budget life, changed into a pair of jeans and a cotton shirt and got the train home to his wife and children.

47

Instantly, I missed him.

So there I was, standing and staring into the great nothingness, the black shack behind me and the marshes before me. There was not a sound in the air, coming either from the heavens above or from the salty earth beneath my feet. It was as if I was in a photograph, caught and trapped within an invisible frame. It was an effort to move, though move I had to. But where to go and what to do? There was no way I could consider, even for a moment, all that had happened to me up to that point; it was all too big. To have pondered longer than a second upon my situation would have been to crumble.

Examining the shack was an obvious option. It was every bit as dirty and gloomy as it had seemed the night before, despite the absence of smoke and the presence of foolhardy sunbeams who peeked through the open door. Dust particles floated in the half-light. There was a dryness in the air, a hardness that crept from the walls, that served to constrict my breathing. Had I shouted with all my might, my voice would surely have sounded no louder than a whisper. I found myself moving ever so slowly as if Zachariah Leonard was still there, perched on his haunches in a corner, watching me, smelling me, bestial and unblinking.

I stood in the centre of the shack and listened to my shallow breath, waiting for my eyes to catch up. After some moments, I made out the form of a rectangular chest in the far left hand corner. I approached it and when I peered closer, it was most definitely just a wooden box. The word 'chest' would have implied entirely more grandeur than it deserved. I lifted the lid and saw within a neatly folded set of clothes.

There was a pair of trousers, or what I would come to know more correctly as britches, and a rough over-shirt made out of some coarse, heavy material. My lack of knowledge of all things textile has never been of great concern to me before, though it would have been pleasing back then to know just for what I was exchanging my faithful baggy jumper. The over-shirt was slightly too large for me and the sleeves only allowed for the protrusion of my fingers. I felt I would be rather too warm in it if the weather continued as it had been, but it seemed I had little choice.

I put my discarded jumper in the box and closed the lid, leaving the britches inside where I felt they belonged. I would stick to my jeans for now.

As the beginnings of a smile began to form upon my lips, darkness entered the shack, an all consuming darkness that laid all to waste. A cloud must have brushed itself against the sun momentarily. This place was undoubtedly, in truth, a tomb, a coffin. Where only the previous evening it had seemed to me to be the birth of the working man, now it was no more than a creaking place of death. I shuddered a little and made for the dim light of the doorway. Had I stayed there any longer, I would surely have fallen to my knees in fear and horror for the gloom was so powerful, so awesome, it could have frozen your heart white and solid. Without its master, it was an unholy place indeed.

The afternoon lay before me. The marshlands bathed in the token offerings of the sea and the sun set itself in the blue of the Tollesbury sky. Was this the same sun and the same sky that had peered in on the darker moments of my life, that had just watched as I fell apart in stages, staggering about wayward and forlorn? Or was this literally a new dawn, a new beginning? Perhaps I was already dead and this was all just some sort of dreamy purgatory.

It was then that I felt momentarily immortal. A contradiction in terms you may think but that is the closest I can come to describing how I felt at that moment. I could not be harmed and death was nothing to me. These thoughts instilled me with confidence and courage – those two elements that I so lacked in everyday life. How ironic that they should have given themselves up to me only when I had decided to eliminate myself from this world.

I turned right from the shack and walked along the edge of the marshes, where one day the winding sea wall beside me would be built and re-enforced. There were all kinds of sailing vessels upon the Blackwater now, some heading towards the harbour and others disappearing into the void of the horizon, off to Mersea Island or London or maybe even further. I had never realised how much a seafaring village Tollesbury actually was or had been, despite the fact that the Tollesbury village sign sported a sailing vessel. The estuary truly could have been the A12, so busy and urgent was it. As I approached the harbour, my soul was filled with humility.

The sound of reed warblers, dragonflies and reed buntings rode on the gentle breeze that caressed the land about me. There was a tang of acidity in the air and I could not help but sigh as I walked. The paucity of my pace was due not to any fear or inherent lowness of mood; it was merely that I was in no rush. There was no place I had to be. The chaos was gone from my world – it was just me and this beautiful Tollesbury day. It was as simple and as lovely as that.

And in time, I came upon several wooden boats bobbing upon the shallow waters, floating upon the very exhalation and inhalation of the living waters beneath them.

Thus I spoke to the sea:

"Let me breathe with you and feel your touch, let me be a part of you, let me be within and without you and may you recognise my presence upon this earth, though it be so insignificant when compared with your wonder."

As I spoke those words, mad as they were, I knew I was in deep. So I did the only thing I felt safe doing – I just kept going, just kept going as Bob Dylan had taught me.

The day was warming and the sky was clear. The sounds of the sea and the land came together like gentle hands clasped and before long I had drifted through the marshes, and arrived at the meeting of a dirt track and the Blackwater. Such was Woodrolfe Road. It was then, as the openness of the area fell upon me, that I heard the laugh of an angel. It was such a combination of giggle and breathlessness that I had no choice but to just stand where I was lest I shatter the delicacy of the moment with my clumsy oafishness. I was entranced.

"Oh Adam, do not fret so! You did well! All will be good with you!"

The sweet voice followed the laugh, grew from it almost, a continuum of brightness and innocence. My eyes could not help but alight upon its source. And I gasped; for a gasp is the response of the heart when the world either falls apart or falls perfectly into place. The thumping of my heart was a Ringo backbeat complete with grinning joy.

Seated on the ground some twenty yards from me was the most gorgeous woman I had ever seen in my life. At that stage, I could only see her from the side yet gorgeous was still the word that exploded into my mind. She just sat there, her right arm across the thin shoulders of a young boy. From where I stood, I could see him shuddering as if he were laughing; or maybe he was just as in awe of her as I.

"I shouldn't have to keep telling you, Adam. You should know by now. I will give you the confidence you need if it be the last thing I do!"

The woman ran her slender white fingers slowly through the boy's black hair and he bent forward slightly as she did so. I could almost feel her nails against my own scalp as I observed the scene before me. I touched the top of my head, breathed deep and found that my eyes had closed of their own accord. I smelled the fish and the hops in the air and took in the natural beauty of all that lay around me – the grass either side of the lane, the smoke from the cottages half way up the road, the dung from the horses even that were tethered to a wooden post just the other side from where this woman sat. All was beautiful, but the gorgeous angel whose voice charmed even the breeze, had heightened my senses, brought my soul to the surface of my being. Yet she was not even aware of my presence on this most magical of afternoons. I opened my eyes wide and vowed never to let them close upon this woman again.

It was the boy who first noticed me. He must have sensed me for I saw him flinch a little as he looked over his shoulder, past the pale neck of the woman beside him. It was the third time I had seen him. He had been there in the village square when I was hauled out of the lock-up and it had been he who had jabbed me with the stick before running into the distance. His broken teeth were bared in my direction and his eyes were as dark as his hair. He whispered something into the ear of the beautiful woman and she turned towards me.

There was a pause in time. That is the only way I can explain it. The first moment I looked upon that face was akin to looking at a portrait in the finest of galleries. It was her fragility that first struck me. There was a grace about her, a gentleness that could only have been the product of a delicate but pulsating soul. No hint of the harshness of life emanated from her. She was all innocence to me. Her hair was so fine that I felt it would fall apart were I to touch it, those red yellow ringlets flowing to her shoulders like some rolling slow motion ocean of flaming wheat. Her eyes were blue green and her thin lips were red and glistening.

I knew I was staring. I just couldn't help it. I gulped with what was left of the wetness in my mouth before drying up completely. She pushed herself to her feet, ruffled the boy's hair and glided over to me. Her light skirt obscured her feet as it caressed the stony ground like a parting lover's stolen kiss.

When she was within a yard or so of me, she paused as if listening intently. Even I could hear the rush of my breath as I tried to regulate it. Without a word, she reached forward with an outstretched arm, placed a finger beneath my chin and gently closed my lolling mouth for me. For the life of me, I do believe I leaned forward a little to allow her to do it. And then she smiled, not just with her lips, but with her whole being. It was as if the sun itself were breaking forth from within her. She warmed me to the point where a spark was lit.

"Hello," she said softly. "You are new to these parts, aren't you sir?"

I couldn't speak.

"My name is Penny. Penny Shoraton."

What a fool I was and what a fool I remain.

Penny Shoraton's eyes surveyed me, as she smiled all the while. I knew she was peering into my very being. Still I remained silent. She had truly struck me dumb.

"I'll just be over there," she went on, angling her head to where the boy sat. He was just looking down ignoring the moment. As the words left her mouth, he began to beat rhythmically upon a stone with a stick he held in his hand – tap, tap, tap. She sauntered back to sit beside him again and he put down the stick as soon as she laid a hand upon his head. She murmured something into his ear. He laughed out loud, looked over at me and leaned into her shoulder.

I took my leave of this incongruous couple and spent the rest of the day wandering around Tollesbury.

Eventually, I returned to the shack and rested. I lay down by the box in which I had found the clothes and pondered my situation. How easily I had come to accept this bizarre chain of events. The world had been simplified for me. It was nature and it was people. My life had been stripped down to what was real. I had been presented with the opportunity, goodness knows how, to start again, to understand life and my part in it. It was a reassuring feeling and one that I clung to through the darkness of that night.

Penny Shoraton came to me in my dreams, parading coquettishly through my fitful sleep. She swayed slowly at the forefront of my mind, skipping across the derelict plains of my heart and making herself at home in the deepest corner. Yet I awoke with a start as the night was at its blackest, thinking only of Zachariah Leonard. A sullen pain crept above my left ear. As I sat up, I rubbed the side of my head before putting my hand down to where I had lain. It was then that I felt the padlock. I had slept throughout with my head upon a door in the floor, a door just a foot square, bolted shut and secured with a small padlock, a door I had not noticed until that moment.

I wandered out and looked up at the Tollesbury sky. Those same stars I knew so well stared back at me. I felt comfort in their rigidity, a momentary relief in their permanence. And I stood there until the red sun broke once more across the endless horizon, wondering at the immensity of this world.

As I sat upon the sodden morning grass, gazing into the water of the marshland, two shadows fell across my vision. I looked up and there stood two figures, one short and one tall.

"Who are you?" I asked, addressing the black silhouettes.

"We pull the strings around here," replied the tall one.

"We pull all the strings," added the other.

"Best you come with us," they stated, in unison.

The two men walked away from Zachariah Leonard's shack and I followed them as they requested. The time to see what that padlock was guarding would come in future days - and when it did I knew it would be more appalling than anything I had experienced up until now.

5. Weepy and Nardy

I sat at a wooden dining table in a house just at the junction of East Street, Mell Road and Woodrolfe Road. I guessed the house stood roughly where Leavett's Butcher's stands today. The tall man and the short man had walked in front and I had followed them without question.

The two men sat down opposite me and thus it was in that small candle-lit room that I first saw their faces. The shorter of the two had a balding head and a grey beard that hung down way past his chin, almost touching his chest. He had blue eyes and a flat nose that may have been pressed one too many times by errant children. And between the strands of his beard was a permanent smile. It was as if the beard itself had been formed purely to stop this squat little man's face from literally falling apart with laughter.

"I am Weepy," he said.

The other, taller man also had little hair upon his head. It seemed all to have gathered above his top lip in a wonderful moustache. He had deep brown eyes set in the greyest of sockets. His forehead was lined like the bark of an ancient tree and his mouth was stern and rigid. All these features contributed to a rueful expression that indicated he had seen more or less everything there was to see and had not been impressed by any of it.

"I am Nardy," he said.

Weepy and Nardy. I was at that stage less inclined to believe they 'pulled all the strings' than when they had been silhouettes looming before me.

"Hello Weepy. Hello Nardy," I ventured. "I am Simon Anthony."

My voice sounded more and more vacuous with every syllable. Even hearing it, I doubted myself. When you spend so much of your time alone, it is always difficult to predict how you will be received by total strangers.

Weepy smiled and Nardy stared. They looked at each other momentarily and then back at me. Weepy leaned forward and rested his surprisingly large hands upon the table. Nardy arched back in his chair in a way that would have made any infant school teacher shudder. He ran a hand slowly down each side of his smooth cheeks, bringing his palms together as they slipped off the end of his chin. Three times he did this before interlocking his fingers and resting his hands in his lap, rocking gently back and forth in his chair.

The only sound was the pop, fizz and sizzle of candle wax and the tiny creaking of Nardy's chair.

"So, Mr Anthony, how have you been?" asked Weepy.

"I'm not sure, to be honest. Things have all been a bit of a whirl lately."

"Well, Nardy and I are here to help you."

Nardy nodded. I glanced at him but was not reassured. He continued to nod regardless.

I made an involuntary sound that was intended to express a combination of relief and tiredness. Whether my inquisitors understood me, I knew not.

Weepy and Nardy just continued to look at me. I assumed they thought that was helpful. In truth, I felt they were analysing me, trying to see through me, assessing me for who knows what. I began to wish I had sat closer to the door. It was different from the feeling I had experienced when I was in the presence of Zachariah Leonard, but no less powerful.

"What makes you think I need help?" I asked eventually.

Weepy paused before answering.

"You wouldn't be here if you didn't need some kind of help, now would you, Mr Anthony? You have no need to be afraid. We are very experienced, Nardy and I. You are in good hands."

"What do you know about me?" I asked, suspicion creeping into my soul. I wasn't sure who to trust. I didn't even know if I could have faith in my own senses. And that concerned me greatly.

Weepy continued.

"We know you have been here for three days. We have reports that you spent one night asleep on the grass and one night asleep on the floor in that shack by the marshes. We know you have had some ale and we know that you have met Penny Shoraton and the young boy. Those are the facts. That is what we know."

"We deal in facts, here, Mr Anthony," added Nardy. "Facts are what we deal in. Isn't that right Weepy?"

"It is indeed, Nardy. It is indeed, Facts," concurred the diminutive Weepy.

Neither had made mention of Zachariah Leonard. I decided then not to bring him into the conversation; if they didn't mention him then neither would I. I felt a rush of embarrassment at the mention of Penny Shoraton and bowed my head though I had nothing to feel guilty about, nothing at all. They couldn't see into my dreams. They were mine and mine alone. Whatever dreams meant to me, I didn't believe they would constitute facts to them.

"What we don't know," began Nardy, now taking the lead, "is what is on your mind, what is inside you. That is what we don't know. And that is precisely what we would like to know."

I resolved at that moment to conceal as much of what was 'on my mind' as I could. It was clear I had been watched, for they knew all my movements. Had Zachariah been spying on me too? Was he in league with them?

"We are going to ask you some questions, Mr Anthony. Please answer them as best you can. We know this is a difficult time for you but please do be honest with us. In that way, we can help you," said Weepy, trying to sound as soothing as he could. "Now, do you know where you are Mr Anthony?"

"In a house in Tollesbury," I replied with as much confidence as I could.

"And what year are we in?"

"I have been told it's 1836."

"I see," said Nardy. "And who told you that?"

I shrugged my shoulders. For two people that purported to know so much, they were asking me a lot of questions. It was I who was lacking information, I who wanted to try and understand what was happening to me.

"What did you mean when you said you had reports, you know, earlier? Who were the reports from? Why are you spying on me?" I asked all these questions whilst trying to sound as casual as I was able.

"Reports is all," replied Weepy crisply. "Just reports."

Nardy leaned across to his companion and whispered something into his ear. Weepy nodded before continuing.

"What do you think of our ale?" he asked.

"What do you mean?"

"You have had some of the local ale. What did you make of it? Did it agree with you?"

"It wasn't bad," I replied hesitantly. "Not what I'm used to, but I could get used to it I suppose. I didn't feel as bad after I'd had it as I thought I would."

"Good, good," said Weepy, glancing furtively at Nardy, before returning his gaze to me. "Very good indeed, Mr Anthony. That's the spirit! And you got a little jab from Penny's young boy I understand. What was that all about do you think?"

I had almost forgotten about that. "It was a bit of a shock I suppose. Didn't hurt too much. He just did it and ran off down towards the harbour."

"Any lasting effects?"

"Not that I know of. Why?"

"No matter, Mr Anthony, no matter."

Weepy and Nardy conferred once more. This time it was Nardy who spoke.

"Do you have any further questions for us, Mr Anthony, anything more before we bid you good day?"

My mind was hazy. I was now even more confused than I was before I had met these two. And still no mention of Zachariah Leonard. Not for the first time, I was feeling drained and weary.

"I just need to lie down, I think, and hopefully clear my head. I'm feeling tired most of the time even though I'm not really doing anything."

"Understandable, Mr Anthony, eminently understandably," said Weepy, nodding vigorously.

There was a silence that lasted some moments during which Weepy and Nardy just sat there with their eyes closed. It seemed as if they were making a concerted effort to inspect my thoughts, to enter my mind. I in turn stared back at them in an attempt to repel their unwanted intrusion into the last part of my being that I could truly call my own. I thought of getting up and leaving but I felt compelled to stay.

I peered into the dark corners of the room, trying to discern what may lie there as yet unseen, watching me, listening to this whole bizarre conversation. For a moment, I felt I sensed movement but as soon as the feeling caught me, so it subsided. I wanted so much to have my back flat against one of the walls so that I might at least know I was not at risk of being leapt upon from behind. My throat was dry and my breathing audible amidst the quiet of it all.

Weepy and Nardy stood up and I guessed I was to do the same. They took it in turns to shake my hand. Their palms were soft and sweaty, like dough that had been kneaded too much. It was as I stood that I noticed two faces pressed against the glass of the window that faced out onto East Street. It was Penny Shoraton and the boy with the cracked teeth, Adam. Their noses were distorted flat against the grimy glass and they were both smiling and waving at me. It was a grotesque scene and I began to feel very ill. The moist hands of Weepy and Nardy, the incessant grinning of the boy alongside the absolute beauty of Penny Shoraton; it was all too much for me. I lurched for the door and staggered a little as I passed the two figures that were still leaning against the window, smiling and waving, even though I was no longer in the room.

The sky was a bruise. The earth was cracked. And a wind began to howl.

When I was some thirty yards away from the house, having crossed the corner of Woodrolfe Road and Mell Road, I stopped to regain my balance for I was truly reeling. I felt simultaneously sick and scared. Darkness was falling in the

Tollesbury sky yet it felt like only a couple of hours had passed since dawn had splashed across the horizon.

Then I heard a clapping beat coming from outside the house from across the road. It began faintly but was then joined by the tapping of another. It was a wonderfully syncopated beat that I recognised at once. It caught me just as it had so long ago when I was but a lonely, worn out boy trying to understand life. The irony was not lost on me, I can tell you.

I looked over and there was Nardy leaning against the wall outside the house that is now the Butcher's, slapping his hands rhythmically against his thighs. The boy, Adam, was joining in with his stick, tapping it against the top of the wall. Penny Shoraton was swaying back and forth, moving only from her waist upwards, her feet remaining planted and hidden beneath her long skirt, like the most beautiful of Jack-in-a-boxes, just swaying and bobbing her head up and down, swaying and bobbing.

Then Weepy began to sing.

"Lover, love me too. You know we love you. So plee-ea-ese, love me to-o."

And as he sang, he walked towards me, slowly, ever so slowly, his back a little hunched, his feet shuffling in the dirt, his arms moving and striking out violently in time with the beat.

Closer and closer he got. I could do nothing but stare.

"Lover, love me too. You know we love you. So plee-ea-ese, love me to-o."

His singing was almost child-like, enunciating every syllable with joy. But when he was just a few feet from me, I could see the anger in his small, blazing black eyes. He glared up at me, a frown cracking his forehead. And this time, he didn't sing, he screamed.

"Love, love me too! You know we love you! So plee-ea-ese, love me to-o! Oh, love me to-oh!"

I was breathing so fast I thought I would pass out. Weepy stood before me, literally shaking, his fists clenched so hard I could see the bones of his knuckles almost breaking through his skin. Penny Shoraton was still. Nardy and the boy had ceased their percussion.

Without thought, I did what I always did. I ran. Down Woodrolfe Road I pounded, turning left just before the harbour and across the marshes towards Zachariah Leonard's shack. My ears were aching and my chest was breaking. My whole being was a-rocking and a-rolling. I was panicking and I was running for my life. The wind blew harsh around me, buffeting me as it would a battered, hollow wreck upon the shore.

At last, I burst into the shack and threw myself to the floor, face down. And I lay like that until my breathing slowed and the fear left me. I could smell the dirt beneath me and was glad of it. A splinter of wood ripped my palm and I couldn't have been more relieved. I did not move, merely seeking comfort in the solidity of my surroundings. I could have lain like that forever, so safe did I feel. This was a broken place and I was broken too. I was a cracked cup, a shattered dream.

But precarious safety does not last. It can not possibly last. I knew that better than anyone.

Then a deep and thunderous voice bellowed from the shadows, resonating through the dark and the wood, a voice that humbled the wind that had been beating upon the door, humbled it until it became a mere breeze that skulked away into the trees.

"What you been up to boy? What have you done?"

There was no further sound but that of my world falling apart.

61

6. A Man Who Needs A Drink

Guilt consumed me though I had done nothing wrong. I hadn't been 'up to' anything as far as I was aware. I had met some strange people, that was all; and wasn't Zachariah Leonard one of the strangest?

Weepy and Nardy had troubled me, yes, and they had played with my mind, without doubt. Zachariah, however, shook me to my very core. It was in the way he looked at me, in the way he moved in so simian a fashion. It was in the primeval potential for horrific violence that emanated from every taut sinew of his grubby, perspiring body. He had asked what I had been up to. I had been equally curious as to where he had been the previous two days.

I manoeuvred myself into a sitting position and crossed my legs, my hands upon my knees. He sat opposite me some six feet away in the exact same pose. Thus I faced him.

"You found the shirt then?" said Zachariah, nodding his head towards me. "Fits you well."

"Thank you," I replied. "Is it one of yours?"

"Not quite, boy; not quite."

"When did you get back?" I asked

"Just before you did. And just in time, it seems."

Zachariah lit his pipe and sucked, his cheeks hollowing as he did so. He looked momentarily imbecilic before puffing out the sickly smelling smoke and lowering the pipe once more. His eyes simmered like pools of hot oil. He was truly indestructible.

"So boy, who were you running from? What put the fear in you? Not seen fear like this since the last time?"

"What last time?"

"Just answer my questions, boy. You know how this works."

I put a quivering hand to my forehead hoping maybe it would in some way steady my mind. Sweat was upon my brow and trepidation was within my heart. I had the feeling

Zachariah knew all the answers, knew exactly what I had just experienced, about Weepy, Nardy, Penny Shoraton and the boy; knew everything and was just confirming to himself to what extent he could trust me; if indeed trust was a concept of which he was even aware.

"I've just been wandering around the village. I went down to the harbour and all around there."

"Just wandering around, boy?"

"Yes, just wandering around."

"So what feared you, set you running so?"

I had to tell him. To delay would likely be to perish.

"I met two men who asked me some questions. I must have upset them. One of them got angry with me and I had to get away. So I ran back here. They didn't mention you and neither did I. I promise."

Zachariah listened and then took a deep breath. I got the feeling he was trying to suppress a burning rage, cooling it with this long intake of stale air.

"Two men you say?"

I nodded, watching as he chewed upon his bottom lip with his yellowed teeth.

"One big and one small?"

I nodded again.

"You did right, boy," he said eventually. "You did right."

At that moment, looking at Zachariah as he in turn stared at me, I wasn't entirely sure where I was safest. I detested this feeling of insecurity, of doubt and foreboding. My situation was as abstract as time itself although exactly what time of day it was would have given me some measure of relief, something for me to at least cling to. The constructs of my existence were fading in and out of vision, the solidity of what I knew to be true crumbling all about me.

And what had he meant by 'the last time?'

"What should I do now?" I asked, meekly.

Zachariah closed his eyes and puffed upon his pipe for some moments before answering me.

63

"They will come for you again," he said. "Maybe not right away, but they will come for you. They don't give up. They never give up. Do what you been doing, boy. You be doing well."

"I don't understand what's happening," I said to him. "I don't understand at all."

At this, he rose slowly, like a house being built, and came over to me. He knelt down and put a thick arm across my shoulders before leaning his face right in towards my left ear.

"Just one thing, boy and you make sure you remember this," he whispered. His voice was as of the sound of a steam train in the distance. "You don't know me, you have never seen me. I don't live here. I don't live anywhere. I don't even exist as far as anyone else be concerned. You understand that boy? You understand?"

I nodded as best I could, staring at the floor, his arm weighing heavy upon me and his stale breath permeating the pores of my face.

"Now you rest, boy," said Zachariah, standing. He nudged me with his monstrously thick leg and I couldn't help but roll onto my side. He fetched a heavy blanket from a pile in the corner by the trapdoor and draped it across me. I do believe it was as kind an act as he had performed since I had met him.

And I closed my eyes to all this, just closed my eyes and slept the ragged sleep of the torn and frayed. Time turned and my heart beat. The despair of the day would not abate and my clothes were as lifeless upon me as if they were the garb of a scarecrow. A sense of hopelessness overwhelmed me as much in sleep as when I was awake.

I didn't dream, though I know not for how long I slept. It was a flat, black sleep that restored neither energy nor perspective, the kind of sleep that just leaves you restless.

I had not even the pleasure of drifting back into wakefulness, for it was Zachariah Leonard who stole that small joy. He shook me alive roughly with a cold, hard hand. I looked up at that gruesome face and he had a finger to his lips. His eyes glared at me from beneath his grimy brow as he

64

slowly moved backwards to the corner by the door, still squatting; a silent and deadly Groucho Marx.

Still prone on the floor, I stared after him. His movement had been stealthy and silent and he merged into the shadows so easily I could barely make him out. And then the wooden door of the shack was rattled by a knock. I was losing control of my breathing as I lay staring towards the door, propped up on my elbows now, my eyes flicking to the outline of Zachariah Leonard perched in the corner like some stone creature from a gothic cathedral, all ready to pounce.

Again there came a knock on the door, harder this time.

I got up as slowly and as quietly as I could. My eyes bored into the darkness, straining to get an indication from Zachariah as to what I should do. As I stepped forward, I knew that only by opening the door would this tortuous moment end. For good or for ill, I pulled it open, careful not to bang it into Zachariah who hid silently behind it.

And there stood Penny Shoraton, framed in the doorway like the full length portrait of a beautiful princess on a castle wall. The evening sun was slipping into the marshland and a purple orange sky bled from the horizon.

I could sense Zachariah tensing. The delicacy of Penny just inches from the barbarity of Zachariah was such a juxtaposition as should never rightfully occur. And just a rickety wooden door between them.

"Hello, Simon," said Penny in the kindest of voices. "Are you ok? I was worried about you."

She was truly enchanting.

I was willing myself to gaze straight at her, though my whole being was drawn to the secreted Zachariah.

"I'm alright, thank you, just tired that's all."

She held out her hand.

"Come with me," she beckoned. "It won't help you to stay in here on your own all the time. "

I heard a small noise as of something breaking from behind the door. It seemed Penny had heard nothing, for there was no reaction on her part. Perhaps it was just the sound of Zachariah's grin cracking his face. I stepped out of the shack and followed Penny as the door closed silently behind me. I did not take her hand for there are some things that you just shouldn't touch. I swear the whole shack shook as we left.

We walked across the edge of the marshes and then up the hill to the village green. In the time it took us, the sun went down and the moon came up. There were a couple of people standing on the green talking whilst I could see several others just ambling along aimlessly. An elderly man was leaning on the wall outside St Mary's Church, staring into the grave yard. White stars spattered the early night sky and I began to feel some sense of safety as I became a part of this quaint English scene.

Ah the perfect blackness of an English country sky is surely the blackboard upon which the angels sketch their heavens.

"Would you like me to introduce you to anybody?" asked Penny, touching my arm gently. "They are all very nice people."

"It's ok. I don't feel all that sociable. Sorry, this is all a bit weird for me at the moment."

"I'm sure it is, Simon. I'm sure it is. You will get through it though, I promise you. You always have done."

Penny Shoraton truly had me hooked, I don't mind admitting.

"Let's have a drink," she said.

I looked down, scratched my neck and followed her into the King's Head. All that was missing was the collar and the lead.

Zachariah Leonard suddenly seemed a million miles away.

The pub was more crowded than the last time I had been in. There was an altogether busier feeling about the place. There was music, of a sort, being played by a lady over on the far side of the bar. She had a guitar propped on her lap. On it were scrawled the words 'This Guitar Kills Psychiatrists'. Though she plucked the strings for all to hear, she sang only to herself. I saw her lips moving and I saw the tears as they eased from her startled eyes. She could have been a hundred years

66

old. Her hair was all yellow and grey and the bones of her face told of a former beauty. Perhaps that was why she was crying.

"One ale for my friend here and a water for me please, darling," said Penny to the young barmaid.

"Will that be a small ale or a large ale, Miss?"

"Oh definitely a large one I think. He is definitely a man who needs a drink right now, aren't you Simon?"

I sighed and gave her my best sheepish look. She smiled, winked at the barmaid and led me over to a table by the fire that burned all red and yellow in the iron hearth.

Penny sipped her water. I gulped my ale. And in that moment was encapsulated the very difference between us.

"Take your time," she said. "There's no rush."

Her voice had an accent I couldn't quite place. I could have listened to it for eternity, though it did little to improve the taste of the ale. I could hear other voices murmuring in other parts of the pub. The lonely woman played on and time, such as it was, passed.

"This is hard for you, Simon, isn't?" asked Penny, breaking the silence that had swelled between us.

I nodded. I found it so hard to talk to her. She must have thought me very ignorant. I drank some more of the ale as she stared at my tankard. She seemed pleased I was getting through it. Even I wasn't as uncouth as to allow a lady to buy me a drink and then not finish it.

"We can help you, you know, Simon – Weepy and Nardy and myself. Even the boy, Adam, has his uses. The serving girl here is nice too. Her name is Carrie."

I still could not relate Penny and Carrie to the others - Weepy and Nardy, Zachariah Leonard - even the boy who clearly hated me. I never wanted to see them again, yet I wanted Penny Shoraton to be with me always. Everyone was trying to help me, it seemed, but help me to do what? To get back home? My recollection of life before waking in the village lock-up was becoming frighteningly vague. It was as if all this were real now and my former life but a dream. In just a few days, years of experiences and memories had shattered into disparate shards that now lay abandoned across the landscape of my mind.

"I don't know how I got here. I don't know what I'm supposed to do here and I don't know how to get home. I don't know who I can trust and I don't know who I should fear." I blurted this out, not in a loud fashion, but merely stating it as undeniable fact. Then I downed the remainder of my ale.

Penny considered what I had just said.

"Do you trust me, Simon?"

I had to say yes.

"Thank you," she said. "That means a lot to me."

"So, do you have any answers to any of my questions?" I asked. Then I sighed. A sigh can hold back a tear, but not forever.

Penny leaned forward and covered my hands with her own. The touch of her fingers upon my skin almost broke me in half. I had never experienced such a sensation of longing.

Was I ashamed? Not at all. In love? Possibly.

"Simon," she began, "I think it might be a little early to answer any of your questions. You have only just arrived, after all. But you need to know that you can trust me and that I will do all I can to help you understand what is happening to you. I can tell you that you have no enemies here. Strange as it may seem, everybody is here to help you - everybody."

The name of Zachariah Leonard was upon my lips. Was he too here to help me in the same way as Penny and the others? I doubted it. And just as the man himself had slunk into the shadows, so his name withdrew once more into the recesses of my mind.

The once beautiful lady at the bar had replaced her mournful song with a wailing that was drawing looks from all corners. Her guitar lay at her feet. Her hands were on top of her head, wrapped in her tangled hair as if she were either trying to tear it out or to keep it from leaving her.

Penny rose from her chair and walked over to Carrie, who then escorted the former beauty from the pub via the back door. It was time for her to go it appeared. The large measure of ale I had consumed seemed to be slowing everything down for a moment. The smoke in the pub from the various pipes and the dwindling fire in the hearth were gathering around me. I wondered if I would be able to stand, let alone walk. As it was, Penny Shoraton returned to help me up from the wooden chair and led me outside onto the village green.

"I will walk with you back to your shack," said Penny, supporting my arm.

She was so close to me. I could smell her purity and her naturalness for they were fragrances so tangible, so real I felt I could reach out and touch them. Was this love or was this madness? I have since come to learn that there is little difference between these two most life threatening of conditions. As we walked slowly in the black night, I swear I could see a glow around her.

When we reached the shack, she bade me goodnight and drifted off towards the harbour.

I pushed open the wooden door and stood there waiting for Zachariah for I firmly believed he had not moved from his hiding place and that he would swiftly be upon me.

A rumbling sound came from the far corner. I could see nothing through the gloom. I closed the door behind me and stood there trying to make out what was happening. And then I smiled with both relief and not a little amusement. The sound was that of a man snoring, the sound of a man in a very deep sleep indeed.

As I approached, I saw Zachariah curled up on the floor. He suddenly looked so vulnerable, a shadow of his waking self. He was a sleeping bear of a man but just as vulnerable to sleep as the rest of us. Whether he dreamed, I knew not. I somehow doubted it. I deemed it more possible that in his sleep, he created my nightmares - and perhaps yours too.

So I lay down in my own dank corner and brought my knees to my chest, wrapping my arms about them both for warmth and security. And with Penny Shoraton in my heart and Zachariah Leonard on my mind, I let the ale do its work.

Angel and Devil.

Beauty and Beast.

If only it were that simple…

7. Man of The Match And King Of The World

There are times in Tollesbury when a mist comes up from the marshes and from the fields. It seems unconnected to any weather system. Be it the heat of the summer or the bitter chill of winter, lawless bands of cold fog will consume the tracts of marshland just as a throbbing guilt will devour the heart of a sinful man. But you do not stop there, oh clouds of hell; you enter my brain, smothering my thoughts and clothing my fragile mind in the raiment of the utterly confused. And I break out, yearning and gasping, into the clarity of the day, believing in my heart that the fog is there for me and me alone.

I cannot recall a time when I ever felt totally in control. Confidence eluded me as I had grown and my understanding of the world had fractured more with each encounter. Nothing was simple except my innate need to comprehend all that happened to me in every waking moment. It might be easy for you but, for those such as I, it is a torture that the word 'illness' can never fully communicate. To understand the look, the inflection, the intention or the meaning of my fellow human being had always been a task akin to climbing the tallest of mountains for poor me.

Poor, poor, pitiful me.

Poor, poor, pitiful me.

Julia and I had met in 1980. I had been drunk in a pub in Chelmsford and she had sobered me up. She had looked upon me as a challenge and began by throwing away my Jack Kerouac books. I believe she saw the future, even then. She kissed me and told me she loved me. I wish I could tell you more about our courtship (as she liked to call it) but I cannot. I remember our early relationship as I do snippets from a really bad sitcom. I was maddeningly unfunny and the only laughter there was came in cans. Our wedding I recall vaguely as being a tawdry affair. I had never been taught how to love. I hadn't known where to start.

The notion of having children had never entered my mind. So self absorbed was I as I grew into adulthood, the idea of settling down in any way had been anathema to me. Jack Kerouac had consumed me in my early twenties and it wasn't long before I threw myself into a life of cheap wine, cigarettes and a broken notion of my place in society, or lack of it perhaps. I adopted the persona of the maligned fool, the misunderstood genius, the perennial recalcitrant. Jack Kerouac, you see, had the eyes of an angel and the spirit of the devil. He mesmerised me and tantalised me, toyed with my mind and led me down paths no young man such as I should have trodden. He was me and I was he. God, I loved that man and in many ways still do. The shimmering vision of a man who is one too many mornings and a thousand miles behind will always be an intoxicating hero to me.

And I was given a little baby boy for my gargantuan, inconsequential, metaphysical struggles. A little baby boy.

My son was born in 1982. He was christened Robin, but I never liked that. It was Julia's choice. All that came to mind for me was the cheesy grin of Robin Gibb or the moronic despair of Batman's sidekick, the Boy Wonder. From the day he was born, I called my boy Robbie.

The year Robbie was born, Graham Gooch took a team of cricketers to South Africa, a country that had been banned from competing in international sport since the end of the sixties because of apartheid. Italy beat West Germany 3-1 to win the World Cup for the third time. The Clash released Combat Rock. John Lennon had been dead for two years and Paul McCartney went to number one with Ebony and Ivory. I hated him then more than ever, or so I thought; the Frog Chorus or whatever it was called was still to come. Oh, and the Falklands War happened. Margaret Thatcher was re-elected the following year on the back of it and England, my England, changed forever. I was twenty-four years old.

Robbie is now twenty five or twenty six. To my shame, I cannot be exact. When he was small, I could never bear to go to that hospital to visit him. My reluctance to see my own son engendered a murderous hatred in Julia and she conveyed her feelings to me with charming alacrity; in essence, she was thoroughly disgusted. I could never make her understand how I felt about Robbie. It all hurt too much. Jack Kerouac hadn't prepared me for having a child with a severe disability, neither had the Beatles or The Clash. Thus my close encounter with the real world merely led me back to the fantasy realm of my mind.

Julia would not let Robbie out of her sight when he was first born. She would barely leave the house except for essentials. Whilst she sat and stared at him as he lay sleeping, I would get the bus from Tiptree to The Recreation Ground in Tollesbury and watch the village cricket team. I would take with me a few cans of cider, a pencil and a pad of paper, always glad to be away from the claustrophobic atmosphere of the house, unaware, so desperately unaware of just how much darkness I myself contributed to that all pervasive gloom.

Whenever I went to The Recreation Ground to watch the cricket, my breathing always slowed. I would greet the scene before me with a deep sigh and lie down at the edge of the chalk boundary. The Tollesbury team was made up of a wonderful mixture of serious children, local drunks and eccentric old men - the first group becoming the second and the second becoming the third as the years drifted by. The games always meandered on through the morning, each game ending in the same result - a communal visit to The King's Head.

I was, and perhaps always will be, a character on the nether regions of exactly where everybody else is at. Were I to be absent, I would not be missed. Present, I am acknowledged and no more. Such is my fate.

Watching cricket, for me, is like wandering around a museum. You are in turns confused, delighted, moved and at peace. Just as there is no other place on earth like Tollesbury, so there is no other sport that matches the oh so English game of cricket. As Bob Dylan (a constant reference point of mine for all truth in this world!) once said, "do not criticize what you don't understand."

Cricket, boring? I smile as you judge and weep as you leave.

And I would use my pencil and pad to keep score, marking off every single run and every dot ball, keeping a perfect record of the game. I say 'perfect', but the names of all the players were merely from my imagination. As long as there were eleven on each side, I didn't care – at least not until the end. For then, having emptied my last can of cider of its final golden drops, I would cross out the names of the batsman that had scored the most runs and the bowler who had taken the most wickets. And in their stead, I would write in my laboured scrawl the name 'Robbie Anthony'.

As my little boy lay back at home, his mum protecting him from all the ills that may further befall him, he would be totally unaware that his drunken dad had once more pronounced him Man of the Match and King of the World, for yet another week. In my ever erratic mind, I was the proudest father on this earth. In reality, I was barely able to look at my own son without breaking in two.

It's all about schisms. There are times when we splinter and there are times when we are whole. Though I have found the more I break, the less whole I am able to become. You can come back, but you can't come back all the way it seems. Life has been chipping away at me for many years, sculpting me roughly into a man whom at times I hardly recognise; a man whom you will ever pass by. I try to kill myself and I end up in more of a mess than ever I was before. Sitting in my nowhere land, making all my nowhere plans for nobody.

"You keep talking to yourself, boy you will be here for a long old time."

Zachariah Leonard had risen. For the first time since I had met him, his stench really hit me. Sweat oozed from his pores as he moved to the door. He hauled the smell of death behind him as if it were in a laden sack. I was beginning to notice these things about him now, my senses becoming ever more keen. For I knew then, as he peered out of the doorway, that this was about more than mere survival.

Looking back at me, Zachariah curled a gnarled finger in my direction and bade me join him. As I crept towards him and stood by his side, I saw immediately what had moved him to alert me. The door to the shack was ever so slightly open and through the crack I could see a dishevelled looking figure asleep in a wooden chair.

"You know what this means, boy?" whispered Zachariah, his very essence blazing into my eyes.

I shook my head, afraid to speak, afraid to move; just plain afraid.

"They have you on The Watch."

"The Watch?"

He nodded gravely, breathing noisily through his nose, primitively exhaling the stale air from his lungs as if he were no more human than a factory chimney.

"They have no trust for you. It is that girl. She has gone back to them and told them of your thoughts. That is what she does. She is a dog, boy, nothing more than a dog that comes whenever Weepy and Nardy call her. She disgusts me and she would disgust you if you had any wits about you. Now they have you on The Watch, your time here will be never ending. You have to prove to them that you can be trusted yet you will never get the chance. Is that what you want, boy? Does that please you? All for a stupid, treacherous girl?"

There was nothing I could say.

"It is time for us to leave," he continued, suppressing an urgency in his voice that seeped out through his wide and staring eyes. "Mark my words, boy, that dolt sleeping on that chair has been there all night. This is what they do. This is what it has come to. When they are desperate, this is what they do. It is for their own protection and no more. They don't all sleep though. We have been lucky. This is our moment. If we don't leave this instant, it will be too late."

For this rock of a man to be so concerned was sufficient for me to act swiftly upon his words. My heart thudded and my thoughts raced like a video on fast forward. I was getting the gist of what he was saying but the details evaded me. Before I could take stock of what was happening, Zachariah had dragged my by the arm and we were wading knee deep through the Tollesbury marshes.

I knew not quite from what I was running and I knew even less about where I was heading. I would like to say these feelings were particular to the situation in which I then found myself but I cannot; for they could have applied to me at any time of my life from early childhood until the present day. Such has been my wayward existence, forever hiding and never in control of anything, not even of my own visions.

Tension was encroaching upon my world with every sodden step I took. It was as if my sloshing feet were pushing the buttons of some fairground attraction for as I forged on, so it seemed all of Tollesbury awoke. Alarmed voices spattered the morning air. Lit torches brought soft light to the fog but the heavy mist dispersed the lights with cool derision. I could just about see Zachariah as he ploughed on ahead with the strength of ten men. I dared not look behind, though in truth I would have barely been able to see a thing, such was the density of the mist that now engulfed all.

"Come on, boy," shouted Zachariah. His voice was ghostly and ominous.

The ground firmed up and I realised we had left the marshes behind us. I guessed we were heading in the direction of Tolleshunt D'arcy for any other path would have led us into the depths of the murky Blackwater. I had emerged from those depths once but did not relish taking that chance again.

We hurtled across the fields, hunted by who knows how many. We were at the edges of the fog now and each time I stole a glance behind me so there were more and more lights in the grey green air. A wailing sound grew ever closer, piercing the fog, startling the birds and striking fear into me. I had heard it in some other time but could not place it. I paid little heed to my erratic breathing and less to the sharp ache in my chest. I knew my heart was breaking but it made no difference. Zachariah urged me on as if I were some old greyhound on whom he had foolishly laid his life's savings. I craved that final bend and that ever lengthening home straight like I had craved nothing before.

As I was about to implode, I was grabbed by Zachariah's huge hands. He had me by the shoulders, stopping me just where I stood. It was like hitting a wall. He then took his right hand and placed it flat across my mouth. I recall to this day that taste of death as I inhaled his odour. At times, I lie awake and that same smell returns. On such occasions, I can do nothing but pace the floor until a less ungodly air fills my lungs.

After some moments my captor removed his hand and dragged me stumbling down some uneven stone steps. The mist was clearing yet a darkness prevailed. I felt cold water dripping upon my head and the smell of salt permeated the air. We were underground.

At last, Zachariah bade me stop and I sank to my knees. I was shattered in every conceivable way, within and without. Silence abounded. I hardly noticed the moment when a light crept up the wall, a light dancing from an oil lamp. When I looked up from the stony floor I saw I was in a small cavern, no bigger than ten or so square feet. I may as well have been in the belly of some vile creature.

"Sit boy. Sit and rest. They won't find us here."

Zachariah Leonard lit his pipe and smoked.

And me, well I just wept. I wept for my son, Robbie, and for hope and for dreams. I wept for John Lennon and for Joe Strummer. I wept for Rick Danko and for the boy I once was. But most of all I wept for Robbie.

Yes, I don't mind telling you, I cried until I could cry no more. And then, do you know what I did? I smiled, grinned almost. I stood up, walked over to where Zachariah sat in some sort of maudlin reverie and I deftly snatched the pipe from out of his hand. Just like that.

He did not move other than to raise his eyes to me, eyes that were so red with his own tears they could have been bleeding. The tears seemed to have washed some of the grime from his face. There was a difference in the way he held himself, a complete change in his countenance. But his stench was worse than ever. It was then that I realised why that sickening smell seemed so intense. For it rose from my own body, not Zachariah's. Interesting, I thought.

I swept a hand through my lank hair and took a puff on the pipe.

"You don't scare me," I said, slowly, choosing my words with reverence.

He continued to gaze at me with those bloodshot eyes of his.

"I should hope not," he said, eventually. "For you and I are more alike than you know."

The thought appalled me but I knew he spoke the truth. I sat down beside him and drew him to me, holding him whilst he shook. I brushed the hair from his ragged face and rocked him to sleep. I did not know whether it was day or night and, to be honest, I didn't care.

Zachariah Leonard was in my arms.

Robbie was in my burgeoning heart.

And I was about to be reborn from the deathly womb of this fetid land.

8. It Has Begun

Time passed.

Blood flowed through my veins and my mind throbbed as if it had taken the place of my heart. Blackness was all about me and the shallow breathing of the fading Zachariah Leonard was the only indication that he was there at all. Though I could barely see him through the density of the gloom, I had a sense that something about him was diminishing - be it his overpowering presence or that indefinable potential for hostility that ever held me at bay.

Well, I'm not a fan of the dark so you can imagine how I felt stuck in that small cavern cold drops of water spattering around me. The only other discernible sounds were the exhalations of two weary men lost in life. Oh to be so adrift, so far from the shores of normality, so alien a creature in so persecutory a world; well such was my fate. To recognise oneself to be so repugnant to society is an acknowledgement that can shatter your very soul. We don't often get the chance to start again.

So where was I to go from here? Zachariah was fading before my eyes, yet I knew that he was more a part of me then than ever he had been before. Strength brewed within me, bubbling and fermenting. My own frailty ebbed. Clarity clattered into my thoughts and brought about a satori, an enlightenment, if you will.

It was time to make a difference.

I had to begin at the beginning.

Instantly, I knew that I had to find some children. Sometimes you just know these things. Don't make me explain it.

I looked at Zachariah, slumped as he was against the wall, and decided to leave him there. I would come back for him, of course, in due time. But for now, I had to concentrate solely on myself. This predicament I was in was mine alone to solve. As I crawled out into the daylight, the sun flooded into my soul. I felt inebriated, drunk on nature and willing to receive all that came into my presence. But I absolutely had to find some children. I was in that groove.

But isn't that just the way? You clamber out of a hole in the ground all set to look for a child and the first thing you come across is an old woman patting a donkey. It's happened to me more times than I can remember.

"Hello, dear," said the old woman. "Would you like to pat my donkey?"

I smiled and patted her donkey. The only advice I would ever dare to give anybody is that if you come across an old woman and she asks you to pat her donkey, just go ahead and pat it. What's the sense in not doing it?

I was here to learn and learn I would. I was blazing inside, just ready to go, go, go. Alive, alive, alive. Be-bop-a-lu-la. Woo hoo! Don't stop me now! The music was with me and there was not a Beatle in sight. I was the drums and I was the bass. I was Levon Helm and Rick Danko, Charlie Watts and Bill Wyman, The Mighty Max Weinberg and Garry W Tallent. You don't need any more than that. Not when your mind is falling apart. Come on!

The sun shone high and the sky was blue, blue, blue. Where this newfound energy within me had come from, I knew not. The only thing that made sense was to keep on keeping on until somebody stopped me. Were I not fifty years old, I'm sure I would have forsaken my lumbering gait for a sprightly skip.

I wandered down to the field where they had held Tollesfest in 2005. Ah, Tollesfest. It had been a mad mini-bus ride from The King's Head, bales of hay, rock and roll, children hurtling around, drunkenness, drunkenness and the stars in the night sky lighting up the way back home. It was olden times and it was pure and it was absolutely beyond the law. May every town and every village have a Tollesfest. And may it be the benchmark for what is right in this world. Amen.

And in that field where once I had seen ramshackle bands and drunks and burgers strewn like fallen heroes, there now was a sight which I must describe for you. A barn strode the horizon, all wooden planks and age and sprouting hay as if it were hair. It was surely creaking a greeting as I approached it. How long it had stood there, I knew not, but there was one thing I felt to my bones - I was meant to be there and something momentous did portend. Never before had I felt so drawn.

As a friend of mine once said, "you can lead a lunatic to the clinic but you can't make him take his medication." He had been wrong, but then haven't we all at some time or another?

Well, well, well.

So I stood there, the barn some twenty yards from me. As I stared at it, I felt as though everything behind me had been painted out of the picture. There was just me, the Tollesfest field and this barn. The sky dangled above me, just the sparse clouds keeping it from crashing right down and splintering across this land. The air was so clear and every line beautifully crafted. And the one smell that pervaded all was that of vitality. You couldn't bottle it, you couldn't wipe it off your brow. For the smell that filled my very being was that of the four elements of our universe sweating, oozing from every atom and every molecule. Frame that and hang it on your wall.

I waited. But I didn't have to wait for too long.

A man approached me. He wore a long coat that came down to the tattered material that covered his feet. His head was bare save for a few wisps of grey and his whole face was dominated by veined, ruddy cheeks. A huge white moustache sprang from below his nose and reached down almost to his hefty jowls. Though his head was bowed as he came towards me, I somehow sensed he was smiling. And when he was but an arm's length from me, he lifted his head and looked into my eyes. I was right. What a smile!

"Hello, lad," he said, taking my arm. "We've been waiting for you."

"Who are you?" I asked, as he led me on.

"I am The Walrus," he replied. He bade me wait as he retrieved a wooden rocking chair from the barn. I sat upon it and rocked slowly, back and forth. Or maybe I was still and it was the sky and the earth that were rocking.

The Walrus winked at me and headed back to the barn.

"Come on children!" he shouted, pulling open two large wooden doors. "The time has come!"

And as The Walrus spoke, nine children sprung out into view. They were grubby and ragged and blinking in the daylight. I knew not for how long they had been awaiting my arrival. It all seemed so surreal even then. Oh but I did not know what was to come. I had no idea how surreal it would all get. The children were each carrying a square bale of hay as they trotted out and lined up in front of me. They placed their bale upon the ground before them and awaited further instruction from their leader. The Walrus exuded such pride and the children literally shook with anticipation.

And my life was at a standstill just exactly when it needed to be so.

There they were, nine children standing behind nine bales of hay, all in a line before me, the old barn in the background. All was still as the heavens took a photograph.

"Being for the benefit of Mr Keats, there will be a show tonight! Of Beauty and Truth and Truth and Beauty!" proclaimed The Walrus. "Well, off you go children!"

The first child in the line picked up his bale of hay and stepped a couple of paces towards me. This was truly his big moment. It was all their big moment. I stopped rocking, comforting though it was, and leaned forward, bewitched.

"My name is John," said the boy. "And I have a tale for you."

The other children sat down, cross-legged and looked at me. I had eyes only for John.

"There once was a poor farmer who lived alone since the death of his wife and child. He had just one field in which he grew carrots and onions and potatoes. He tilled the land and toiled from dawn until nightfall growing his own food from the soil. And each evening he would sleep upon his straw bed pleading for the dark night to take him in peace to the loved ones he had lost so long ago. He refused to join them of his own free will for his love of life far outweighed his fear of death. Though life be hard, it be life after all.

81

One night as the poor farmer was about to eat his soup, a soup made from the carrots, onions and potatoes of the field, the old wooden door of his home was beaten asunder, splintering before him. He shook not at all though his heart throbbed within him. For what is a door but a barrier to experience?

A starving stranger stood quaking in the doorway, ragged and reeking. The stranger lunged forward and grabbed the poor farmer's bowl of soup, snatching it from him in an instant, drinking it down like an animal, leaving the poor farmer hungry for the night. And the stranger did leave.

As the years passed so the stranger fell upon good fortune. He grew rich and wealthy and decided one day to visit the poor farmer whom he had been told was close to death. When he arrived, the poor farmer beckoned him to come close as he was too frail to stand. He then said that all he required of him was that he sit down and share some of his home grown soup; for when you are alone, to share a meal with somebody is a true pleasure of life.

'But you must forgive me!' pleaded the stranger.

'I forgive everybody everything,' replied the poor farmer, 'And for all those that take advantage of me, there will be one such as you who may learn the strength of forgiveness and will then go out into this rotten land and do as I do.'

'But what of those who will not do as you do, who will use the kindness of others to their own end and will go to their grave rich and obese whilst others do starve?'

'Pity them for they will have lived their lives merely upon the surface of experience. They will have tasted but not indulged, lusted but never loved. Pity them just for a moment though for pity can be in itself akin to arrogance. And arrogance is the final refuge of the truly troubled of heart.'

And the poor farmer did then pass up into heaven.

And what of the stranger. Well he went off that day and changed the world."

The little boy, John, took a deep breath when he finished. He then turned over his bale of hay and stood upon it, his arms by his side. And emblazoned upon the front of the bale was the letter 'F'. His mouth was open as if he was still speaking and his eyes were turned to the Tollesbury sky.

Before I could say anything, The Walrus called out from the side:

"F - Forgive everybody everything."

And all the children clapped. Except John, who remained steadfast and unmoving atop his bale.

And so it had begun.

The next child, a girl, stood up behind her bale of hay. She had big blonde pig tails, the ends of which danced upon her narrow shoulders. When she spoke, I was heartbroken by how few teeth she had in her mouth. All I could think was that when asleep she must look beautiful.

"My name is Louise," she said. "And I have a poem for you."

She licked her lips, smiled, looked over at the other children and winked slyly. And then, in the most sultry of voices, surely not that of a child, she recited her poem. What I write is word for word, for that poem keeps me, inspires me even to this day.

"From the day my wet body
flopped onto this earth,
I've tried to discover
what all this is worth;

the struggling and hiding,
the shouting and crying,
the creeping and running,
the need to keep trying.

So one day I fell
to the floor in distress,
to think of a way
to get out of this mess.

I closed my sore eyes
and hugged myself tight,

83

'til truth became me
and I became light.

There was my answer!!
so joyful and free!!
Beauty itself
surrounding poor me!

For every being,
from here to the moon,
lend me your ears
(I'll give them back soon!)

In truth the same fields
I had known all my days,
now are quite wondrous
the wheat and the maize.

I no longer see
with pretty girl eyes,
for my heart now has vision;
a mighty surprise!

I see glory in dirt
and wonder in rain,
magnificent rivers
where ditches have lain.

Fallen down ruins
are history bare;
a small meal for one
Is for two now to share.

The sky is not blue,
it's purple and green;
the sea is a creature,
dark and serene.

The plants are alive,
church bells do sing;
love is amongst us -
ring a ding ding!

So my fine stranger
do one thing for me -
recognise beauty
wherever it be"

As she finished, she grinned such a wide grin I thought it would break right through the sides of her face. She overturned her bale to present the letter 'R', before hopping upon it. She then performed an elegant curtsey and breathed deep. The little 'F' boy, John, tapped her on the shoulder and whispered something into her ear. She blushed a little before looking straight at me beneath heavy lids.

"R - Recognise beauty wherever it be!" announced The Walrus.

A round of applause burst from the remaining children.

Clouds spread in the sky. And my fragile mind overflowed with wonder.

"Thank you, children," said The Walrus, striding towards me. "You may go inside now, into the barn, come now. For I fear a storm be a-brewing." He clapped his hands and the children hopped and skipped into the shelter that awaited them. But John and Louise remained on top of their bales of hay as if they were sculptures.

The Walrus slapped me roughly on the shoulder and led me into the barn. I looked behind at John and Louise as they awaited the impending downpour, standing still upon their respective bales of hay. And I saw them hold hands as the first cold drops of summer rain began to fall.

9. Raggedy Fury

We sat around a long, gnarled wooden table constructed from battered planks that had been stripped from the trees of the English earth, such swirls and patterns as you never before saw in your natural life. I was at one end, The Walrus at the other. The seven children sat either side, heads down and hands clasped all ready to pray.

Outside, the skies raged on in all their raggedy fury and I could not help but think of the two children out there alone. Perhaps they had vanished as soon as we had all entered this hovel, just slipped into the soil, ready only to bloom again should some other lost and burned out wanderer emerge from a hole in the ground and come upon them.

The smell of charred potatoes hovered in the air and intensified as a boy emerged from the shadows into which I gazed so mournfully. He was carrying a large wooden bowl that had the same effect on the other children as would the most whizz bang of fireworks. The Walrus quelled the excited murmur by clearing his throat as the bowl was placed in the middle of the table.

"Now children. We have a guest," he said, the eyes of the children falling back to their clenched palms.

Such solemnity. Charred potatoes. Gone are those days. We are in Happy Meal times or so it seems. But days are still days and nights are still nights.

The sun and the moon still stare down upon this hallowed and broken earth, still oversee my magical Tollesbury times. They are the great constants, the wonderful keystones of the cathedral that houses our lives. But it is in minds such as mine that break, that fold in upon themselves, that drip, drip with each woeful and inexplicable experience, that those constants - the sun and the moon - stand out as beacons of hope.

"Our guest has fallen upon us this day and for that we should give thanks," said The Walrus.

The children turned my way and grinned, all dirt and sparkle and red cheeks and natural brown dishevelled cool. Each one winked at me in turn and gave me a thumbs up. It rippled round the long table like some whooping jazz wave, black and white and wailing. And when the last child winked and thumbed (even The Walrus had joined in!) I held out my hands in supplication and said the words those children had so longed to hear.

"Let's eat!"

And, as you can imagine, they all dived in. I know I have said the fare before us smelled like charred potatoes, but it tasted like nothing I had ever tasted before. The mouthfuls of food almost became a part of me the moment they entered my mouth, dashing and splitting to all organs, supplementing and reinforcing, giving me just what I needed, rounding me off so to speak. It was the finest meal I ever ate, or indeed ever will eat; for it was just what was necessary and it was eaten in the company of the kings of this earth. For to see a child hungry transform into a child full and smiling is to see the elevation from poor man to king. No crowns, no; but majesty? Oh yeah, man.

When the plates were emptied and the children quietened, the same boy that had brought out that wonderful meal returned to clear the table. I couldn't make him out too well but there was something about him, an aura of some kind that caused my heart to beat that bit faster. He was heavily built and clumsy in his movements, his head remaining bowed as he worked, his chin ever upon his chest. I could not see his face and I didn't even know if he was aware of my presence, so keen was he upon his task. But I sensed an anger from him, a throbbing of soul and spirit that pounded in my direction, beating like the wings of a sullen bird trapped within a cage. I looked away for a moment to see what the weather was doing and by the time I had looked back he was gone.

"Children," said The Walrus. "The skies are clear and our stomachs are full. We must get back to our task!"

The children yelled hooray and stood up at once, forming two separate lines by the door from whence we had come, The

Walrus taking the front - the conjoined spearhead of two arrows. It was then that I noticed the serving boy sitting on the floor in the corner. He was scraping the leftover potatoes out of the big bowl with a crude wooden spoon. He lurked there in the shadows, both of this hovel and in the dark and sombre outpourings of my life.

The Walrus began to weave back and forth, swaying on his bandy legs, feet absolutely still, but rolling his body, writhing like a giant John Lee Hooker crawling king snake. And as he did so, the children behind him in their two rows clapped out a beat, swaying too in unison, a great slap beat clap beat blues beat, slow and as serious as you like. Though the clapping remained cool and rhythmic, the power with which one hand hit the other began to increase, clap, snap, clap, oh yeah, clap, snap clap, oh yeah, CLAP, SNAP, CLAP and it moved and it grooved like some primeval roaring rattle of a train, slow and angry and full of beat up hopes and woes just a-rolling out that shambling station - CLAP, SNAP, CLAP and a CLAP, SNAP, CLAP, moving and a grooving into the moaning mixed-up world…

And The Walrus led them out into the sweating rainbow green fields growling loud from deep within the great gravel pit of his belly, roaring to the sweet skies of all our heavens wherever they may be…

CLAP, SNAP, CLAP
Oh yeah…
"When you got nothing
You got nothing to lose
DAMN BANG
When you got nothing
You got nothing to lose
DAMN BANG
But you always got something
'Cause you never can lose the blues
OOOOOOOOOOOOOOOOOHHHHHEEEEEE…….
CLAP, SNAP, CLAP
Oh yeah…

So you get yourself something
And it's yours all yours
DAMN BANG
So you get yourself something
And it's yours all yours
DAMN BANG
Lock it deep inside you and
Barricade your doors
NANA-NA-NANA-NA-NANA-NA NAAAA!
So what do you do with your
New possession?
DAMN BANG
What do you do with your
New possession?
DAMN BANG
Just add it to the bottom
Of your full confession
OOOOOOOOOOOOOOOOOOOHHHHHHHHHHHHH
HH YAAAAAAAAAAAA!
You are the servant and
Mother Nature is your Queen
DAMN BANG
You are the servant and
Mother Nature is your Queen
DAMN BANG
She's more beautiful than
Anything you ever seen
OOOOH YEAH YEAH YEAH!!!!
A rolling stone
Boys it don't gather no moss
DAMN BANG
A rolling stone
Boys it don't gather no moss
DAMN BANG
You gotta understand the nature
Understand the nature of loss.
BANG BANG
DAMN BANG

And there we were, standing before the two children on their bales of hay, both dry as plaster and steady as the beat that had just cracked off across the fields.

The Walrus was bent down now, trying to retrieve his breath. But there are some things that once you get out, you can't get back and don't get back for it should be shared with the world. The two children were poised atop bales F and R and The Walrus stood behind the next bale. He turned it over to present a U.

"U," he said, proudly. "Understand the nature of loss."

He didn't stand upon the bale of hay as the two children had, but walked slowly to where I stood, waving one of the other children to stand upon it instead. He sat down, cross-legged upon the sodden ground and I did the same.

"It's just wet grass," he whispered to me. "It's just life. How fine is that?"

I looked briefly over at him. No words were necessary.

That blues had just belted me in the gut just as it should. The Walrus had known nothing of my losses, be it my mother and father, my wife, my son, my chance of a rational life - yet he had given me of himself, blasted out from deep within him some ancient scream of understanding that we were both men here together trying to work out what the hell was going on in the fundamentals of this mad, mad, mad world. It must be said though, that he seemed a little further down the road of understanding than I. For he was conducting this show; I was merely the non-paying audience of one.

So there in front of me were the letters 'F-R-U' scrawled in red paint, or maybe blood for all I knew, on three bales of hay. The Walrus breathed heavily beside me. It was all he could do to point at the pale young boy who eyed him quizzically from behind the fourth bale of hay. The Walrus nodded as vigorously as he could and then coughed some more. The young boy politely waited for the air to clear and for The Walrus to be breathing a little easier before starting his

poem - a poem he recited with such gentleness, I ended up
kneeling before him staring into his big brown eyes.

"There is a witch
who lives in the woods
she lives there alone in the dark.
Nobody's seen her,
nobody's heard her,
except once by the edge of the park.

Somebody said
she was holding a bag
whistling a strange little tune;
that when she was seen
she returned to the trees
like a shadow kissing the moon.

There was talk in the fields
about the witch in the woods,
but go see her? No one would dare.
So I thought to myself
I'd sneak out one night
to see what I could find there.

I slipped from my straw,
jumped over the gate,
a candle alight in my hand.
I went to the woods
at the edge of the park
as the moon fell down on this land.

I walked through the trees,
so scared and alone,
though with hope in the back of my mind.
As I saw a small light
and smoke rising high
I wondered what I would find.

I walked up to a door
but before I could knock,
it opened with a creak and a squeak.
There stood a woman
all dressed in white;
I felt completely unable to speak.

I sat on a chair
by the side of a fire
whilst she looked fondly at me.
'Are you a witch?'
I asked her at last.
And she said 'I may possibly be.

But don't be afraid
I just prefer it out here
Away from experienced minds.
I live with my innocent,
simple, sweet thoughts
That are pure and gentle and kind.'

I was a little confused
So I said to her now,
'How do you even survive?'
She said to me softly
'Just love, my young man,
It is only on love that I thrive.'

'What can I do?'
I said to her now
'So I can be just like you?'
'What, wearing a dress?
Clad only in white?
I'm sure you'd look better in blue!'

'No,' I said, laughing,
'To feel just like you
Where everything seems so right.'

She thought for a while,
And closed her deep eyes
As the full moon shed its fair light.

'All I can say
Is open your mind,
The world is more than you know.
Look deeper than deep,
Be a dreamer, my boy,
And give love wherever you go.

When others hurt you,
Accept that it hurts,
Have faith in the bad and the good.
Walk with the soul
And the eyes of a child
You will always be safe in these woods.

As for the world
That lies there outside,
Remember the words that I've said.
Keep them inside
Your heart and your mind
And by them may you be led.

Soon others will see
There is no such thing
As being too nice or too kind.
And then one fine day,
When more are like you,
I can leave this sweet glory behind.'

So when I got home
I thought of the woman
That had entered my life that dark night.
I will walk tall forever
With the eyes of a child,
To the blackness of life I'll bring light."

The children clapped, nodding their little heads in agreement. The Walrus smiled and coughed, bringing his fist to his mouth as if to play an invisible trumpet; instead he just deposited a good glob of phlegm in it which he then wiped on his trousers. Mysterious ways indeed...

"G - Give love wherever you go," he pronounced. "Nearly half way there!"

The young boy turned over the 'G' bale and stood upon it. I was never great at scrabble to be honest, or any other word game; FRUG was a new one on me.

It was in the silence that followed that I heard a rhythmic pulsing sound coming from round the back of the barn where we had eaten our potatoes. It was like gock, pause, thwack, gock, pause, thwack, over and over again. Either it became louder or I was just listening to it more intently the more it went on. I could tell that The Walrus heard it too, for he looked over his shoulder in the general direction of the gock, pause, thwack and I saw him appear to smile.

The children shuffled a little in uniform manacled discomfort as they too became aware of the gock, pause, thwack. But The Walrus definitely had a twinkle about him.

And I thought of the boy who had served us our meal and of the rage that seethed from him. His absence from the proceedings gaped before me like the mouth of a great whale whose form I could not see but whose teeth created the very shadows around me.

10. And Swiftly On

I know, I know. This is all sounding a little too mad, but this is how it happened, and this is how it was. The children, the bales of hay with their ragged red lettering, and the gock, pause, thwack. And through it all, Zachariah Leonard lay drained of everything, clinging to such life as was his in some dank cove by the great Blackwater estuary.

All I ask of whoever reads these words I write upon the walls of my little home is that you believe me. That is all I ask.

How do you know if what you have just seen doesn't vanish the moment your eyes are averted, that what you have just heard does not disappear into nothingness the moment you are out of range? If you could not smell, would those wonderful fragrances of this fragile land still emanate from every plant and living creature? And if you had no sense of taste, would sweet, sweet love be quite the same?

It was with such questions that I wrestled on this, the most endless of endless days.

The sun was now high in Albion's sky, pouring forth its warmth in invisible droplets of pure heat, transforming the gargantuan oceans from translucent to azure blue and breaking through the ice at the very top of the world, turning it to life blood water to flow mercurial through the veins of my earth. I have learned since all these experiences that I recount that every moment is a moment of wonder, from the clicking nick nock knees of the grasshopper to the millennium breaking of the cracked old stones that hold us all together. And if it is all in the mind, then so be it. It matters not to me.

I wanted so much to investigate the gock, pause, thwack, but, as they say, the show must go on. The Walrus, now seemingly fully recovered from his exertions, wonderful though they were, addressed me thus:

"I hope you are still with us my boy. We have all waited a long time to perform for you."

"Thank you," I replied. "Please go on."

The Walrus bowed. I should have asked questions but I knew I would have received no answers, not at least until all the children had finished their respective turns.

"You will see at the end of the performance what we are revealing to you - by that time you will know the truths of this life; and may you carry these truths into your own life."

He then called out to the children:

"Isn't that the cold hard truth, my darling young ones?"

The five children who were yet to perform uttered various yeps, yups and yesses and fell silent once more. Those who stood on top of the bales moved not a muscle. I settled into my spot upon the grass and waited for my enlightenment to continue.

A young boy, maybe no more than four or five years old, was the next to speak. I leaned forward to listen but soon realised I needn't have done so. He had the voice of one who has spent years drinking and smoking and screaming and crying. He didn't so much say each word as spit it out.

"A hunk a chunk
O' burning bread;
Come on desire -
Douse my bed.

YOU'RE A
DOWN
RIGHT
LIAR

These words go through my head;

And so
I whisper
Low...

(*and he did - in a sing song murmuring lilt*)

'how are we today sir?'

'won't you take a seat sir?'
'how'd you like your hair sir?

FUCKERS..."

The boy, red raging through his cheeks and eyes, turned over his bale of hay and stood upon it, the letter 'A' at his tiny feet.
There was a silence in this Tollesbury day.
A hiatus.
I wasn't sure if I was to speak or not. The Walrus eventually intervened, clearing his throat as he did so.
"A," he pronounced. "Anger Devours The Soul."

The children applauded though in a somewhat muted fashion. It seemed this boy had affected even them.
And swiftly on.
The next child, a girl, voice loud and confident, stood behind her bale just bursting with a child-like energy. She clasped her hands behind her back and bellowed like a good old Romford Market lass:

"Come gather round people,
come look at my wares!
You've seen nothing like it
at your fetes and your fares!

Come here my lovely,
you know that you can;
get right up close
my number one fan!

Whatever you want,
you can have it from me;
you can have it for dinner,
you can have it for tea!

But what's that I hear?

I'm selling fresh air?
Ah, cynical lady -
just you beware!

But on one thing
I must surely agree -
what I have to give
is not easy to see!

Keep your eyes closed
and my heart will call;
you've got to look deep
or not look at all.

You've got to look deep
or not look at all.

Pfff"

And at that, the girl turned over her bale of hay and leapt
sprightly upon it.

"L," proclaimed The Walrus. "Look deep or do not look
at all."

The children clapped this energetic performance and the
little girl bowed in a thank you, thank you type of way. It
seemed the pall cast by the 'A' boy had been well and truly
dispersed.

It was all buzzing now, buzzing and a-whirring just like
my mind when it gets into the fundamental deep down
doingness of it all, away from the temperate life of drudgery
and non-existence which we are led to believe is real - not just
real, but normal. Ah, the greatest, most dastardly deception of
them all.

F-R-U-G-A-L

Well now at least that was a word I understood – or so I
thought. But no time to pause now, they just kept piling it on
me, with their stories and their songs and their poems.

Madness, madness, madness!

Up stood the next boy, chest out and proud, blood pumping and heart thumping - thump, thump, thumpety thump.

"I am your imagination. Simple as that mate. I whirl and swirl and break through every boundary you try so hard to put in front of me. You can't keep me down, no way. And do you want to know why? Well I will tell you anyway. Your eyes lie. Your ears lie. Your nose lies. You have no sense of touch. In fact you have no senses at all. The only reality is me. Without me, you are just a shell, a box of bones and skin. Yes, yes, yes! I am your imagination and you don't know how lucky you are. You see a colour and I make your eyes glow in wonder. You hear a song and I am the one that drops your jaw and brings forth the tears from your heart. And I am the one that tells you that you are in love."

I nodded. Well what else could I do?

"Love, big man, you think that has nothing to do with imagination? Let me tell you that is all it is. The life that you are led to believe is real is nothing but sticks and straw. It has no depth and can go up in a blaze with the slightest spark, whether that be a spark of hatred or a spark of joy. A spark is a spark and no more. I AM LIFE. I give form to your thoughts and your dreams and your desires. I am the next step from what you are thinking right now. Without me there is no future so don't you ever deny me. The dreamer is king for it is only he who truly appreciates my majesty. The cynic and the pragmatist are but rats upon this dire earth, scrabbling for one plus one in the hope that it will equal two and they can go to bed with a sigh of relief and a restful disposition. But you and I both know that numbers are mere fiction, just a tool to bind together all the other superficial inventions of man. The days of the week, the months of the year? All artifice and no more!
"

I shook. My mouth was dry as stone. Each word may as well have been an iron bar crashing down upon my flaccid body, so powerful were they. And I didn't want him to stop.

"Imagination is me and I am life and I am you! When you are awake I give you hope and when you sleep I give you dreams. I am the fuel that services the furnace of your soul.

99

Without light the sky is not blue, nor is the sea green. Nonsense - it is all my doing! I burn, burn, burn so that your very essence may strike out into the firmament and be consumed by the stars that are surely just the bright smiles of all our heavens."

I began to cry for I knew this boy was right. I had always been castigated for being a dreamer, for believing in things other people derided. I had in my life spoken honestly of what I felt and what I heard and what I saw and, in return, I had been shunned by society. And scrawled upon the ragged wooden cross of my despair had been the word 'schizophrenic'. Not only had I been told I was wrong in all that I perceived - I had been diagnosed with a severe and enduring mental illness.

So bring on imagination, boy, bring it on home to me-e-e.

Whoosh! The boy upturned his bale of hay! Boom! He leapt upon it! The letter 'I' was struck through the face of the bale as if it were dividing the whole world in half, between those who believe and those who dare not.

"I," said The Walrus in a sombre tone. "Imagination is life."

Wow!

Wow indeed!

I sensed this show was coming to an end in the same way that I had always been able to predict two doctors and a social worker coming to my house. There is an inevitability to the end of wonder just as the turning of the sun from yellow to orange doth foretell the coming of the black night.

"As you can see, we have two children left. We are nearing the conclusion of our performance. It has been momentous. You will stay with us for a while after we have finished?"

"How do you mean?" I replied.

"Stay with us. Stay here. For as long as you need."

I remembered the gock, pause, thwack and knew I could not leave until I had seen that serving boy again. Not only seen him, but confirmed to myself that he was the very reason I was

100

here at all. For that was my suspicion. I nodded to The Walrus that I would indeed be staying.

"Good, good," he said. "Continue my lovelies!"

And continue the next little girl did. She was sweetly spoken and her voice had a certain husky quality that soothed me with every syllable.

"There were once three men who lived in the same small village. One fine night each was called by an angel to gather at the edge of a cliff. They were, at heart, good men and they spoke freely amongst one another whilst they awaited the arrival of the angel. The moon was hidden by the clouds thus there was a darkness upon the earth. Yet the men were more curious than afraid, for when an angel calls you, surely good things do portend.

Now waiting for an angel is a little bit like waiting for dinner. You look forward to it because you know it is going to be great but then once it is in front of you, you want it to last forever. Just as some have a hunger for food, so others have a hunger for angels and the like. I, myself, being a little girl who is often hungry, would humbly suggest that food is better; you can't eat an angel, and to be honest, you shouldn't really try.

Anyway, it was as the night was at its darkest and the air at its most still that the angel arrived and stood before the three men, his heels almost overhanging the cliff edge. He must have been a brave angel, but then I suppose he had wings, so perhaps it was a little less scary for him than it would be for anyone else.

'Welcome,' said the angel in a voice indescribable. 'I thank you for meeting me here this night. It is good of you to come.'

The men did not speak, but listened with the wonder of us all.

'I have a simple request for each of you.'

There was a pause as the earth itself stopped to listen.

'I want you to step forward and jump over the edge of this cliff.'

101

The men were aghast. They made as if to protest but their astonishment at what had been asked of them stifled the words in their gaping mouths.

'If you are not to jump, I request only that you tell me why; and then may you be on your way.'

One of the men spoke almost immediately.

'I can tell you forthwith that I shall not be jumping, angel or no angel.'

'And your reason?'

'I trust nobody. We are born alone and we die alone. In between we strive to be the best and overcome our fellow man. It is in this way that we achieve earthly reward. What may come after, I care not. So that is it. I trust nobody, not even an angel. So I shall not be jumping.'

'Very well,' replied the angel. 'You may go back to your home. Just remember that I love you.'

And the man did leave.

So that left two men and an angel in the quiet of the dark night. Nobody spoke, not the angel, nor the men for each was thinking his own deep thoughts.

Finally, the second man sighed and spoke.

'I trust some people and I mistrust others. We are born with choices, be that to lead the life of a good man or to lead the life of a bad man. It is by having faith in the good and dismissing the bad that we can lead a life of harmony and peace. And that knowledge comes only with time and with experience. I know you not angel. You do not make sense to me. There is no logic to your being or to what you ask - therefore I am sorry but I cannot trust you. So I shall not be jumping.'

'Very well,' replied the angel. 'You may go back to your home. Just remember that I love you.'

So that left the last man. And had you held a candle to his face, you would have seen bright eyes and a smile as he stepped forward to stand at the edge of the cliff, staring into the blackness of it all. As he spoke, he did not direct his words to the angel but to you and to me.

'I trust everybody, ' he said. 'We are all born good and we all die good. In between, we will make mistakes for which we should be forgiven. If I am wrong, then so be it. But I don't believe I am.'

And then he jumped into the night.

As the man leapt so the stars exploded and the moon shone great upon this earth. The angel returned to the firmament and the man who had jumped lives now forever. He is the smile upon your lips, he is that missed beat of your heart when you fall in love and he is the hope that will ever endure."

The boy upturned his bale of hay to display the letter 'T'.

"T," said The Walrus, sounding weary now. "Trust everybody for, at heart, people are good."

Then the smallest child of all, grinning so wide, clambered onto the last bale of hay. He then got a nudge from the boy beside him and he realised he hadn't turned it over to reveal a letter. He giggled, stepped off and tipped the bale to show the letter 'Y'. He then counted in a gorgeously delicious voice.

"One, two, three!"

And all the children pointed at me before yelling with joyous abandon the words,

"YOU ARE WONDERFUL!!!!"

As their voices danced across the fields, the smallest boy winked at me before closing the whole bizarre production by shouting:

"And don't you ever forget it!"

"Y", said The Walrus, reverently, "You are wonderful."

And I don't mind admitting that I wept for a long old time.

11. The Gock-Pause-Thwack

FRUGALITY.
FRUGALITY.
I closed my eyes and thought of corner-shop sweets, steaming hot chocolate and Airfix models. I thought of cowboy wallpaper and digging holes in the garden, of books about bees and a misshapen teddy bear. And when I opened my eyes, the children were gone. The Walrus was gone too. The barn was before me looking as deserted and ragged as my own poor soul. It was neither day nor night. The sun was red, the sky was blue. And the earth could have been made of marshmallow, so unreal did all this feel. For what had I just sat through if not the unravelling of my very mind?

The show was over and the bales of hay with their red lettering were the only sign that anything had occurred at all. If they were real, I reasoned, then I was not completely mad. I sat on the last bale in the line, the 'Y' bale, I guess you could call it. I did not fall straight through it and that was good enough for me at that point. It was all moment, by moment by moment.

And there it was again - gock-pause-thwack - echoing from around the back of the barn, calling me on, drawing me in. I stood up and with a sigh, ventured up the hill and leaned against the right hand side of the barn, leaning against it like Cool Hand Luke himself. A bird crossed the sun, turning from white to black and then white again, bringing life to this desperate watercolour vista. It was all so scripted, so planned and so inevitable.

Row, row, row the boat gently down the stream. Merrily, merrily, merrily, merrily, life is but a dream…

So on bended knees like an old plastic toy soldier, I peered around the corner.

And there was the source of my curiosity, the aural author of the gock-pause-thwack. It was the serving boy, standing some ten yards from the rear of the barn, a flat piece of wood gripped in his hands, his eyes upon an object that hurtled towards him. Then he swung the piece of wood at the small blur before him - gock - silence as it travelled fast through the air - pause - and then - thwack - as it crashed against the wooden structure only to return, bounce and then be hit again by this startling boy. And on and on without relent. Gock-pause-thwack...

Mesmerise me, mesmerise me. I was mesmerised. That sound of summer, the sound of my youth, the sound of my dreams - oh leather on willow in the gorgeous English field of my wonder so perfect, so sonorous; swing low, sweet chariot across this green and pleasant land into which I was so preciously born.

The boy did not notice me at first. His concentration was magnificent. I had read how the old cricketers used to practice with a stick and a home-made ball against a fence, how they used to just go at it over and over again. And here it was before my very eyes. I was in awe of this boy who had served us our meal with such sullen distraction. I would soon learn that the cause of his sadness and anger was much more complicated than merely being deprived of a spot of rudimentary batting practice.

Gock-pause-thwack.

Pause...

Stop.

The boy laid his crude bat upon the ground and turned to look at me. Had I not been leaning against the barn, I'm sure I would have fallen, for as he raised his head and stared at me I was reminded instantly of my son. It was Robbie - kind of.

Robbie had always been vulnerable in the eyes of my wife, a baby swaddled, entombed in the desperate arms of his mother, hidden, protected and defended from the world of man. Not only was this boy in front of me now ten or twelve years old, he had none of the characteristics of Downs Syndrome with which my Robbie was burdened. I use the word 'burdened' for that is how I saw my son, a burden to his mother, and himself burdened with an affliction about which

105

he could do nothing; but for which the world would judge him nonetheless.

And if using the word 'burden' wasn't bad enough, I find myself using the word 'affliction'.

Shame on me.

"You're not my dad," said the boy. "And my name's not Robbie," he added, before I could even say a word.

Before I could even say a word.

"What is your name?" I asked glibly.

"People call me W.G."

"What does the 'W' and the 'G' stand for?"

"Just W.G. is all."

W.G. walked over and picked up the ball which I saw now was constructed of what seemed to be rags wrapped around some sort of wooden block. The wood was visible in places where the rags had begun to tear. The boy stood there and tightened the pieces of material that had come loose, tucking them into the folds, doing his best to make a sphere out of what was ostensibly a cube. He worked on the ball for some five minutes, appearing to forget that I was even there. When he was satisfied with the shape of the ball, he placed it on the ground and stood before me, his hands on his hips, waiting for something to happen. I waited too. Nothing happened.

Neither a sound nor a smell was present. Movement ceased and the light was still. It was just me and W.G. and this earth of ours, this earth that had both spawned and sustained us.

Phew! What a wonder is life, what a veritable conundrum is the mind and what a suspension of belief is required to even make sense of any of it! At that moment, I believed not that the sun rotated around the earth but that the heavens themselves were in thrall to me and this strange boy. We were, at that moment, the axis upon which the whole world turned.

"Best you come with me, Mister," said W.G. finally. "Best you come with me."

He led. I followed.

And you know what it's like when you're stressed and you're down and the world is too big? What do you need at those times? What do you most require? I always thought I needed a woman to hold me, to tell me she understood, to make me understand that the confusion I felt was nothing but a phase in the miraculous turning of my days. For that was love to me - the compassion that one has for another in those darkest seconds, the drawing of breath, the tolerance and the moment of sympathy that is followed so swiftly maybe by a spark of humour or a burst of affection. But it wasn't love I needed.

Light up my days and banish the fractious winds of gloom that do infuse my depression.

In that moment, when I was pulled along by that angry boy known as W.G., I suffered an enlightenment. Suffered indeed! For it is not the glow of love that breaks the darkness, but movement itself. Keep on keeping on, my hero once said. Keep on keeping on.

And off to work we go…

When troubles look big, you have to go small. And thus I found myself peering through a dirty window, W.G. whispering in my ear.

"Tell me what you see," he murmured, simmering with a rage unshackled, a rage unbound. "Tell me what you see."

I saw red bleeding into orange and orange fading into white. And then the perfect darkness of silhouettes stamped themselves onto the scene. All black upon white, just like the pictures I once made in infant school where the teacher had shown us how to carve shapes in halved potatoes before dipping them gloriously in whatever colour we chose. Then bang, bang, bang onto the pristine white of the paper - a cross, a smiley face, an indeterminate splodge.

Dead bird swinging in the black of night…

Through the small pane of glass I saw the shapes of several small beds, each one topped by an unmoving bundle - surely that of a sleeping child; they must have been the children that had worked so hard that evening to help me understand FRUGALITY. They deserved their rest no doubt.

As I gazed upon the scene, the glass of the window began to mist up, giving the impression that the sleeping children were being engulfed in an unholy smoke. It was W.G. standing beside me. As my breathing had slowed, so his had increased. I was at peace - he clearly was not.

Take these sunken eyes and learn to see. All your life,
You were only waiting for this moment to be free.

W.G. led me down an incline that fell steeply from the back of the barn in which the children slept. He moved in a clumsy, heavy footed fashion, leaning forward as he walked, his head bowed and his arms swinging more than perhaps they ought. There was an aura of determination about him, a determination that could clearly be employed either for good or for bad - as things stood, my senses having been suitably heightened, it seemed this boy was capable of anything.

At the bottom of the incline, the field levelled out. By the time I caught up with W.G. he had already begun to add some sticks to a burned pile of wood that scarred the grass. Blankets lay folded neatly nearby along with a pan and a wooden plate. W.G. had placed the ball and his crude bat between them. This, evidently, was home for him. He poked at the pile until smoke sneaked from beneath it and tainted the air. What had ignited it, I knew not; maybe it was the anger that seethed within him so vehemently. Seeing the sparks grow into flame, I felt the cold for the first time and sat by the burgeoning fire. It was an orange crackle fire that somehow warmed me from the inside. It was magnificent.

Leaving the fire for a moment, W.G. brought his blankets over to where I sat, handing me one and keeping the other. He set about the task of covering himself with an earnestness that befitted his serious nature. With his body thus covered and just his head visible, it was so clear to me that he was indeed just a small boy. In such a short space of time I had already begun to view him as so much more. I sat closer to the fire and wrapped the blanket about my shoulders, wondering just what was going to happen next. I didn't have to wonder long.

"Those children, all asleep, the boys and girls, together in the barn," muttered W.G...

I turned to face him. He was lying on his side and seemed to be speaking as much to the cold grass as to me.

"I saw them," I replied. The grass answered with more dignity than I. It said nothing at all.

Flames flickered. The sky breathed. And the earth turned ever so slowly.

"They have it all," W.G. continued. "The Walrus looks after them. He keeps them warm. He makes sure they don't get hurt. He makes them laugh and when they cry, he tells them everything will be all right."

I listened to his words and tried so hard to say the right thing. When I think too much, all I can ever express is the obvious.

Sometimes I think too much, some people say so. Other people say no, no; the fact is, you don't think as much as you should.

Hmm.

"Why don't you stay in the barn with them; let The Walrus look after you too. Surely it's better than being down here all on your own?"

The fire crackled and popped.

"There's a little one there now," continued W.G. almost as if I hadn't said a word. "He hasn't been there long. He can't even walk, just crawls around. They have to feed him because he doesn't even know how to use a spoon like I do. And when they tickle him he laughs. It's just a laugh but they all go mad saying how great he is."

All this said in a monotone voice directed just at me and the world.

"I've seen him up close. He's nothing special. His eyes aren't even right but none of them says it to him. And The Walrus picks him up sometimes and dances with him and tells all the others to be quiet when this little one is trying to sleep. Sometimes The Walrus even sleeps on the floor next to him like he's the little one's dog or something."

W.G. just stared ahead, maybe just waiting for sleep to take him. He sounded so bewildered, so utterly unable to comprehend how things were.

"Why don't you just stay up there in the barn with the others?" I ventured, again doing my best to offer some kind of succour. "The other children could be your friend and The Walrus could look after you too. There would be a bed for you to sleep in, I'm sure. He is nice, The Walrus. He would do for you what he does for the others. Then you would be happy."

W.G. sat up so quickly that even the flames backed off a little.

"Why would I ever do that? He's not my dad is he? My dad left me when I was a baby, just left me. He may as well have left me in this field as anywhere else. He wasn't there to listen to me crying or to clap his hands when I did good things. When I was scared, I stayed scared and when I was angry, I stayed angry. And that little one, he is the worst of the lot."

I was becoming weary now and decided to lay myself down upon the grass to sleep. I covered myself with the blanket as best I could and let the fire run its course. The night was dark except for the dwindling flames. The birds slept in their nests and the foxes slept in their holes. And I was just too tired to make the connections.

As sleep finally began to overwhelm me, W.G. spoke again, one final time. He had shuffled over to where I lay and whispered into my ear in a voice so much deeper and more coarse than befitted a boy of his age.

"That little one," he said, "that little one's going to get it."

12. The Splintering of Minds

In 1836, the Marylebone Cricket Club, better known as the MCC - that crotchety old magistrate of my wonderful game, was one year away from the fiftieth anniversary of its formation. To put that into context, the Football Association still had to wait another twenty seven years to be formed, with the Rugby Football Union coming into being another eight years after that, in 1871.

Cricket itself had long been a gambling game, with various land owners pitting their best fellows against one another, and sometimes even deigning to compete themselves. To see the middle-classes, as they would come to be known, throwing themselves about in attempts to catch the ball or charging up and down the wicket foregoing all attempts to retain their decorum, would be a pastime much enjoyed by your average plebeian.

Ah, cricket! I do believe you are my finest friend! That feeling of hitting the ball so sweetly off the middle of the bat must surely have heralded a perfect sense of enjoyment whether that ball was struck either by a young farmer in the early nineteenth century or by one of the modern day twenty-twenty dynamos. And to catch a catch in the deep - the anticipation as the ball drops from the sky and the relief when it is pouched - well that is a pleasure of life indeed.

Such were my thoughts as I greeted the day at the foot of the incline. I was somewhat stiff and damp, but refreshed nonetheless.

W.G. lay in the exact same position as last I saw him. He looked intense even whilst in sleep. There was a pain that crept from the frown lines upon his forehead like smoke smouldering from the embers of a fire that will never burn out, a pain that seemed desperate to leave its source without waking it. When pain is scared, there really is a problem.

I surveyed the field around me and ambled up the hill to where the barn was, seeing as I approached that the land to the right of the building levelled out over quite a considerable area. And when I see a large expanse of grass, I hear the sounds of the finest music never written - the metronomic sound of bat on ball, the percussive clapping of gentle people and the deep woodwind section comprised entirely of my own sighs. Such an overture will turn a field into a pitch in an instant. And that was when I saw a way into W.G.

Gock-pause-thwack…

"I have an idea, W.G." I said to the boy when he finally awoke.

I had returned to the foot of the incline following my ramblings and had waited for over an hour for him to awake. By the expression on his startled face, I may have been a little too eager and a little too close. He did not reply, but merely rubbed his eyes and looked around as if to remind himself that he was still on this earth. He seemed disappointed when he realised he still was.

"W.G. I have an idea," I repeated.

He nodded, more forlornly than I may have hoped, giving me consent to continue. By now, he had shuffled over to a tree and had his back against it. He just stared at me, blankly.

"Well, when you were hitting that ball against the side of the barn yesterday, that was really good. I mean you never missed and that stick you were using wasn't even that wide and certainly not as big as a real bat."

I could hear myself sounding patronising and forced myself to slow down so as to be able to choose my words with more thought.

"Do the other children ever play with you?" I asked.

I watched as he breathed deeply. He made as if to stand. The anger that had been less prevalent upon his waking was surely rising to the surface again. I felt I was about to lose him.

"Will you let me play with you, W.G? A game of cricket on the field up there, just me and you. What do you think?"

The sun edged up into the sky and the birds began their whitterings.

"Play with you?" asked W.G. "Hitting the ball?"

"Yes, yes. Cricket. We could have a game of cricket. What do you think?"

W.G. sat back now and stroked his hair slowly.

"I never played with no-one else. Cricket is what they do in the town I heard. I ain't never played no cricket. Just hit a ball against a wall is all I do."

"I will show you, W.G. I will show you!"

Looking at his changing countenance, I could tell that my enthusiasm was clearly beginning to reach him. I wondered how many times anybody had ever given him the idea that he felt needed, let alone begged him to play with them. I don't know what I would have done had he declined my offer.

"I will be back for you later," I said, getting to my feet. "Where will you be?"

"At the barn with the others or down here," replied W.G. as he pulled his braces over his shoulders. "Only places I go - up there with them or down here on my own."

I let the moment pass and headed to the barn.

The Walrus was out the front, near where the FRUGALITY play had been conducted. He was sitting on the grass, cross-legged, whittling on a stick. He greeted me warmly when I approached.

"Hello, my friend. And how are we today?" He looked up at me, continuing to work away on the piece of wood in his hand.

"I'm good, thank you," I replied, eager to get the pleasantries out of the way. "I wonder if I could ask you a favour?"

He stopped his whittling. "Ask away, young man. Ask away"

"Well, I don't suppose you have any shears? Garden shears really but anything like that. It's just I need to borrow them if you have. If that's alright of course?"

"Mmm. Garden shears. I never had call for them. I do have some big scissors though that I use to cut cloth for the children's clothes. Would they do?"

"Yes, yes. That would be great."

He went into the barn and returned moments later with a large, rusty pair of scissors. I thanked him and rushed to the level piece of field on the other side of the barn. The groundsman had his land and his tools and the whole morning ahead of him to prepare his wicket. At that moment, I don't believe I had ever been happier or more imbued with purpose.

And so with the Tollesbury sun on my back and the English air filling my lungs, I made a mark in the earth. I walked twenty two paces and stopped, forging another mark with the blade of the scissors. I laid on the grass vertical to the mark I had made and stretched my arms above my head. I figured this to be about eight feet and holding the scissors in my outstretched hand made another mark. I reversed my position, made a further mark and joined them with a long score in the earth. I repeated the exercise at the other end of the twenty two yards. Having done this, I scored a long line down each side, joining the two shorter marks I had made. I looked upon my long rectangle and considered myself satisfied.

A child brought me over a cup of cool water, patted me on the head where I sat, and skipped away. I drank the water slowly, using every sensation available to me to appreciate it. I tasted its wetness and listened to it as it entered my throat and imagined being able to see it as it made its way to my stomach before sustaining me in all sorts of ways. We are as plants, needing nourishment to grow and continue, the natural fuel of the land and the sea being our most abundant benefactors. God, when life is that simple, no worries need impinge upon the perfection of Albion's mighty horizon.

The morning wore on and I continued on my mission. I worked a small area at a time, bent over, using the old scissors to trim the grass within the rectangle, taking it almost back to the soil. Various children came and went either to replenish me with water or to stare and giggle at this strange man on his knees cutting the summer grass with the same implement that fashioned their meagre garments. I saw nothing of W.G. that morning. Where he was, what he was doing and what he was thinking, I knew not. If I had known what was truly occupying his soul, I may well have ceased my work. As it was, I was all joy and optimism, as child-like as my fascinated and frequent little visitors.

I don't know how many hours it took me to finish my work. I had begun to lose track of time during the preceding days and was glad of it. For what is time but an unhealthy imposition on the natural flow of existence? It prevents us from fully immersing ourselves in THE MOMENT. It urges us on blindly and leads us not to fulfilment but to one more point of stress after another. The land is in darkness or the land is in light. That is the only approximation of time we really need. Yet we hurtle from one day to the next, trapped and inhibited by the ticking of the grand clock of society - that ticktockticktock rhythm to which our hearts meekly comply. To have time is said to be a luxury. I would contend that the opposite is true. But then, having just described how I had used a rusty old pair of early nineteenth century scissors to create a cricket pitch, you may well be stepping slowly away from me at this moment, looking over your shoulder for the nearest available exit...

Well, onwards.

I stood back and surveyed what I had made. It was most definitely a batsman's paradise - flat, not a crack in sight and bereft of any of the morning dew. Pity the poor bowlers on this track! But a cricket pitch isn't a cricket pitch without stumps.

I do believe The Walrus had a deal of fun making my stumps and bails. He knew of cricket but had never seen it played. He did a fine job and, before long, my masterpiece was complete. It may not seem much to some, but making my own cricket pitch was a dream that had long lingered in my disordered mind.

I located W.G. at the back of the barn. He was leaning against the wooden building, his crooked bat in one hand and his ball in the other, as if he had been waiting for me all day. Looking past him through the window to the sombre dining area, it seemed he had just cleared up the children's afternoon meal - some were still seated at the table, whilst others were on the floor, cross-legged in front of The Walrus who stood before them, laughing and gesticulating.

115

"Hi," I said to W.G. "Ready?"

"I suppose," he replied.

I should imagine my odour was not one that would inspire anyone to uncork an empty bottle with which to ensnare it and I must have looked flushed indeed, toiling as I had been in the field for most of the day. Me, toiling in the fields. Imagine that!

W.G. followed me to my cricket pitch as if he were walking out to bat at Lord's. I was proud of my achievement and he treated it with due deference, turning to me and smiling. It was the first time I had seen him without an ounce of either bitterness or anger. He actually looked like the child he was and not the weary, encumbered soul he had so evidently become. He threw the ball to me and strode to the crease. I made my way to the bowler's end, paced out a run-up and took a deep breath. And I knew then that no moment in my life would ever compare to the one I was then experiencing.

"Play," I announced.

W.G. didn't take guard, he just stood there in front of the stumps gazing in my direction, his make-shift bat at the ready. I ambled in and looped up a half-volley. The boy dispatched it over my head without even moving his feet. He grinned and nodded in my direction.

"So that's how it is," I said to myself as I walked some thirty yards back to fetch the ball. But before I could get there, a small boy picked it up and lobbed it to me, positioning himself, rather sensibly I might add, at mid-on.

"We'll call that a four," I yelled to W.G. when I reached my run up.

"Call it what you like," he replied.

Now I have never considered myself to be competitive in any way. But then, up until that point, I had never had a ball smacked back over my head by a boy who had put no more effort into the shot than he would have done swatting a fly. My fielder was in position, all five years of him, and I bowled the next ball, short and fast. It reared up past W.G.'s shoulder and on past his left ear. Did I feel at all guilty? Not a bit of it. Did I smile as W.G. glared back at me? Indeed I did. The beaten batsman turned to get the ball, but there was no need. The Walrus picked it up, threw it back to me and took up his position as wicket-keeper. Where he had come from, I did not know, nor did I care. Every bowler needs a safe pair of hands behind the stumps and it seemed I had mine.

And so it went on. Each time W.G. seemed to be dominating my bowling, I managed to get in a sneaky off-break (no mean feat on that pitch!) or a faster ball that beat him for pace and bounce. But I was never even close to getting him out even though, all the while, my options in the field were increasing. One by one, the children took up their places with minimal guidance from me, appearing unbidden as if from the earth itself. Before long, I had a mid-off, a mid-on, two slips, a wicket-keeper, a gully, a cover point, a square leg, a short-leg and a third man (or rather a third small girl to be exact.)

Occasionally I pointed to one of my team mates to just move a few yards to the left or to the right, or maybe to come in a bit from the invisible boundary - not for any other reason than I had always wanted to do it; the demon bowler directing his field in order to out-think the in-form batsman.

The little fielders charged around the field like flies in an empty jam-jar, chasing after the ball and returning it to me in a ramshackle, hickledy-pickledy display of clumsiness and glee. On more than one occasion, two of the fielders collided, only to roll around laughing at the glory of it all and filling the air itself with joy.

I was having the time of my life.

W.G. hit the ball to all parts, jogging a single here, hitting a boundary there. In truth, he was unbeatable and I was tiring. I had bowled a thirty over spell after all. The sun was creeping towards the back of the barn and the little girl at third man was asleep on the grass. One of my slips came and told me that the small boy fielding at gully had possibly wet himself.

I was on the verge of considering a bowling change when The Walrus left his place behind the stumps and walked up the wicket towards me. He ruffled my hair, shook my hand and called a halt to proceedings. He lifted the bails off the stumps at the bowler's end, did the same at the batsman's end and pulled the stumps out of the ground. W.G. stood there resting his bat upon his shoulder. His performance had been legendary. I laid down my set of stumps and the ball and clapped heartily. All the children joined in as W.G. walked off the field and down the incline and out of sight. I like to think he had a tear in his eye on this, his finest day. I know I did.

A feeling of elation coupled with absolute weariness overcame me. I could have slept right there on the wicket of my own devising and would surely have done so had I not spotted a figure sprawled on the ground some sixty yards away at what would have been the cover boundary. I stood up, wiped the sweat from my grimy forehead and looked around. The Walrus and the children were long gone. I walked achingly across the field and soon saw that it was none other than Zachariah Leonard. It just had to be, didn't it?

Zachariah looked more invigorated than last I'd seen him. He had regained that indestructible demeanour that had not so long ago shaken me to my very soul. The purity of the day was brought to a close; for Zachariah Leonard brought dirt to the occasion, granite to the party. He was the thud in the gloom, the depth to the darkness. And instantly I saw that he was a part of me. I smiled. My smile turned to a grin. Zachariah's torrid face was ablaze with smoulder. A part of me was complete. A part of him was fulfilled. He stood up. I was already standing. Now that was easy.

"Hello," I said.

He nodded. But I was not so distracted as to fail to notice how he screwed up a piece of paper in one of his hands.

"What have you been doing," I asked.

"Nothing, boy. Nothing that need concern you."

We stood looking at one another. He was dirty and hard and charming as ever.

"Let's go," he murmured, putting a big hand upon my shoulder and nudging me with it. We walked away from the cricket pitch and down the incline.

W.G. seemed to have disappeared in the same manner as The Walrus and the children. So there I was, at the foot of the incline once more, this time though not with a disturbed young boy, but with a brooding Zachariah Leonard.

"Sit," he ordered. So I sat.

It was reminiscent of that first time I had met him, the two of us seated on the grass, side by side, eyes upon the bold horizon. The Tollesbury sky was dark now, black and still.

"Tell me what has passed," said Zachariah, finally, just as I was beginning to settle into the silence.

So I did.

"Forgive everybody everything. Recognise beauty wherever it be. Understand the nature of loss. Give love wherever you go. Anger devours the soul. Look deep or do not look at all. Imagination is life. Trust everybody, for at heart, people are good"

I turned at last to look at him, having intoned the previous words with neither excitement nor emotion, for as I spoke them, they seemed too naïve, too trite to be uttered in the presence of such a man as Zachariah Leonard. But then I saw the tears upon his face, edging their way through the centuries of grime, filling the deep grooves and crevices, bringing water to that arid land of his countenance. He didn't shake or rock or move at all; just those tears easing from his heart and his mind, flowing out into the night.

"You are wonderful," I whispered.

He closed his eyes. And the tears stopped. I had the feeling he was using all his might to keep his eyes shut and wondered if he would ever open them again. He was absolutely like a rock. The piece of paper I had seen him with earlier was on the grass by one of his crossed legs. Without thought of consequence, I leaned over and picked it up. It was rough in my hands and the marks upon it had been made with what could have been a piece of coal, so dark and deep were they. I blew upon the sheet and cleared the debris. The words beneath were thus revealed. The beating of my heart was the only sound to be heard from miles around as I read.

'W.G. - 100 not out - Man of the Match and King of the World.'

As I read that last word, the silence of the moment was shattered, broken in a most terrifying fashion. His eyes still closed and remaining perfectly still, Zachariah opened his mouth and screamed. It was a sound like I had never heard before - high-pitched and never ending; such that would break this whole world in two. It was a dog in its death throes, a train screeching into a wall, the grinding to a halt of the rusty iron wheel of our times, the shriek of the abused, and the roar of the risen. And he just kept going - it was an avalanche, an earthquake, the fracturing of nations, the splintering of minds and the cracking open of the skies, the panic of the new-born, the explosion of adolescence, the gurgling rattle of the dying. It was all these things. It was all these things.

And it was happening. It was happening now.

From behind, I felt the ground shudder. I stood and whirled around. It was W.G. charging down the incline. He came to a halt just a foot in front of me. Whatever Zachariah had used to mark the paper, may well have been used to forge the eyes of the young boy. I stared in horror at the blood that spattered his face and the red juice that dripped from his crude, home-made cricket bat that he held tightly in both hands. It was as if the blood were seeping from the wood itself. We stared at one another, both of us struggling to control our breathing.

"That little one," W.G. finally said. "That little one got it."

Zachariah Leonard ceased his screaming, fell back upon the earth and just lay there, silent, slumped and spent.

13. The Child-Killer

I was still staring in shock at W.G. as he moved away from me and sat beside Zachariah Leonard. Zachariah lifted his arm and enveloped the young boy with it, gently holding him close. Such a display of affection from him shook me still further. He made no attempt to wipe the blood from W.G.'s face and spoke not a word. The bat lay on the grass, its job done. The night was cool and aloof.

I could stand no longer so returned to the earth. Gravity had never felt so unwieldy.

There are no rules.

"What have you done?" I asked W.G. "What have you done?"

"The little one got it," he mumbled, his words directed more into the dirty folds of Zachariah's grubby over-shirt than to me.

That much I had understood. But only that much. What a trio we were. It was so hard to work out the time, with no clue from the sky. I knew I had to stay awake. No sound came from up the hill so I could only think the body of the stricken child had yet to be discovered. I was thinking as calmly as I could about how to resolve this whole situation, yet this 'situation' involved a small boy having been battered to death by a piece of wood and the young murderer dozing beside me in the arms of Zachariah Leonard.

And I could think only of my son, Robbie.

He was four years old when last I had seen him. I had decided to leave some months previously. I thought I had been kind in giving my wife a date of departure, reasoning, perhaps foolishly, it would make my abandoning of her easier to take. It was almost like I had handed in my notice - I don't want this job anymore. Reason for leaving? Self-centred, dream-world living, whiskydrunk fool. I was miserable. My wife was constantly intense. Our lives were nothing less than painful. It's not that we abused one another or were even offensive to one another. It's just that we had come together at a time when we just could not be accommodated into our own individual concepts of life. All these excuses had precipitated my decision to leave. I reasoned that it was better for all of us.

To give up your child, to give up your child.

In the story of my life, there is a vague smudge of ink, a disastrous undoing of logic. I left my son for reasons that now make no sense. I did indeed forego seeing him every night and every morning. I wilfully excepted myself from his smiles and his tears and his wonder. I didn't see his face the first time he saw snowflakes and I was absent when he experienced the grand display of fireworks night and I was not there to comfort him when the dark scared him just a little more deeply than he could understand.

Robbie's first day of school had been the last time I had seen him. He was up so early and so excited. My wife had tried to explain to him, in the preceding days, what school was all about and he had seemed to accept that it would be nothing less than brilliant. He would have friends to play with and he would learn things and be all grown up. It used to break my heart when I thought of what it would really be like for him, a boy with Down's syndrome in a mainstream school in the middle of Tiptree. Not that there's anything wrong with Tiptree, you understand.

So that morning, my wife got herself ready as if she were going out on the town. She wore make-up, something which it seemed she hadn't done for years. She painted her nails red and looked beautiful. It was then that I realised this wasn't just to hold her own with the other parents in the playground; for she was losing her little boy to the big wide world of school on the same day that her husband was deserting her. Joni Mitchell used to sing to me "you don't know what you've got till it's gone" and Tom Waits would tell me "you never seen the morning till you stayed up all night." They were both right. And yes, I was indeed tangled up in blue. God, she looked beautiful that day.

Julia stood in the small lounge doing the buttons up on Robbie's shirt but a look of great concern was on his round face. He didn't really do subtle.

"Mummy, you've got blood," he said.

"Where, darling?"

"Your fingers."

"That's just my nail varnish. It's supposed to be pretty."

"Does it hurt?"

"No darling. Now stand still."

I sat in the back of the car with Robbie as Julia drove us the short distance to the school. Robbie was soft and round and impossibly unaware of the life that faced him. It seemed to me then that the car was as much a womb as the one in which he had been carried prior to his birth. The world that he had experienced until this point had been a deceitful one of Disney videos, cuddles, warmth, chocolate and Julia's Elvis records; she had never really been a Beatles fan. There are some barriers, I guess, that only the best of relationships can overcome.

Robbie's departure from the car at the sound of the bell would truly herald his birth into the cruel life of which I was only too familiar.

By the time we had got to the school, Robbie had succeeded in undoing all the buttons of his shirt, his chubby fingers having worked tirelessly to achieve their aim. He lifted his vest and patted his belly, giggling. My thoughts being far away, I had sat and watched him, unblinking, for the duration of our journey.

When Julia opened the back door to let Robbie out, she tutted, buttoned up his shirt again and lifted him out of the car. It was almost as if that episode alone had confirmed the disappointment she had felt the entire time she had known me.

"You can leave now," she said to me, without as much as a glare in my direction. Not even a glare.

"Ok", I replied.

I had got out of the car and watched her take Robbie's hand and lead him into the playground; the playground of fears, the playground of dreams - sandpits and grass and

123

concrete and fences. Her back was straight and she walked proudly. Robbie tried to keep up with her, looking back at me all the while. I slunk off. And that was that.

I had left my son and my wife so that I could pursue what? Dreams, fantasies, a brighter future? I didn't know then and I don't know now. It happened. That was all. Had I known of FRUGALITY then, I may have made a different choice. But here I was, years later, in a field with a decision to make.

The clarity of what I had to do was like an epiphany. A light shone down upon me, from maybe the only star in the sky. Without any conscious thought other than what I was doing was right, I stood, picked up the blood stained cricket bat and walked up the incline towards the cricket field. I passed through the nights of Robbie crying, through his terrors and his worries, through his anger and his despair. I climbed over the barriers I had erected for him and I pushed through the disgust I felt in myself.

W.G.'s face was large in my mind, his grin when he hit that on-drive, his loneliness and his rage. The two became one for me - W.G. and Robbie. So now you see there was only one thing for me to do.

The sky was pink when The Walrus found me. I was lying on the cricket pitch, curled up like a baby, cradling the bloodied bat as if I had fallen upon it in battle. I had been awoken some moments earlier by the shouts of children and had spent the intervening time readying myself for who knows what.

"You need to come with me," said The Walrus, sadly. He looked deep into my very being and sighed, nodding as if in that moment he understood everything.

I rose stiffly, leaving the bat on the pitch and followed him. My gait was awkward and my back ached as I walked behind him. It was as if iron shackles had already been clamped about my ankles. The cricket pitch disappeared into the earth and the stumps became mere twigs once more as I left them behind. I had no idea what form of justice I was about to face, only that I deserved it. And it felt so good.

When I got to the front of the barn, the children were waiting for me. Each had their head bowed and their hands clasped behind their back. On command, they stood behind The Walrus.

"In front of me Simon, if you will," The Walrus said to me.

I did as I was ordered.

"Where are we going?" I asked.

"Back to where you came from. It is time for you to return now."

And thus did I arrive in the village square once more.

It was a bright day, with the sun gaining height in the Tollesbury sky. I breathed in the air and felt it drift down into my lungs, simultaneously moist and dry, filling them up before being expelled again. In and out. In and out. This motion, I realised, was all that kept any of us alive - this automatic function of drawing air into the body only to breathe it back out again. I tried to hold my breath but my body would fight against me until I had to relent and allow the air to return once more to the world. In and out. In and out.

I could hear the birds warbling and I felt for a moment I could taste England. The sense of belonging I had at that instant was absolutely palpable; belonging to this village, to this country, to this time. Love flowed through me, washed over me, dabbed my brow, dried me softly and left me cleansed.

The door to the village lock-up was already open. I stepped into the dark space and turned as the bolt slid across with a deep clang. It was a pleasing sound and I continued trying to listen to it as it faded away, seeking the vibrations as they drifted into the earth and the trees and the souls of all those that stood outside. Even the smell of urine and vomit and the odour of men that emanated from every crack in every piece of wood that housed me, even those things brought pleasure to me at that moment. They were signs of life, of the past, of the inevitability that all things must transform and temporarily end before evolving and going on and on and on.

Just urine, vomit and sweat to many perhaps. But not to me - I was savouring all.

I sat down and closed my eyes not caring for a moment if I ever moved from this spot. My world consisted then of just four old walls that were just large enough to contain me. I understood such small proportions. Everything was within reach. There was no movement that was not initiated by me. And, most reassuring of all, there were no people, no-one with whom I felt compelled to interact, no judges, no conspirators, no thieves, no lovers. Just me - the Child-Killer - a man simply awaiting his fate - the confirmation he required that he was indeed not meant for this world.

Sleep did not take me. I was awake yet drifting between one world and the next, a trance like state within which I could not be harmed. I could see my internal organs, how every part of my body worked. I could feel my liver, touch my lungs, smell the fragrance of my mind. These were deep sensations, incalculable in their meaning, incontrovertible in their evidence that life was all an illusion. My eyes see not what your eyes see - not really. We are all sentient beings encountering our own entirely unique experiences, floating in time, suspended in moments which we are taught to call life-times; taught by those who strive erroneously to make sense out of all of this.

Before I knew what was happening, there was a loud crack that shook me instantly. I covered my ears as the noise continued. It gradually came to my consciousness that somebody was hammering upon the door in front of me. I stood once more, tremulous.

"Out, drunk!" called a guttural voice.

The door to the village lock-up opened and I fell into Tollesbury village square. As I looked down, trying to gain my balance, I noticed I was kneeling in filth and straw. There were cattle wandering in front of The King's Head and several people ambled about all dressed in dull, loose clothes. A smell of dung plunged into my lungs and I could do nothing but try to cough it out. A small boy walked towards me and leaned

126

over my confused frame. I was on all fours, more akin to the cattle than the people.

"What's happening?" I asked the boy. A graveyard grin cracked his grimy little face in half and I expected one of his few remaining teeth to tumble out of his mouth and imbed itself in the dirt before me.

"Away boy!" shouted a large man who now stood before me. He held a wooden baton in one hand. It must have been he who had rapped upon the door of the lock-up and he who had yanked me out.

I stayed on the ground and leaned against the closed door of the lock-up. Before me, on two old armchairs, sat Weepy and Nardy. Penny Shoraton was standing behind them looking achingly beautiful. I could look no further than her.

"Where have you been, Simon?" asked Weepy.

In considering my reply, I could only smile. For where had I been indeed?

"It would help if you could tell us, Simon?" added Nardy. "It would assist us in helping you."

I was truly in a state of bliss.

Weepy and Nardy exchanged a serious glance and then addressed me in unison, their voices intertwined, even their gestures mirroring one another.

"You have destroyed the life of a child. You took away his hope, his chance of a life of fulfilment. You valued your own foolish dreams above the wonder of an innocent. That child did you no harm. For all we know, he loved you, thought of you as a hero, a saviour, a superman. You have denied him the anticipation of birthdays, happy Christmases, the applause as he crosses the line in the sack race, the pat on the back when he is substituted at half-time, the confirmation that he is loved. You contradicted the absolute belief of a child that there is no evil in this world. And there is no greater crime than that."

I think, at that moment, they expected some kind of response from me. I gave them nothing but a wink.

"Do you really believe what happened to you when you were a young boy gave you the right to ruin the life of another?"

They knew nothing, man, nothing. They wanted me to please, please, please them - I knew that much. But things were all just too far gone.

Penny Shoraton sang to me in a high pitched shimmering crystal stream voice "She loves you, yeah, yeah, yeah! She loves you, yeah, yeah, yeah!"

I ran my fingers through my hair, looked at her as seductively as I was able and replied in a dirty street John Lennon growl, "Why don't we do it in the road?"

"Enough!" shouted Weepy and Nardy, standing simultaneously as if strung by the same puppeteer - for even they had strings it seemed.

"Simon Anthony, you have taken the life of a child and shall hence forth be known forever in this village and beyond as 'The Child-Killer'. Parents will use what you have done as a means of disciplining their children, of educating them in the evil that men do. Now leave us. Go to where you will end your days. And may you never return."

I was led by a crowd of people, away from the village square and down Station Road, arriving eventually at Zachariah Leonard's shack. It seemed even darker than I remember, more ancient and so much more like the mouth of death than ever it had been before. A rough hand pushed me in and someone closed the door behind me. I was nearly home.

The brightness of the sun had left me unprepared for the all encompassing gloom in which I now found myself. I crawled on my hands and knees to reach the other end of the room and it was then that I felt three short wooden legs. I guessed it was a stool of sorts. I stroked the smooth wood as if it were a cat. The movement soothed me. And as my eyes grew attuned to the darkness, I saw that there was a square piece of wood protruding out of the floor in the far corner. I slithered over to it on my stomach and saw that it was the trap-door. I sighed in disappointment, thinking that I was being offered one last way out; for in truth I wanted no escape.

I reached my hand into the aperture that had presented itself to me and, to my surprise touched earth. This was not some tunnel to freedom but merely a hole in the ground. I felt around and my hand enclosed a piece of what appeared to be rough cloth with holes in it, three small holes. I put it back and awaited what some may consider to have been my doom. I did not have to wait long, although I suppose it may have been hours.

The door to the shack was flung open and a beautiful corridor of sunlight yawned into the room picking out the stool in silhouette. The Walrus entered, followed by the FRUGALITY children. They all formed a semi-circle in front of me. And next came Zachariah Leonard. He pushed through the children and strode to the hole in the ground where he retrieved what I then saw was a hangman's hood. He put it on and I realised of course that he had been forever incomplete without it.

My eyes turned back to the doorway where the light was at its brightest. And there were W.G. and Robbie, arms about each other's shoulders. I couldn't tell whether they were laughing or crying. All I could be sure of was that their little boy shoulders rose and fell, just rose and fell like the pistons of a machine. It was as if the light was bursting from them alone and it was the motion of their shoulders that powered and sustained the universe.

Zachariah is before me now and beckons me to stand upon the stool. Once I have done so, he unravels a rope that has been secured to the ceiling and forms it into a noose. The noose complete, he turns to The Walrus, who nods and begins to clap rhythmically, a 2/4 beat for a few bars and then a 7/4 beat. He repeats this twice before the children begin to sing:

"Tollesbury Time,
Nothing is real
And nothing to get hung about.
Tollesbury Time Forever."

Zachariah puts the noose around my neck and secures it tight.

"Tollesbury Time,
Nothing is real
And nothing to get hung about.
Tollesbury Time Forever."

Zachariah kicks the stool from under me and it falls to the ground.

"Tollesbury Time,
Nothing is real
And nothing to get hung about.
Tollesbury Time Forever."

There is a wailing sound in my head but still I can hear the children singing. The sound in my head turns into the claxon at Ford's that signals the changing in shifts. I see my dad coming into my bedroom to say goodbye to his little lad. He then leaves to go to work. Then I see my uncle coming in. He has dark grease on his hands. He steps out of his overalls and approaches my three year old self who just lies there on the bed unmoving. The monster from Ford's lifts me without effort, turns me and buries my cold face into a tear-stained pillow.

And there is an angel before me now. Her name is Penny Shoraton.

All is silent.
All is black.

Tollesbury Time,
Nothing is real
And nothing to get hung about.
Tollesbury Time Forever

PART TWO

.....but I say it just to reach you

14. Incident Report No: 1050491/2

A. Nature of incident: NEAR MISS
B. Individual involved in the incident:
Name: SIMON ANTHONY
Gender: MALE
Date of Birth: 8th JULY 1958
Ethnicity: WHITE BRITISH
Patient Number: PN65738
C. Treatment received:
Received oxygen and placed in the recovery position until the paramedics arrived, who then took him to A&E.
D. Injury suffered:
Red mark around the neck made by the belt. No breaking of skin. Bruising evident.
E. Location of incident: BLACKWATER MENTAL HEALTH UNIT
Primary Location: CRIMSON WARD
Secondary Location: BEDROOM 11
Clinical Speciality: ADULT MENTAL HEALTH UNIT (ACUTE SECTOR)
Date of incident: 15th JULY 2008
Time of incident: 17:25pm
F. Circumstances of Incident:
Mr Anthony was found hanging in his bedroom, secured by a belt from the wardrobe door.
G. Remedial action taken following the incident:
Mr Anthony was taken down onto his bed and basic first aid given. He had a pulse. He was placed in the recovery position and given oxygen until the paramedics came and took him to A&E. He had a mark around his neck that had been made by the belt.
H. Witnesses: PENNY SHORATON, STAFF NURSE

15. Witness Statement

Name of person making Statement: Penny Shoraton

I have been a qualified psychiatric nurse since April 1997. I have been a Staff Nurse on Crimson Ward at Blackwater Mental Health Unit since October 2002. I have known Simon Anthony for the last four years in a professional capacity during several admissions to Crimson Ward. During this current admission, I have been his Keyworker.

On 16th July 2008, I was on a late shift. I was the nurse in charge throughout the shift, which started at 13:30pm and finished at 21:00pm.

At handover (sometime between 13:30pm and 14:30pm), I was informed that Simon Anthony had been returned to Crimson Ward by the police. They had apparently found him in a field between Tollesbury and Tolleshunt D'Arcy. On return, he was placed on Level 3 (continuous) observations due to a risk of absconding from the Unit and due to the previous suicide attempt that had led to the current admission. As nurse in charge, I allocated the periods of observation to the staff on duty. The staff rotated each hour as per the Observation Policy.

At 17:25, I was in the nursing office speaking on the phone to the relative of another client when I heard the emergency alarm. I terminated the call and went immediately to the ADP (alarm display panel) in the corridor. The alarm had been sounded from bedroom number eleven and so I ran to that location. When I arrived, the door to the bedroom was being held open by Pauline Zuma (Agency Support Worker) who had been on level 3 observations with Simon Anthony between 17:00pm and 18:00pm. It had been she who had activated the alarm.

When I looked into the room, I saw that Simon Anthony was hanging by his belt which had been fastened around his neck and looped around the top corner of his wardrobe door. A chair was on its side on the floor. His CD player was playing music at a very high volume. According to Pauline Zuma, the

Beatles' song "Strawberry Fields" had been played continuously over and over since she had commenced her stint of observation at 17:00pm.

I was joined then by Isabel Summers (Staff Nurse on Crimson Ward) and Steven Benson (Support Worker on Crimson Ward). Steven Benson supported Simon Anthony's bodyweight whilst I undid the belt. All three of us then manoeuvred Simon Anthony's body onto the floor.

On checking, I noted there was a faint pulse. I sent Isabel Summers to the Nursing Office to contact the paramedics and to bring an oxygen cylinder. With the assistance of Steven Benson, Simon Anthony was put in the recovery position. When the oxygen cylinder arrived some moments later, I applied the mask and Simon Anthony received oxygen until the paramedics arrived at 17:45pm, at which time they took over. They removed Simon Anthony to an awaiting ambulance and he was taken to Accident and Emergency. He had maintained a pulse throughout the immediate first aid procedures but had been non-responsive to verbal interventions. Steven Benson accompanied Simon Anthony to the Accident and Emergency department.

Signed

Penny Shoraton
(Staff Nurse)

16. The Mental Health Review Tribunal (Act I)

(The author recovered this transcript from Simon's house - the words in italics were written across the pages and in the margins. The author has inserted them accordingly.)

15th August 2008
Present:
Simon Anthony - Client
Peter Middleton - Solicitor
Dr Weepy - Responsible Medical Officer
Penny Shoraton - Staff Nurse (Crimson Ward)
David Cromwell - Social Worker
Iris Pearson - Tribunal Chair
Dr Khan - Medical Representative
Raymond Lister - Layperson
Donna Watkins - Mental Health Act Administrator

Big long bing bong table stretching on in out of perspective perspective. Chairs down each side like a rectangle round table of yore. This is it and this is it. Suits and form and fragile frugals. Sun is in the windows and the wind is on the rise. The time is here and the static is pure. I sit me down and wait for servings. Obladi. Oblada. Life goes on. Life goes on.

IRIS PEARSON (TO SIMON ANTHONY) - Thank you for coming here today, Mr Anthony. My name is Iris Pearson and I am the Chair of this panel. I am a barrister by profession and, as such, as well as being the Chair, I am also the 'Legal Member' of this panel. As you know, you have appealed against your detention under Section 3 of the Mental Health Act (1983) and this Tribunal has been convened to hear that appeal. We will be making a decision today; a decision

135

which we will inform you face to face in the first instance, with confirmation of that decision in writing to follow. You will also receive a transcript of the proceedings. If at any time you need a break, please indicate to your solicitor and we will break and reconvene when you are ready. Now do you have any questions, Mr Anthony, before we do some introductions?

SIMON ANTHONY (TO IRIS PEARSON) - No. It's ok. Thank you.

Thinking thankings. Cokey dokeys up the hokeys!

IRIS PEARSON - Very well. (SHE NODS TO HER RIGHT TO INDICATE TO DR KHAN THAT HE IS TO INTRODUCE HIMSELF)

DR KHAN - My name is Dr Khan and I am the Medical Member of this Panel. I am a Consultant Psychiatrist specialising in Forensic Psychiatry.

Forever in sync with my psychic tree. Now that's nice. Stripy shirt don't hurt me. The sheer arrogance of the purring, self-professed king of the jungle! Ah, sheer Khan!

SIMON ANTHONY - Hello.

RAYMOND LISTER - Hello Mr Anthony. I am Raymond Lister. I am the Layperson on this panel.

Lay Raymond Lay. Lay across my big brass bed. Loody loody, lady lady.

SIMON ANTHONY - Hello.

IRIS PEARSON - Now, please, for the benefit of the panel, could you all please introduce yourselves; beginning with you, Doctor.

DR WEEPY - I am Dr Weepy. I am Simon's Responsible Medical Officer.

Responsible. Indeed.

PETER MIDDLETON - I am Peter Middleton. I am a solicitor from Middleton and Fowlers. I am here today representing Mr Anthony.

Wonderful Peter the middle son of all the flowers of this earth. Presented to me from the tillers of the fields. Wonderful Peter.

SIMON ANTHONY - Hello. I'm Simon.

PENNY SHORATON - And I'm Penny Shoraton. I am a Staff Nurse on Crimson Ward. I am also Simon's Keyworker.

Beauty queen oh beauty queen. I am the grim son you never had. Lord I'm so keen it hurts.

DAVID CROMWELL - I am David Cromwell and I work for the Blackwater Community Mental Health Team.

Too much monkey business. Deep dark purple and a shade of grey. Colours in the sky of the pie high high.

IRIS PEARSON - Thank you. Just to let you know, Simon, that the other person here, over there with the notebook, is Donna. She is the Mental Health Act Administrator for this Unit and she will be taking notes of the session.

Now she is barmaid nice and blibs and blubs. Cheeky reds and Thelma orange roll-neck jumper as expected and dejected. Wink at me and wink at you. Castigate and flush, ruminate and vegetate. Like you. Like you a lot.

SIMON ANTHONY - Hello.

IRIS PEARSON - Now if we can begin with you Dr Weepy. Could you please talk us through your report? When you have done so, the panel will ask any questions they would like answered and then Mr Middleton will have an opportunity to question you on behalf of Mr Anthony.

Cough up doctor. Clear the throat and smote the groat, Sing it loud and proud from the heartstops of your thuddings and the needlings of your knowledge. Go doctor! Go doctor!

DR WEEPY - Thank you. I will give a summary of Simon's background history before going onto the current admission and the treatment plan that is currently in place.

Simon was born in Dagenham, Essex in 1958. He has no brothers or sisters and both his parents are deceased. He was delivered by caesarean section and, as a child, met all developmental milestones. The family moved from Dagenham to Tollesbury when Simon was very young. His father, who was an alcoholic, left the family home two years after the move to Tollesbury and Simon was thereafter brought up solely by his mother. Simon attended Tollesbury Infant and

137

Junior School, towards the end of which, at around the age of nine, there are reports of aggressive behaviour towards fellow pupils. He was also at times reported to be incontinent of urine. This continued until his early teens. Indeed, night-time enuresis has continued to be a problem for Simon throughout most of his adult life. He left school at the age of sixteen with no qualifications.

Simon's first contact with mental health services was in August 1975, at the age of seventeen, when he was brought into Blackwater Mental Health Unit by the police. They had found him lying on the pavement in Tiptree High Street, screaming. He became aggressive towards them when they attended and they needed to use handcuffs and a van to bring him in. He was detained under Section 25 of the Mental Health Act (1959) and diagnosed with Paranoid Schizophrenia. During that first admission, Simon spent almost a year in hospital, finally being discharged in June 1976.

Subsequent admissions followed, the majority under section, over the next three years. Between 1979 and 1985, Simon was maintained in the community, although his mental state remained brittle throughout and he grew heavily dependent on alcohol. In 1980, he got married and in 1982, he had a son. The boy had Down's syndrome and evidently was cared for very much by Simon's wife, Julia.

When his mother died in January 1986, Simon suffered a further relapse and was detained in hospital under Section 3 of the Mental Health Act (1983). During that admission, consideration was given as to whether a return to the family home, now in Tiptree, would be beneficial for Simon, or indeed the child. He spent seven months in a rehabilitation unit which addressed both his insight and his dependence upon alcohol. During this period, his relationship with his wife deteriorated, but she continued to visit on a regular basis and remained in constant contact with the care team.

On discharge Simon returned to live at the home once owned by his mother, in Tollesbury. He continues to live at that same address to this day.

In June 1989, following a suicide attempt where he had taken an overdose of his prescribed medication, Simon was admitted once more to hospital under Section 3 of the Mental Health Act (1983). He had been found by the milkman who had been alerted due to the front door being open. During that admission, Simon had his first course of ECT. A period of stability followed, largely due to Simon being compliant with his Depot medication and he began to see a psychologist on a weekly basis. It was during these sessions that the sexual abuse perpetrated by Simon's uncle was revealed. The uncle had shared the family home in Dagenham and had worked with Simon's father at the Ford's plant. It is not clear as to whether Simon's parents had ever been aware of the abuse, which continued until the move to Tollesbury in the early Sixties. It is my opinion that Simon's mental health problems and subsequent addiction to alcohol have their base in this sexual abuse.

Pause and take a sip good doctor from your water glass of water essence. Let it soothe and cool and rest your soothings. Replace the face of fractured flubbing. The monster of Ford's is in and out, here and now and broken flax that wheels and burns from top to trim, heating and blurring the visions of breath. Take a sip good doctor. Take a sip.

Simon had two brief admissions to hospital, both under Section, in 2001 and 2004. It seems that as time has gone on, he has gained a degree of insight into his illness when stable, which has allowed care in the community to be more effective. I will now go on to the details surrounding the most recent admission and detention.

This admission began on 5th July 2008, when Simon was brought to A&E following a suicide attempt. A passer-by walking his dog had discovered Simon face down in the marshes in and around Tollesbury. Simon received emergency treatment at the scene. When roused, there was a larger than normal degree of alcohol in his blood and it was clear, judging by his reported speech content, that he was suffering from a relapse of his paranoid schizophrenic illness.

139

When medically fit, he was transferred to Blackwater Mental Health Unit and admitted to Crimson Ward. He was largely incoherent in his speech and was reportedly disorientated in time, place and person. We restarted him on his depot medication on admission but both myself and Dr Nardy felt he had not shown sufficient insight to ensure he would stay informally. He had, for example, been given his depot injection without even giving any sign that it had happened. He spoke at the time only of horses and a boy with no teeth.

When I first saw Simon, he displayed elements of paranoia consistent with previous relapses and both myself and my colleague, Dr Nardy felt detention under the Mental Health Act may be inevitable. This was confirmed when he left the review prematurely, running back to his room with his hands over his ears. We placed him initially on continuous observations for a twenty four hour period during which we intended to discuss further whether he could be managed as a voluntary patient. This decision was made for us however when he absconded from the unit the following day. On his return to the ward on 15th July, having been Absent Without Leave for three days, he attempted to commit suicide in his room by hanging. Thankfully, he survived and was detained under Section 3 of the Mental Health Act.

Since his return to Crimson Ward, Simon's mental state has steadily improved. We had planned for a course of ECT but it seems this may no longer be necessary. He continues to comply with his depot medication with an adjunct of an oral anti-psychotic and an anti-depressant. I am hopeful that he will continue to maintain his current progress.

Double eyes removed spectacular spect-a-cular. Close your mind good doctor and lap up the cooling air to brace your ice. Head so bow wow wowed and then retrieve your gusto and gaze upon your jury.

IRIS PEARSON - Thank you Dr Weepy for that comprehensive summary. Now, if you don't mind, I will ask the panel if they have any questions before giving the opportunity to Mr Middleton to question you on behalf of Mr Anthony.

IRIS PEARSON - Dr Khan?

Oh rise Dr Khan from your petal covered nub, flower and be seen whilst tingle touching your fingeroos.

DR KHAN - Thank you Dr Weepy. As I understand it, Mr Anthony has been treated for many years on depot medication. Is that also the current treatment plan?

DR WEEPY - Simon is on a Depixol injection every two weeks. He has been on a variety of depot medication over the years, but Depixol seems to suit. He is also currently taking 300 mg of Quetiapine daily as well as Venlafaxine, which, as you know, is an anti-depressant.

DR KHAN - You alluded earlier to the fact that Mr Anthony had engaged in psychological therapies in the past. Is this something that is currently still under consideration, or are you content that medication alone will alleviate the current symptoms and sustain him in the community?

DR WEEPY - Well, as it is, Simon is responding very well to the current medication regime. If he continues to be compliant with it, I am hopeful that he may remain well when he is eventually discharged from hospital.

DR KHAN - Thank you, Dr Weepy. I have no further questions.

IRIS PEARSON - Raymond?

RAYMOND LISTER - Thank you madam chair. Dr Weepy, thank you for your summary and also for your report. All very informative, I'm sure.

DR WEEPY - Thank you.

RAYMOND LISTER - What I would like to know, Dr Weepy, is have you discounted the psychological therapy option entirely or is it something that you are still considering?

DR WEEPY - One can never discount anything when it comes to mental illness. Simon Anthony is suffering, and has in fact suffered from, a severe and enduring mental illness that has blighted his life. Medication has helped him to achieve a certain level of well-being and in time, with appropriate psychological therapy, I feel he can look forward to a relatively stable future. The importance of the timing of psychological therapies can never be under-estimated.

RAYMOND LISTER - So you still have plans to pursue psychological therapies?

DR WEEPY - Yes.

RAYMOND LISTER - Thank you.

IRIS PEARSON - Well thank you, Dr Weepy. Nothing from me; so Mr Middleton, you can address Dr Weepy with any questions you may have.

PETER MIDDLETON - Thank you.

Pretty Peter pose and scribble. Sniggle it over to me. Well I see your words but not your point. I will nid and nod my head anyhow to smooth your brow and plaster your cast. Continue!

PETER MIDDLETON - Firstly, Dr Weepy. Could you please confirm on what basis you are currently detaining my client. Is it in terms of Nature or Degree, or, if you deem it so, both?

DR WEEPY - Simon is suffering from a mental illness, namely Paranoid Schizophrenia, which is of a nature that permits detention under the Mental Health Act. His illness is currently at the stage where recovery has only just begun. There has been little sustained evidence of insight. I would therefore argue that he is being detained on the basis of both Nature and Degree.

PETER MIDDLETON - Nature and Degree?

DR WEEPY - Yes.

PETER MIDDLETON - You mentioned earlier the sexual abuse suffered by my client when he was a child. Could you please clarify whether the medication addresses the trauma that arose from that terrible experience?

DR WEEPY - When people suffer such a trauma, mental illness can evolve. Some may experience periods of depression; others such as Simon, may experience hallucinations and delusions, which, although distressing, may in some ways protect the mind from facing up to what has happened to them. The medication seeks to dull the emotional impact of these psychotic features and thus limit the problems

142

they cause in day to day to life. From that perspective, I believe medication in Simon's case has, and will continue to be, effective.

PETER MIDDLETON - And in terms of addressing the deeper psychological issues?

DR WEEPY - Well, that is a very long process. Simon needs to first accept that he is suffering from a schizophrenic illness before any progress can be made in that aspect. During this admission, he has been of the belief that he has been in Tollesbury back in the early nineteenth century or some such. He has had many delusions over the years which, when untreated, have made it impossible for him to live in the community. When a patient is disorientated to that degree, it is necessary for us to bring him back to reality with the use of medication before he can begin to explore what has happened in his childhood. Surely that much is obvious?

Pleadle plaudle with your dove-like hands good doctor. You can vious your ob any way you like and plore your imp to all that will listen. 'Tis your frightful right good sir!

PETER MIDDLETON - And whose reality is that, Dr Weepy, to which you seek to bring my client? Your reality or his?

Dun dun daaar!

IRIS PEARSON - Dr Weepy?

Well, well, weeeeellll?!

DR WEEPY - Well, I don't think it is actually that helpful to labour this point. The fact is that if somebody thinks they have gone back in time then, to me, and to society at large, that is surely the product of a mental illness and it is my duty as a Consultant Psychiatrist to lead that person back to the real world. It would be cruel not to do so, wouldn't you agree?

PETER MIDDLETON - I wonder if you could tell me at what point, Dr Weepy, you would consider my client to have gained sufficient insight to warrant you discharging him from Section 3? Assuming of course he is not discharged by the panel today.

Puppy dog eyes my Peter to cajole and shlurp the spaniel paniel. Ah but the eyebrow of the lady jerks and jumps over the

143

hurdle of her eye and her chin sinks into swampy pulpy neck flesh. No dice, man. No dice.

DR WEEPY - Insight is a key component, maybe the key component of any patient's recovery. Without insight, a patient may discontinue medication which will in turn lead to a relapse. Without insight, a patient may neglect to meet up with their Community Nurse or Social Worker. They may even refuse to attend Outpatient Appointments with the Consultant Psychiatrist. In short, without insight, a patient will inevitably disengage from all attempts to help maintain them in the Community with, just as inevitably, disastrous consequences.

PETER MIDDLETON - So if I understand you correctly, Dr Weepy, insight is gained when a patient does what the mental health system tells him or her to do, without question. Is that what you are saying?

DR WEEPY - Let us not be trite Mr Middleton.

PETER MIDDLETON - Please forgive me. I am just trying to ascertain as to what, in your opinion, my client needs to do to prove to you that he has, as you call it, developed insight.

DR WEEPY - Well, he would need to understand that he suffers from Schizophrenia and that he needs to take medication. He will also need to assure me that he understands the need for community care and to show sufficient commitment to engage with community services.

PETER MIDDLETON - Not an easy task, I'm sure. Could you please tell me briefly how the medication works? I would just like to understand it a little bit more.

DR WEEPY - Anti-psychotics work by increasing or reducing the effects of natural chemicals (called neurotransmitters) in the brain, including dopamine, serotonin, noradrenalin and acetylcholine. These neurotransmitters regulate numerous aspects of behaviour including mood and emotions, control of sleeping and wakefulness and control of feeding.

PETER MIDDLETON - Thank you. I think. Is it true that one view would be that such medication dulls the emotions and impulses of an individual to the point where they no longer have the motivation or energy, mental or otherwise, to do anything other than the most basic of daily tasks? And that's without even considering the side-effects of such medication. And furthermore, could that reduction in energy, emotion and motivation then perhaps limit the opportunity for others to be aware of the thoughts someone such as my client may have purely because one such as my client would be spending the majority of his time, well, asleep.

IRIS PEARSON - I think, Mr Middleton, that such a debate could go on indefinitely. If we could just stick to why we are here today, namely whether Mr Anthony warrants continued detention under Section 3, then I would be much obliged.

PETER MIDDLETON - I'm sorry. It is not my intention to keep the panel here any longer than is necessary. I would just like to make the point that the fact that my client is currently complying with medication is evidence alone of a degree of insight into his condition and that surely he does not need to complete a test in physiology to prove that. When my GP tells me I have a chest infection, I do not ask the ins and outs of how it develops and he does not grill me as to whether or not I understand what is wrong with me or whether I will comply with treatment. I just take the antibiotics and hope things improve. And my GP trusts me to do so.

DR WEEPY - My point exactly.

Plinky plonk ker-plunk. Pull your straws and lose your marbles. Tickety, tickety BOO!

PETER MIDDLETON - But we are not talking about mere chest infections, are we Dr Weepy? We are talking about a man's thoughts, his emotions, his moods, his connection to society, indeed to the world. We are talking about the sensory experience a man has of his life - and if that experience is too dissimilar to that of the rest of us then we call it an illness - and the cure for that illness is to subject the transmitters or whatever they may be to drugs which debilitate the workings of the mind to the extent that a fog, a vacuum, develops; the only way out being to agree that you are mad and that the venerable Dr Weepy is right.

145

Sigh miles high Mr Peterman and raise your hands to the venerable amongst us. Tolerate their frown with a stoic tinge and seek not to vanish into the antiquity of it all.

IRIS PEARSON - Thank you Mr Middleton. And thank you Dr Weepy.

Nodding head Weepy wibbly wobbly leaning back recline and sink into the form of all our souls the power turning twixt and thus into the spirals of my mind.

IRIS PEARSON - Are you ok, Mr Anthony? We can stop for a moment if you like?

In the name of love! Before you break my heart - think it oh oh ver.

SIMON ANTHONY - I am fine thank you. Well, in a manner of speaking, of course.

IRIS PEARSON - That's good. I am aware that these kind of things can be very stressful so please do let me know if things are becoming too much.

SIMON ANTHONY - Thank you. I will.

IRIS PEARSON - Now, if we could come to you please Miss Shoraton. A summary of your Nursing Report if you please.

Quivering quaking in your shakings redden up as your lamp arises bringing forth the fundamental shift of the soul to the surface, breaking the mighty tensions with which the gentle of heart must forever contend. The beat of my heartness, the heart of my beatness and the twanging of your memory strings combines to fill the VOID with musical delights and absent smitings that behold nothing but the glory of the future and the nebulous hammerings of the past.

PENNY SHORATON - Thank you. I have known Simon for about four years. In that time, he has had three admissions to Crimson Ward. On the current admission, I have been his Keyworker. He was admitted informally having just tried to drown himself in the marshes in Tollesbury, where he lives. When he was admitted, he was disorientated in time, place and person. He walked around the ward constantly with little communication to others. He was noted to be responding to auditory hallucinations whilst in his bedroom. It wasn't clear as to whether he was experiencing visual hallucinations as well.

Simon initially complied with oral medication which was given in liquid form due to him having secreted tablets during previous admissions. He took his depot from one of our student nurses but continued to present as confused and disorientated. There were initially no signs of him being a suicide risk or a risk to others.

When Simon was seen in ward review by Dr Weepy and Dr Nardy, he became distressed and was placed on continuous observation. This was mainly due to the fact that on previous admissions he has attempted to harm himself when distressed. It was the following day that he absconded from the ward. He was found after three days, asleep in a field near Tollesbury. It seemed he had cut a narrow strip of grass about a foot long and placed matchsticks in the ground at each end. According to the police, it looked like some kind of miniature cricket pitch.

When Simon returned from AWOL, he was taken first to the Section 136 Suite and then to his room. It was there that he tried to hang himself and I was one of those who found him. In his pocket, there was a selection of scrabble letters - nine of them from what I remember although I can't remember which ones they were. I think there was an F and a Y and perhaps a G.

IRIS PEARSON - I am not sure we expect you to remember such unnecessary detail, Miss Shoraton. Do go on.

PENNY SHORATON - Sorry. Thank you. Well when Simon returned from A&E he was placed again on continuous observations and began to comply with his medication. Over the last few weeks, he has become orientated to reality and there has been no evidence of responding to visual or auditory hallucinations. He is now on intermittent observations. He hasn't had any periods of unescorted leave but does currently have one hour escorted leave per day around the grounds.

Beauty is as beauty does and we all stand together! The lady of all our wonders sighs and touches so gently her own cream hands and her eyes enter mine with the gargantuan fullness of the steamer departing from the shores of Albion's purity. There is nothing like the deep ocean look of the majestic love that throbs within a fairy woman's soul and the splendour of its radiance when it encompasses your whole entire earth. Penny Shoraton you are not only my angel but the fulfilment of all my misshapen logic and blunders. You stream into me and take apart all that is treacherous in the mountainous regime of my powerless worth. I am yours, in madness, your friend and your lover - Simon Anthony.

IRIS PEARSON - Thank you. Are you ok to continue Mr Anthony?

SIMON ANTHONY - If it's alright with you, I would like to just take a breath in the garden. Only if that's alright, of course?

IRIS PEARSON - In that case, we will adjourn for, say ten minutes? Thank you everybody.

The leaves depart and the light ascends, flowers pulsing through the veins of time. The breath of all is upon me now weaving and meandering in and out of my mighty heart and dishevelled mind. The arras awaits to save me once more. Falling apart is so much harder than keeping it together, the crimble crumble of my stony pony brings about a gathering of unfortunate miasma that can lead only to a debacle from which there is no escape. But I know all that and knowledge alone is what will keep me strong. It's a quarter to four and the bell doth ring clanging me home from school into the greasy arm slithering dreams of a grim decaying monster.

Love me do, people. Love me do!

17. The Mental Health Review Tribunal (Act II)

Well, from behind the arras I do now reveal myself and once more am I to be subjected to the jestery tinklings of adultspeak; but, ah, the light in which I will submerge my fine self is that which gushes forth from the angel of all my heavens and pours over my big old aching soul. All else is but shadow to me now.

IRIS PEARSON - Thank you for returning on time everybody. So, if we can continue? Before we adjourned we had just heard the evidence of the nursing team. Now I will ask the panel if they have any questions.

DR KHAN - Do you consider, Miss Shoraton, that Mr Anthony is currently a danger to himself?

PENNY SHORATON - I don't think so, though it's difficult to say. He has obviously tried to kill himself in the recent past and you can't rule out him trying to kill himself in the future I suppose. But right now, he is really well - probably as well as I have seen him for a long time.

Love is in the air! Every time I look around it seems I'm bound to have found the sound that leads ever to the ground, that deep dark bass that throbs and fathoms the ultimate assuaging of the tortuous rhythms of my heart. I love you, Penny Shoraton.

DR KHAN - Well, going on from there, do you consider that Mr Anthony warrants continued detention under the Mental Health Act?

PENNY SHORATON - That's not really for me to say, I don't think. All I'm saying is that Simon has been very unwell and now he's getting better. Whether he needs to stay on a Section is really up to you. And the others of course.

DR KHAN - Thank you.

IRIS PEARSON - Raymond?

RAYMOND LISTER - Could you please explain to me what you mean by Mr Anthony being 'well'?

PENNY SHORATON - When Simon first gets admitted, he is always very deluded in terms of time and place. This is the first admission where he has not worn sunglasses the entire time. When he is unwell, he can be very unpredictable. When he is well, he seems just like me or you. You can have a normal conversation with him and you wouldn't know there had ever been anything wrong with him. He really does go between being incredibly ill to more or less fine.

RAYMOND LISTER - So it is your professional opinion that he is now, as you call it, more or less fine?

PENNY SHORATON - Well, yes. More or less.

More or less and twist and shout, roust the boutings and beat me dry. The world doth take its chaos and ram it into sidings and skirtings to sculpt and mould the eternal freeform thoughtness of it all into yesses and nose and right and wrong and thisem and thatem so everyone can feel the safe carousing and wondrous extensions of intimated intimacy and beauty beholded in the eyes of HE WHO IS KING. You treat my thoughts with your contempt and your medicine but judge me by my words alone. I can believe I am Jesus or Buddha as long as I don't tell you, yet you can freely admit that there is a God that speaks to you and you could become the president of the united states - is that not the cold hard truth? Oh broken hearted simpletons of this vacuous void you call the civil west, the archetypal homespun society that ingratiates itself with the firm and the angle, the sharp and the crangle, the pinpoint and the needle, the cross and the bearer - do not ever truly delve too deep inside my mind lest you yourself go mad. I'm in love with her and I feel fine, I'm in love with her and I feel fine...

IRIS PEARSON - Now do you have any questions for the nurse, Mr Middleton?

PETER MIDDLETON - Hi Penny.

PENNY SHORATION - Hi.

PETER MIDDLETON - So if I understand you, Penny, you do not currently believe Simon to be a risk to himself or others?

PENNY SHORATON - He has really improved over the last few days which is great to see. He is spending more time out of his room and interacting appropriately with the staff and some of the other patients. I know that, in the past, he has been aggressive to nursing staff, but on this admission there has been nothing like that.

PETER MIDDLETON - I understand it was you who found Simon hanging a few weeks ago. Was there any indication that something like that was going to happen?

PENNY SHORATON - Not really. I mean he was on continuous observations more due to his risk of absconding. We were all obviously aware when Simon returned to the ward that he was very unwell. He hadn't seemed upset though. If anything, he had been very calm. He was playing his Beatles music like he always does and seemed fairly settled. It was definitely a shock when he tried to hang himself.

PETER MIDDLETON - Have you spoken to him since about why he did it?

PENNY SHORATON - Well he was initially taken to A&E. When he returned the following day, he was very subdued. It was difficult to get anything out of him. It was as if he was kind of in shock about what he had done. As Dr Weepy said, ECT was considered but Simon started to pick up as the days went on. As is consistent with previous presentations, when Simon is in his psychotic phase, he doesn't really remember very much which I suppose maybe just as well.

Or is it more about what I don't tell you than what I don't remember? But of all these friends and lovers, there is no-one compares with you. Some are dead and some are living. In my life, I've loved them all.

PETER MIDDLETON - I take it you do not currently consider Simon to be a danger to himself.

PENNY SHORATON - No, not as he is at the moment.

PETER MIDDLETON - Thank you, Penny.

151

What a lovely couple they would make - the fragile fleetings of paleface Peter and the boundless chasm of beauty that is my Penny. I look and observe and see all from a position just a little further back than you could ever believe. I am here upon my cinema seat, popcorn down my shirt and coke too cold watching the film of my life as it is played out before me. There is little I can do but to muse upon the variations of theme and the lightening of darkness, the exquisite contradictions that fuel every waking moment where power and might meet the meek and the mild. I sit back and view all for that is all I can do. Play on, good people, play on.

IRIS PEARSON - And now over to you Mr Cromwell. I understand that the report submitted from your Community Mental Health Team was not written by you, but that you are representing the author due to sickness?

DAVID CROMWELL - That's right. And I would like to confirm that this is the first time I have met Simon.

IRIS PEARSON - I see. Not a very good show, is it? Anyway, we must proceed. Do you have anything to add to the report?

DAVID CROMWELL - No.

IRIS PEARSON - Dr Khan?

DR KHAN - No questions.

IRIS PEARSON - Raymond?

RAYMOND LISTER - None from me.

IRIS PEARSON - Mr Middleton?

PETER MIDDLETON - Just one question, Mr Cromwell. Could you please confirm what level of support Simon will receive from your team were he to be discharged today?

DAVID CROMWELL - One of our team will visit Simon on a regular basis. It will probably be one of the nurses, seeing as he is on a depot. They will keep an eye on him to see how he is and help him with anything he needs help with. It might have been me, but I'm a social worker. I don't do depots.

PETER MIDDLETON - So you don't know as of yet who will be Simon's Care Co-ordinator?

DAVID CROMWELL - I'm sorry. I don't. I can check for you after this if you like?

PETER MIDDLETON - Thank you. But I'm not sure that will be necessary. Suffice to say, there is a plan in place were Simon to be discharged by the panel today.

DAVID CROMWELL - Yes.

PETER MIDDLETON - Thank you.

Hurrah! Hurrah! Support for little old me to keep my eyes on the prize and keep me keeping on like a bird that flew. Mister, Mister Raymond Lister, you and your friends are always welcome in my humble abode fireplace ablaze and wooden floor scuffed with the bootmarks of the downtrodden man. Come in, come in!

IRIS PEARSON - Now, Mr Anthony. I want to thank you for your patience to this point. It must be very difficult to be the subject of such a discussion. Now it is your opportunity to have your say. In your own time, could you please tell the panel what your thoughts are with regard to your current detention under the Mental Health Act.

Step onto the stage young sir. Cross that white, white touchline of your shame and jog onto the park to try and dazzle in so little time, to make a mark, to cement a place, to raise an eyebrow and to make them realise you are worth more than all of this. Carry the drinks no longer for that sweaty, putrid middle order batsman who doesn't even like cricket yet gets in every week whilst you sit there at home working out averages and gazing at black and white photos and wondering what it would be like to stride out in confidence, to swing a bat with authority or to bowl a ball with venom. Stride out fine man and jingle jangle with the best of them.

SIMON ANTHONY - Err. Thank you. What would you like to know?

IRIS PEARSON - Just please tell us how you feel about your current detention. Anything you would like to add to what has been said, to what you have heard.

SIMON ANTHONY - I think everyone has done a really good job. They are all very nice and very kind. I don't really know what else to say. If Dr Weepy thinks I need to stay here, then maybe I do. I wouldn't like to disagree with him. He has a wonderful beard. I think he cries more often than I do. But then crying is good. It's just the way the soul squeezes out its squeezings.

PETER MIDDLETON - Simon, Simon. Perhaps it would help if I ask you some questions?

SIMON ANTHONY - Ok.

PETER MIDDLETON - You have heard many things said about you this morning. I would like to clarify a few points with you. Firstly, do you recognise that you suffer from a mental illness for which you are required to take medication to remain well?

SIMON ANTHONY - I do.

PETER MIDDLETON - And are you prepared to continue with that medication if you are discharged from the Section.

SIMON ANTHONY - I will

To love, honour, cherish and obey sweet Weepy so that you may sleep safe in the knowledge you have cured the incurable, fixed the unfixable and ticked the tickables of all that is required of you. Til death do us part. And may it be mine, not yours.

PETER MIDDLETON - In terms of the support available to you in the community, Simon, are you willing to engage with whatever is offered, visits from a nurse or social worker etc?

SIMON ANTHONY - I will.

PETER MIDDLETON - I have no further questions.

IRIS PEARSON - Dr Khan?

DR KHAN - Hello, Mr Anthony. Could you please explain to me how you understand the illness with which you suffer? I am very pleased to see you seem to be recovering by the way.

Here goes the goes. That old question. It's all perception and lack of perception. I see things that you don't see and I feel things you do not feel. I experience sensations, smells, tastes, terrors and hopes and dreams and absolute doodle dandy wonders. When I express them, I am ill. When I keep them to myself, I am well.

SIMON ANTHONY - I was first diagnosed with Schizophrenia when I was about seventeen or eighteen. The medication helps me to be more like other people. Sometimes, at times of stress, I have to come into hospital. The nurses and the doctors make me better and then I go back home. I can't thank them enough for the help they give me. That's it really. I'm sorry that I can't be more exact.

DR KHAN - Please don't apologise, Mr Anthony. I understand you very well.

Like you understand gravity and the movement of light and centrifugal force and atoms and car engines and all those other concept driven quantifiable elements of life. You are a very bright man, Dr Khan. But have you smelled the baking of potatoes in early nineteenth century England or lain upon a cricket pitch gazing upon the snow white sky of ultimate heaven? Have you listened in awe to the gock-pause-thwack or felt the power of the fundamental belting blues that roars and soars from the soul of the absolutely wretched and departed? You understand what I think you can cope with. That is all, my friend. So let us both live our lives in the way we choose untouched by such sensorial admonishments as rank and class and pride and wellness and illness and await in complete dismay the final denouement.

IRIS PEARSON - Raymond?

RAYMOND LISTER - None from me.

Nice smile Raymondo, just short of patronising but with enough kindness to infer a depth of wisdom of which you may be entirely unaware.

IRIS PEARSON - In that case, Mr Middleton, all that remains is for your summing up. I shall now hand over to you.

PETER MIDDLETON - Thank you.

Deep breath, scratch your chin my Peter, pick your pretty thoughts from the wonderful fragrant garden of your mind and present your posy to judge and jury. And may you impress yourself more than all others here for you are a man who takes care of the lost and the broken, you suit and boot

155

and toot the toot for the down of trodden and the fragments of our bizarre human race. I would have liked to have been your bestest friend at school, to share my packed lunch with you and to dream my dreams with you. I had never the opportunity, not merely because we are of different ages and attended different schools, but moreso because my waking hours dripped ever with grease and oil. And I pray that yours did not.

PETER MIDDLETON - The panel have heard the evidence here today and I would humbly submit that my client should be discharged from Section 3 of the Mental Health Act. We have heard from Dr Weepy who confirmed he is continuing to detain my client in terms of both Nature and Degree. I would contest that the Degree element has not been proven.

You have heard confirmation from Penny Shoraton that my client currently is well and presents no risk to either himself or others. Dr Weepy himself confirmed the improvement my client has made over the past few weeks. Were my client to be discharged from the Section today, Mr Cromwell from the Community Mental Health Team has confirmed there is a support plan in place. My client has confirmed that he is more than willing to comply with the aftercare arrangements, just as he has been complying with his treatment on Crimson Ward. He has also indicated that he would consider staying as an informal patient should Dr Weepy feel discharge from hospital to be premature at this present time.

My client has conducted himself today with humility and good grace. I do not dismiss however, the seriousness of the attempts he has made on his life over the last two months, the one that led him to come into hospital in the first place, and the hanging attempt that occurred on his return to the ward following his three day unauthorised absence. It is absolutely apparent, however, that these attempts on his own life were not a product of depression or a rational attempt to kill himself - they were the culmination of an untreated psychotic illness,

156

which is now, I'm sure we would all agree, thankfully in check.

Detention under the Mental Health Act is supposed to allow for illnesses, such as the one my client endures, to be treated effectively even when the very person who suffers that illness is oblivious to the need for treatment. I would submit that treatment of the acute phase of his illness is now complete and a period of supported stability in the community, in his own home, in the village he so clearly loves, is what is now required. It is the logical step in the patient journey. Continued detention in hospital under Section, against his will, would, I humbly posit, go against the very spirit of the Mental Health Act. I have no further remarks other than that I know you will fully consider all the evidence you have read and heard and come to a wise judgement. Thank you.

Ah my Peter, you poor angel, you entirely beautiful man, you. I could tell you so much more but it would blow your black and white mind. I want you never to know of ones such as Zachariah Leonard, or of oil hair and greasy sheets and a big dirty hand over the cherry red mouth of a cherry red child, of the most searing of pains, the deepest of guilts or the broken shards of a young boy's crystal amazement. It is not you that is protecting me, my Peter, but I that is protecting you.

Exeunt

18. Plosh, Mooom, Plash, Aaahhh

I was told on the afternoon of 15th August 2008 that my detention under Section 3 of the Mental Health Act had been rescinded by the Mental Health Review Tribunal. I received confirmation in writing two days later and at my next ward review, the following week, with Dr Weepy and Dr Nardy, I was discharged from hospital, back to my home in Tollesbury. And all was well in my world - or so I believed.

When your thought mind thought thinkings lead you down their woe begotten tracks, upturning briars and brambles and unseen colours, you can't just dismiss it. So the first thing I did when I returned home was to take out the scrabble letters from my pocket and arrange them on my sturdy old wooden table. F-R-U-G-A-L-I-T-Y.

I could see the little children in those small square tiles, hear their voices, feel the beating of their boom-boom hearts and smell the fragrance of how things once were and always should be. And I knew instantly it was my task to apply the diamond white lessons I had learned, apply them to my own existence.

An opportunity for fulfilment had been presented to me by the erratic meanderings of my fractured mind. I just needed to tie the knot, to buckle the braces and to snap that final piece into place that would make my life worthwhile indeed. I needed what I should never have forsaken. I needed to see my boy. But first I needed to be worthy of him.

As I thought on, the indomitable presence of my wife, Julia, edged into my Blakean vision. She was a colossus and I but a fool. I knew that. But our lives had once become entwined and we had produced Robbie. It was time for me to stand up. It was time to do what a man does.

It was about half past two when I got to The King's Head. I got my pint and sat over by the book shelves in the far corner. I could see the world from there - both yours and mine. I have always adored looking at the photos on the walls - those pictures of old sailing boats - wondering where the sailors had been and where they were going; and wondering whether they knew all along that it was not they who had control but the great rolling dark ocean beneath them. And above that the sky and the moon and the firmament, all majestic and immovable, historic and forever, governing the flip and the flop of the boat upon the waves.

Plosh, mooom, plash, aaahhh.

The cider sparkles golden in my glass and slowly begins to focus my mind. This can happen even when I just think about drinking. The alcohol gives hard edges to my thoughts and imbues them with greens and blues and reds. It welcomes me home and fixes me ever in place in the universe. It is my sigh and my deep breath, the whisper in my ear, the stroking of my matted hair. If you can replace what it gives me, then please feel free to remove it from my life. Until that moment, please leave me to my immaculate soothings.

Plosh, mooom, plash, aaahhh.

"How goes it, Jim?"

"Not bad, Bill. Not bad."

"Guinness?"

"Good of you, Bill."

From my corner, I couldn't see either Jim or Bill, nor could they see me. I guessed it was just the three of us in the pub, except maybe the barmaid and the glamorous lady to whose photograph the bacon fries were attached. I felt relaxed, ready. There was a stillness in the air such as when you first awake from a dreamydeepsleep.

"How's the wife, Jim? Doing her womanly duty?"

"She's ok. She's ok. Roasties still the best in the world and she doesn't snore half as much as she used to. Who could ask for more than that at my age, eh?"

"Ah, the roasties. I wish she would give my missus the recipe. Finest roasties I ever tasted, mate."

"I'll drink to that."

And they did. Slurp, gulp, savour, numbness, life. Roast potatoes, warm wives, gravy, the Sunday papers, heating that

159

works, a glow, a glow, a glow. To sigh so right and not so wrong. Cider do your duty.

"Kids ok, Jim? Behaving and all that?"

"Funny you mention that, Bill, but yes they are. Bloody adolescents, you can never work out why they do what they do. Bet they don't know themselves half the time, what with all the hormones and that."

"Ah, the hormones. The moaning whores we used to call them. Funny buggers. But at least they're behaving mate. That's good that is. Did you do the old child-killing thing on them like I said?"

Pause. Possible gulping. The Child-Killer is here lads, in the corner, by the books, his head in cider, his heart in the world. He did what he did and he knows what he knows. It comes around and around. Nobody is bad - all is good. Don't be afraid and let not your children be afraid. It's all FRUGALITY and that's all.

"No, Bill. I didn't do the bloody child-killing thing on them. At times, you're an idiot. Now get me a drink."

The window behind me was open and I could hear clearly several voices, affable and teasing, comfortable and utterly of this village. And, yes, doctor, the voices were all outside my head and, no doctor, they neither commanded me nor persecuted me - they simply were. They came from what I suppose would be referred to as the beer garden but which was, in reality, merely a paved area crammed with benches bordered by a fence.

"I was working on Mersea Island with this other bloke last week. This fella has himself a kebab for breakfast..."

"Don't put me off kebabs you bastard!"

"For breakfast? What sort of twat is he?"

"Works with numbnuts there - what do you expect?"

"Shut it, all of you. Anyway. He's having this kebab when he realises there's a bloody moth in it! A real one, wings and everything. He was already halfway through it when he realised, poor bastard."

"Half way through the moth? Had a couple of wings and then decided he didn't like it?"

160

"Wouldn't that be two thirds - what with the body?"

"Depends on the size of the body and if you're talking about size or weight I reckon."

"Half way through the kebab, you piss-taking fucks; not the moth."

"Chilli Moth - tasty!"

"Four for a pound in the supermarket in Tiptree."

"Serves him right for having a fucking kebab for breakfast."

"I got some raspberries from that shop in Tiptree once. Bloody caterpillar in the middle of one of them!"

"Do you know the average English male eats thirty five to forty spiders every summer?"

"You don't half talk some shit."

"Have a liking for the human mouth do spiders."

"Fuck off."

"Spazzer."

And round and round the world continues to turn. Time moves and tears fall. Laughter explodes and hearts stop. I will never get the hang of how all this goes on at once, how each and every wondrous one of us perceives every moment so differently. It rains for some, the sun beats for others. When I freeze, you thaw. When you scream a scream, I dream a dream. And when I am in my darkest moments, you are so madly, so smadly in love. Love is all you need. Love is all you need.

I hadn't spoken to Julia for some years. Though Tollesbury is just a bus ride from Tiptree, I had never made the effort to reach her. When she had told me that morning outside the school that I had to leave, I had done just that. Robbie would now be twenty-six. More than twenty years had passed since I had seen him fumbling with his buttons and he had seen me fumbling with my life. Yet I still felt he was a part of me, that we had shared moments we could not possibly have shared. Tiptree. Julia. Robbie. It was time to get on a bus.

I left The King's Head by the back entrance, out to where the benches are and did a staggering afternoon right turn down the High Street, passing the side of the pub and fully believing that the figures of Bill and Jim were merely etched upon the window pane and were not real at all.

For what is reality but that which is corroborated by more than you or me? I have heard birds talk to me and I have seen flowers bow down to one another in greeting. I have seen colours that have yet to be invented and I have bathed in the glory of the nineteenth century open air blazing orange sun. An etching for me may be motion for you. Neither one of us is right. The only fact is that during that moment we are both alive.

The bus stop in Tollesbury is a simple brick shelter comprising two sides and a roof. The children of the village gather there at times, the young girls with their make up and the lads longing to be old enough to enter the marvel of adulthood that is The King's Head. The chip van parks outside there a couple of nights a week and a hearty meal is had by all. The same woman that serves the chips also runs the hairdresser's which is more or less opposite where I live. She has a hard charm. I have never tasted her chips nor felt her hands upon my head. I should imagine though that she cooks magnificent roasties.

But despite the conglomeration of the aged, the young and the infirm, the bus did not come. A silence descended and the awaiting group wandered off alone and together, splintered and shattered yet replete with hope. We will not let it get us down. Chin up and queue up. The chip van will be here soon, so all is not lost. God what a wonderful nation.

I gave up on my impulsive notion to hop on a bus to Tiptree and instead shiddled and shaddled my short way back home. Within mere minutes, I was back in my old front room, sitting in my soft, low armchair, so aware that I could not rest now, that my thoughts had put into motion a series of events that I must follow. FRUGALITY was here and it was here to stay. And there was not a horse in sight.

The telephone rang. I didn't answer it. I never do. I suppose I should get rid of it one day. But in my darkest times, I guess when it rings it reminds me that I am at least connected to the world in some sense. I see it not as someone trying to get in touch with me but as a bell ringing to alert me that I will never, and perhaps should never, be totally free from this deep dark earth of ours. And just to prove it, there was a knock on the door.

Creak.

"Hello Simon. I'm Frank from the community mental health team. Here to give you your depot injection."

"Ok."

"May I come in?"

"Sorry, yes."

Creak. Click.

"I hope I didn't disturb you, but I think we did have an appointment?"

"It's fine. Really. Where would you like to do it?"

"We can have a chat first if you like?"

I sat back down in my armchair and Frank sat on the settee. He was about my age, wore glasses and was unshaven. I had never seen him before. He had a yellow box in one hand and a blue tray in the other, which, from experience, I knew contained a syringe, a plaster, a medical wipe and a glass vial of medication. All covered in a paper towel so as not to scare me!

"So how have you been since leaving hospital, Simon? It's been about a week hasn't it?"

"I've been alright, thank you. It's good to be home."

"I bet it is."

Silence.

Uncomfortable silence.

St Mary's bells chime.

Uncomfortable silence resolved.

"Well, I'll get your injection ready and then I can leave you in peace."

Frank proceeded with his work. I had seen it done a hundred times or more by perhaps a hundred people or more. They each have their own way of doing it, of introducing the act, of constituting the paraphernalia, of delivering the drug, but the result is always the same - a sharp needle inserted into the upper outer quadrant of either the right or left side of what

163

I believe is called in their training, my gluteus maximus. And through that needle is pumped a solution developed and sold by the pharmaceutical industry that is designed to make my thoughts and experiences more like everybody else's.

The nurse cracks open the vial with a 'pop', screws a green based needle onto a 2ml syringe and inserts it into the vial. The liquid is sucked up into the syringe and then the needle is swapped over for a clean one. The nurse pushes the liquid up until a small bubble forms at the tip of the needle. Weapon loaded. All good to go. Deep breath, mind-blank time. It's the only way. Some try to distract you with small talk. Others just line up the drill to the wall.

Sometimes you feel a sharp sting, sometimes it's in without you even knowing it. But when it's in, your whole world stands still. The syringe pumps the drug slowly into the fatty tissue - slowly, slowly, oily, oily. I somehow think that the fatty tissue is the dimmest, least intelligent part of me. Thus it does not resist, nor does it remember. It consumes and disseminates without question. Think of a drop of paint in a glass of water - it spreads until the water is no longer translucent, the paint takes over, it taints and consumes and changes all irrevocably. As the paint cannot be removed from the water so the drug cannot be removed from the body. You can't vomit it up. It is instantly a part of you, a mysterious dark and spreading web that is designed to impact upon your thoughts and your emotions. How it works, I do not know. Over the years, it has led to my hands having a subtle tremor. When I walk, I feel awkward, as if I am at times being manipulated by the strings of a puppeteer. Yet I continue to accept stranger after stranger into my house to fill me with this stuff.

Sigh for me please kind soul, for I am all sighed out.

"Well, Simon. I must be off now. Another three of these to do today. I may see you next time or it may be one of my colleagues. Take care."

Creak.

Click.

"Goodbye."

164

So there I was, medicated and treated. The sun would soon be going down and the moon would soon be rising. After my injection, I have always found that forced sleep is the only thing to keep me sane. Tomorrow would be the start of my reunification with my son. With such thoughts did I seek repose. And with such thoughts did I awaken the following morning.

You can prescribe this and administer that, but love will never be darkened and spirit will never be quelled. You may call me schizophrenic if you like, if it so please you. But my life is not about what you call me; it is about how my heart beats.

19. Forgive Everybody Everything

In order to prove to myself that I was worthy of my son, I needed to put into action the lessons I had been taught. The FRUGALITY children had been my teachers and I their student. But what value is knowledge if it does not change your life?

So I began at the beginning - Forgive everybody everything.

Not to forgive is to load your heart with a burdensome smouldering from which it can never truly recover. Bitterness, resentment, anger - all are emotions that weigh a soul down. I went initially for the easier forgivings, knowing that I had to start somewhere.

To kick off, I forgave Paul McCartney for The Frog Chorus and I felt a little lighter almost immediately. Just that little bit of forgiveness started the process. I then forgave Graham Gooch for going on the rebel cricket tour of South Africa. This was swiftly followed by forgiving Joseph Heller for everything other than Catch-22, Kevin Costner for The Bodyguard and Bob Dylan for Under the Red Sky.

Following these forgivings, I reflected upon how much better I felt in my soul. And through this process, my regard for Paul McCartney, Graham Gooch, Joseph Heller, Kevin Costner and Bob Dylan had somehow intensified.

I then began to believe that the act of forgiveness not only lightens your own burden but enhances your view of those that you have forgiven. Maybe that's true. Maybe that's just me. These were the easy forgivings.

I found it simple to forgive misjudgement. It sat well with me. Forgiving harm knowingly done was going to be so much more difficult. This led me initially to Diego Maradona and then to Margaret Thatcher. It was like a psychological equivalent of Dante's nine circles of hell. It was about damage done and how you try to minimise the effect of it upon the rest of your life. The moment is horrid but it need only be a moment. With forgiveness, I was realising, you could regain control, withdraw the dagger from the wound, staunch the bleeding and continue in goodness.

Diego Maradona. The hand of god. Peter Reid and Terry Fenwick with concrete boots and Peter Shilton despairing. The greatest player in the world at the time not only felt the need to cheat but to claim the hand that punched the ball into the goal was manoeuvred by an all powerful deity. He not only betrayed his unbelievable talent but he betrayed the beautiful game itself. He robbed me of a dream and he broke the hearts of children (admittedly only English ones for which he probably had scant regard.)

When genius has to resort to theft, it is a woeful time indeed. I remember feeling so angry at the time, not just that England had lost, but that a single man had deceived us all. But I now forgave him. He did what he did in a fleeting moment. And once you set out on the road of deception, it's so hard to come back. I should know. Thus was my dalliance with football over.

On the subject of being robbed, how about being robbed of the chance to work, the chance to hope, the chance to feel part of this world?

It was the voice that first alerted me to what was to come, that strident, man-woman-man voice whose dialect was from no place I know - the villain that Doctor Who never faced - perhaps the only one that could have truly left him floundering. Margaret Thatcher. Mrs Thatcher. Prime Minister. I guess to this day you do not truly know what you did to the likes of those such as I. I like to think you were maybe just dragged along on the tide of change, of the charge to 'progress' - first female head of the government and all that.

But when you decided the Falkland Islands were worth killing for, well that is when I lost faith in lots of things. I felt alone in my own country, cast aside by my own people and condemned by my own naïve sense of what is right in this world. You made me a stranger and you perpetuated my alienation. John Lennon would have been appalled. William Blake would have screamed at you, defied you and been undoubtedly, violently shunned by you. But I had neither the courage of the former nor the visions of the latter.

I just sat in my room during the eighties, wherever that room be, and shook, regaled from within and without by hurt, pure hurt. You took away my years. Yet I forgive you. I forgive you. I forgive you.

As I thunk my thoughts so I began to lose a hold upon them. I knew they were drawing me with inexorable beauty to the source of it all, the pivotal moment that led to all that was to follow. My thoughts slipped and slupped upon the muddy waterslide of my rundown holiday park memory, leading as they should, to the reservoir of my pain. The Monster of Ford's. My dad's brother. My uncle. I could not deny that it was he that had to be forgiven for my soul to move on.

But how do you forgive a man who raped you when you were three years old?

How do you even begin?

It was not a trauma that I could sit at home and think about. I felt ill at ease bringing a memory as sordid as that not just into my house, but into Tollesbury itself. It's not something to which this corner of my earth should ever be subjected. I would have to travel where Uncle Len lay.

Well if you ever plan to leave Tollesbury
Take the 91A to Witham from the square
Close your eyes and you'll be there.

Get the train from Witham to Shenfield
Taxi then to Brentwood, pay the fare
Close your eyes and you'll be there.

Train goes from Brentwood to Harold Wood
Stops at Gidea Park, all is good
You'll see nothing much but Gallows Corner roundabout
Tesco Superstore, don't forget The Plough
Raphael's Park, Marshalls Park, train slowing down right
now

168

Now you cross over to platform four
Fall off the train, run down the stairs
Close your eyes and you'll be there.

Train goes from Romford to Upminster
Slip your ticket in the slot, out you go
You're out on the street, not far from the cemetery
Park to the right, shops to the left
Left right, left right, darling come along with me,

You get on the bus number three-seven-oh
Your childhood is about to be laid bare
Close your eyes and you'll be there.

And there I was at the gates of Upminster Cemetery, the gates to Heaven, the gates to Hell; and all was silent in my world. At that moment, the universe did not exist save this corner of Essex where the dead are buried. Some were set adrift and aflame in the stone crematorium that stood, shoulders shrugged, in the centre of the whole green set-up; others were just put in wood and dug into the cold, cold English ground.

I felt as if I were surveying an ancient battlefield, a war between armies of stone and armies of flowers, a battle for the domination of this sacred earth. As my eyes flickered over the scene, I had a sense of movement, a feeling that as my gaze turned so the object I had just regarded, be it stone or flower, had altered slightly, had momentarily parried a blow or tightened a grip on a helpless victim. Dullness and colour, death and life grappling in perpetuity, there never being a victor except for motion itself.

In terms of where to look for Uncle Len, I left that purely to chance. I knew he was buried at Upminster Cemetery because my parents had brought me there for the funeral. They had been separated for about three years at the time and never saw each other again, as far as I knew, after that day.

I had been eleven years old and had chosen to sit outside the gates for the duration of the ceremony. I believe my

169

parents thought it was due to an overwhelming sense of loss on my part that I could not face seeing Uncle Len being buried. I was overwhelmed, it's true - but with what I perhaps still cannot say. I just remember the rain falling so hard upon my young self as they buried him, trying frantically to be entirely drenched by it, to be cleansed of him, to be drowned in God's tears, to be rid of the smother of oil and grease.

So now my fifty year old self wandered around the cemetery like an old ghost, drifting in and around the gravestones, floating about them like some drunken spectre, fiddling with his keys, looking for the front door to his end of days home. And like the inebriated fool I am, I eventually found what I was looking for - Uncle Len's grave. I sat before it, cross-legged - a child back in his first ever classroom.

There were no dates marked upon the stone - just the inscription:

Here lies Zachariah Leonard 'Len' Anthony

Well, well.

No dates - no birth, no death, just the assertion that there he lay in the dirt. But I knew he was not there, had perhaps never been there. For he lives in my mind, in my ether, in the stars, in the damp, in the marshland country around my home and in the bubbles in my stagnant beer. He moves when I move and he awakens when I sleep. He is the sweat of me and he is the absolute peak of my pain. He is the silent end to my screams and the crack in the pot of my gold. He is not in the ground at all. I knew when I saw that stone that it was a lie. I couldn't even convince myself that the flowers had won. Though the day be sunny and clear, I could feel nothing but ice cold rain smacking down upon me.

So there I sat waiting for forgiveness to come to me. But how do you forgive a man like that who has done you such wrong? I started to think it was impossible. And it would have been impossible indeed had I continued to hate him. For in that moment, I realised that true forgiveness can only consume you if you can find it in yourself to love the one you are forgiving - yes, love. So as I stared at the words chiselled into the stone, I became my Uncle Len and I entered the soil to rummage around in his bones in search of his soul.

"Working at Ford's is a fuck of a job. You're on the line like a fucking machine, covered in oil and grease. I never thought that would be my life, not that I had any dreams mind, what with any chance of childhood happiness being blown away by Hitler, my dad disappearing in a tank in Egypt and my old mum taking in bloke after bloke as if they were washing. And the odd one or two of the bastards took more of a fancy to me than her, did stuff to me they said was normal. When I told mum once, she hit me and accused me of trying to ruin any chance she might have of a new life. And my older brother, he worked at Ford's with me, he had it easy - got himself a bird early on, moved in with her and her parents soon as he could, give her one too many and got her pregnant.

Then this perfectly perfect baby appears from out of her a few months down the line. They called him Simon. Me and my brother did opposite shifts at Ford's. His wife worked during the day as perfect Simon got a bit older so I helped out taking care of him. I would go round there to that house of bliss, me with fuck all except for a shit job and all this hatred. And I would see perfect Simon all white and sweet and like a fucking angel. And I would see what should have been me, what I could have been like, the hope and the future, the childhood, the life - all those things that were denied me. So I would give him a big hug and lose all control.

I never hurt him mind, not in a way that anyone would have noticed. He would struggle the first few times but then he just wouldn't say a word. It was like he wasn't even there. And I would go back to work on the factory line and all I could feel was the most intense shame and disgust for myself. I wanted to go and tell everybody what I had done, to break the cycle, to get what was coming to me. I had become the worst a man can be but I just could not stop. If I did give it a break for a while, my whole fucking wretched body would shake with rage like a fizzed up corked up bottle. And I would have no choice but to go back and release the tension.

Part of me began to think that everyone, every fucking person that knew me or worked with me or passed me in the street, knew what I was up to yet I still could not stop. I thought often of killing myself but the devil wouldn't allow it. I had lost the power to end my own life from the time that bastard American GI cripple put his empty cock up my seven year old arse. It was just the devil now in control of me. I lived in form only. And I thank the lord that my brother and his wife took Simon to the back of fucking beyond to go and live in the country.

I got myself a bed-sit and held myself in contempt the remainder of my life. I never did what I did to Simon to any other kid. Not that that makes me in any way deserving. Death is the best thing that ever happened to me and that's the fucking truth of it. At least instead of all that oil and grease I now have flowers upon me."

Well that's what I heard anyway. It could have been the whispering of the cemetery grass or the conjoined spirits of the corpses beneath me or maybe it was just in the air that only I breathe. I uncrossed my aching, ageing knees and stood as best I could. As I did so I felt for a moment that I would be taken away by the breeze so light did I feel. I was a balloon, the head of a dandelion, a bubble ubble, a breath of warm mist. I was upon this earth but floating all the same. I leaned forward and stroked the top of Uncle Len's gravestone.

May he rest in peace.

Forgiven.

20. Recognise Beauty Wherever It Be

Beauty, beauty, beauty.

There have been times in my life when I have glimpsed beauty, when it has sought me out for a brief moment, only to flitter away into the world that only others inhabit. I once heard a regular in The King's Head exclaim to one of the barmaids that beauty is in the eye of the beer-holder and that as she must hold more beer than most during the course of an evening, she must therefore be the most beautiful woman in the world.

She had promptly dropped the pint she was passing to him, and for which he had just paid.

"And how beautiful do you think I am now?" she had asked.

Beauty, beauty, beauty.

Beauty isn't a face or a painting or a meal or a house. Beauty is the wonderful coming together of all senses at once in a specific, undeniable, unrepeatable moment. And moments, as I was beginning to learn, are all we really have.

Beauty is nothing but that which is beyond the shadows of this mortal life.

And so it was that I came to write a letter to my wife.

Juuliaa
Juuuuuuuuliaaaaaaa
Juuulia
Half of what I say is meaningless
But I say it just to reach you...
I know it's been twenty years or so that I last saw you and Robbie, but I need to see you both as soon as I can. If we could meet up, that would be so great. I would understand if you didn't want to.
I'm not sure if you are still at this address. I do hope so. That means, not only will you get this note, but you might be

able to meet me at Mo's Café in Tiptree any time on Saturday 30th August. I will be there all day.

A change has come upon me, Julia. It's a long story.

Simon

PS I Love You
You
You
Yoooouuu…

The Post Office in Tollesbury is at the top of Station Road, opposite The King's Head. It consists of a counter at the back of the Corner Shop. The Corner Shop itself is best described as an off-licence which sells some other general goods. It was taken over recently by a chain of shops and the sign 'Boozebusters' was erected big and bold. The people of Tollesbury have a Parish Council that represents them who decided that such a sign was not in keeping with the village ethos and it was thus quickly removed to be replaced by the name of the chain itself.

Imagine driving into a lovely country village and seeing The Hope Inn on one side, the King's Head on the other and opposite that a quaint old fashioned shop called Boozebusters. What a scandal! The fact that if you go further into the village you will find The British Legion Club (selling beer), The Sailing Club (selling beer) and The Cruising Club (selling beer) could perhaps make the casual visitor think that perhaps Boozebusters is not the name of a shop but of the village itself!

Ah Tollesbury - I raise a glass to thee!

I had learned from experience that Mr Postman does not come and collect letters that need posting no matter how much you say please, yet he will at times deliver unwanted correspondence unbidden. He won't stop to make me feel better once he's delivered a card or a letter, not even for a minute. There was nothing for it but to go to the post office with my Julia note, buy a stamp and post it. I owed my wife that much, at least; and a walk in Tollesbury can only bring

174

you closer to beauty - even if it's just up to the corner shop and back.

The heat hit me like a cartoon spade the second I stepped out of the house. Tollesbury seems to have a weather system independent of all others. When it's warm elsewhere, it is sweltering here. It's pointless listening to the weather man, you just have to go out and experience it. And I can think of no finer pleasure.

So, envelope in hand, I intended just to go to the Post Office and post my letter to my wife; but there was more required of me than that. It was my task to recognise beauty wherever it be and that is what I did. The result humbled me. I will explain it as I felt it, for that is all I can do.

Stepping out my side door front door concrete ground in
plinkle colours
of stones and chips and pebble heads
all hard unblinking despite the sun

- and shadows fall just where they ought -

My plastic glass door clicks so shut unlocked
Enter thee who feel the need
no need to plead just click and enter
don't break it open
mine is yours
and you are welcome to it.

From dark to light the flight is flit
I'm in the world now
not my houseworld but yourworld
that opens up to me like the hollow black mouth of a
leering creature
Yet

I SEE ONLY LIGHT -

could be the glinting of the teeth

175

or perhaps
I have been in the gurglebelly
and am in fact
on my way to heaven!

Neighbour's brick wall faces me all crazy shapes of deep
design
yet sturdy strong unfurling
so unique in every aspect of divine mish-mash
holding up the slates that
but for its own robustitude
would scramble down to meet my feet and bury me deep
in a clattering curvy crish crash
pile.

The dits and dots of weather tracks
that have impaled the mighty brick
strike me now as but tattoos
upon the human form;
marks of mystery rent by Gods
part now of the majestic whole.
I tell myself it's just a wall
but I'm learning now it's
Much
More
Than
That.

And now the gate that squeaks and creaks
to me goodbye hello
depending upon which way
I deign to go.
This fine day I, the unhinged,
unhinge the hinge
and turn and pat it on the head,
latching back the naked latch
back into its cosy bed.

So all is safe at my castle home -
the door is closed,
the gate is shut and there I am
Exposed
to the waiting world.

East Street is before me now left and right
one way down towards the sea
the other to the
very edge
of Tollesbury
where all my sense of safety stops
where far beyond in little towns
that you may feel are rather quaint
but
to certain ones like me are nothing
but barbarity where looks and stares
and wayward glares
bang like nails into the lid
that houses both my heart and soul;
the very thought doth make me shake
with trimble tremors and pimple goosings
that mark me out as a man who is
at mercy to the strong straight lines
of every single machination.

I don't mean to decry the earth for I find it wonderful
It's just that my experience
Has led me to a criss cross road
Where all the traffic
Moves
So
Fast.

So I do a right eyes to the ground
my shuffle legs and schoosh schoosh shoes
softly schoosh schoosh as I move

177

like a jazzy drummer with his sch-toom-sch-toom
brushes
backbeat to the light and heat
shuffle feet
shuffle feet.

And there I am in a wild west town,
the green print shop next to the razor's edge then onto
the grave graveyard
- paper, scissors and stone if ever I saw it
all in a row upstanding and
just
there.

Then the old congregational church
on the other side
demure and aloof
with trees for ultimate protection
of
the ultimate perfection.

But this is not the wild wild west,
not even the wild west end,
'tis Tollesburyville
and that is all.

The smell of baking bread is with me now
it is all of me
consuming me
I breathe it in and I breathe it out.
Past the corner shop I am drawn,
The King's Head gasps as by I slip
and there into the bakery
through its tiny door I bend myself
and enter.

I have no money in my pocketsses
but am just content to stand in that tiny corner

close my eyes
and get high

Not a soul asks me to leave;
Unlike the baker, I have nothing to prove…

And I floated down from the low ceiling
in perfect silence and
merged into the day.

And that is what I did.
My feet sighed so soft and most unneeded
for
the scent and beauty of the village whole was what
carried me
back
home.

So there I was, in my haven-heaven
Sanctuary
relieved.

And the letter
Well
that was still in my hand.

Bugger.
That's a problem I have you see. The wayward
meanderings of my mind will at times, and indeed more often
than not, inhibit my ability to complete even the most simple
and necessary of daily tasks. Some may call that a symptom
for which medication could be the answer. I prefer to see it as
just one of those things.
I was standing in my kitchen, a little bemused when a
shadow knocked.
It was the Postman.
"Hello Mr Anthony"
"Hello"

"I was just passing and wondered if you had anything you wanted me to deliver today?"

"Just this letter here. Well it's more of a note really."

"Do you have a stamp for it?"

"Sorry. No."

"Not to worry. I just happen to have one right here."

"Oh. Ok."

"So if you would like to hand me your mail?"

"There you go."

A pause.

"You know what, Mr Anthony?"

I shook my head - for so many reasons.

"It is such a wonderful day, I think I will take a stroll to Tiptree. Let's save that stamp shall we?"

Beauty, beauty, beauty.

It's here, there and everywhere...

21. Understand the Nature of Loss

So Saturday 30th August soon came around. As does the man, Mr Cash. And I thank you for that and so much more.

I arose as the dawn birds chirruped and I squinted through my bedroom window at the blue sky morning. I have my curtains open always and the windows too for to be awoken as the light of the sun doth appear in the sky and to be alerted to the fact by a vibrant orchestra of unseen choristers is a pleasure of life indeed. I had begun to notice in recent times the softness of pillows and the coldness of sheets. Again, pleasures of life, sir. And when you notice such things, life can seem just that little more bearable.

What to wear, what to wear? The denim shirt, the Beatles T-shirt or the checked lumberjack shirt? It has only ever a choice of those three since I lost my baggy jumper. I went for the Beatles T-shirt after a moments thought. I have long had a belief that when the Fab Four are with me, I always need to say just a little less about myself. It gets tighter on me as the years go by. One morning I will wake up and the T-shirt and my skin would have merged into one - and what a fine morning that will be.

The bikers that at times congregate at The King's Head claim that Mo's Café in Tiptree does the best full English breakfast in the land. Praise indeed. I used to go to Mo's when I first met Julia, though I had never met Mo at all. The café was cheap and clean and it accepted us. The anticipation about going there and hopefully seeing my wife again after all these years was tempered by the fact that Mo's may have changed, lost its way, given into the charge of progress. But if Mo's had become a different place, my Beatles T-shirt and I would perhaps represent those that still had a foot in the everpast.

One busridedream and I was there. It was eight o'clock in the morning and the sun was already climbing. Tiptree High Street was clear of the take-away debris and the underage supermarket discarded cans of a village Friday night. And

Mo's was before me smelling of a bacon, sausage and hot coffee paradise.

The first thing that hits you when you walk into Mo's Café is the very greenness of it all. It is as if the ridged carpet were a patch of grass around which has been erected four walls. The wooden panelling that reaches about a third of the way up each wall is a lighter shade of green than the carpet yet a darker shade still than the pale green of the rest of the walls. The four out of five square lights that work in the suspended ceiling act as gentle suns that shine wanly down upon this genuine corner of a struggling man's heaven. As I stood at the door and looked around, I felt like I was the lead character that Roald Dahl never wrote - Simon and the Giant Apple. He missed a trick there.

"What'll it be sweet 'art?"

The lady that had addressed me spoke with the assuredness of one who was in charge. She was tall and sturdy and had the name Mo tattooed on the top of her left arm. Nothing else - just Mo. Though this was not a pub, Mo was most definitely the landlady of this place.

"Sweet 'art?"

"Sorry. Erm. A black coffee and a sausage sandwich please. Thank you."

"Ok my darling. I'll bring it over, love."

I went and sat down at the table nearest the counter and faced the door so I could see when Julia arrived, if indeed she would. I have learned during my times that sitting with my back to people, whether it be in the day room of a hospital or in The King's Head, engenders in me an anxiety and fear that is difficult to suppress. It's in the learning of such lessons that I have for periods of my life been able to cope. Of course, the tablets and injections help, Doctor, of course they do. Although if you could just prescribe me a sausage sandwich and a steaming mug of coffee every Saturday morning, I'm sure I could manage the rest of the week free of your ingenious concoctions.

Clonk.

"There's your coffee, my dear - butty on its way."

"Thank you."

A woman with her back to me, behind the counter, was pushing sizzle crackle sausages around a big open hob and there were three other customers beside myself in Mo's Café that Saturday morning in August.

The other table beside me was vacant, as were the four tables positioned end to end down the centre like some sort of primitive tennis net. On the other side, both tables were occupied, one with a man tucking into a huge mound of food; at the other sat a bald man with a much older gentleman. Both looked forlorn. They looked not at one another but at their respective mugs. I could not see if they were empty or full. Every now and then, the younger man would reach out and squeeze the squeezy ketchup bottle in the centre of the table until a bubble of red appeared at the top of the nozzle. He would then relent and the ketchup would return with a sigh to its plastic home. The older man seemed not to see what I saw. If he did, he made no comment. Perhaps the action soothed them both.

My sausage sandwich was plonked in front of me by Mo and this disturbed my reverie.

"Do you have any sauce?" I asked timorously.

"Yes, sweet 'art," replied Mo. "And plenty of cheek," she added, smacking her own ample behind and returning moments later with two bottles of ketchup. "The cheek's not available though, darling - not on a Saturday." She smiled and returned back to her post.

Mo was formidable indeed. I felt that were the most persistent of criminals to have entered the café, they would have left only with a handful of change having broken like a wave upon Mo's defences. Instead of robbing the place, they would have just ordered a bacon bap to take away.

As I sipped my coffee, a white haired man bespattered with paint pushed open the door.

"Anyone 'ere got an Audi Quattro?" he asked, all East London accent and blue eyed grin.

The assembled customers, such as they were, either shook their heads, mumbled 'no' or looked down at their respective tables hoping he would go away. I was the latter - for I was waiting only for Julia. Time was ticking.

"Then I reckon I've probably got away with backing into it then! Cheers people!"

And he was gone. Bowling, bowling, bowling.

As the door closed, the man who had been sitting by the window approached the counter with his empty, bean-stained plate.

"Cheers Mo - gorgeous as ever!"

"And did you like your breakfast, Clint?"

Clint? Brilliant!

"To be honest Mo, give me a bucket next time and top it right up!"

The cook turned at this stage, mock aghast in her gentle eyes and interjected.

"I just don't know how you can eat all that at this time of the morning, Clint! I feel sort of guilty cooking it for you!"

"Did a forty mile bike ride before I got here, love. Left at six this morning. Gives a man an appetite that does, Shirley!"

The old man who sat with his ketchup-squeezing companion turned round in his seat and addressed the people at the counter.

"I did forty miles myself this morning. Going round in fucking circles."

Clint laughed. Mo knew better.

I then glimpsed a small boy shoot out from behind the counter on roller skates.

"You be careful in here, Lee. If you want to go that fast, you go outside," instructed Mo.

And so he did.

"Be the next Robin Cousins, your boy, Mo!" Clint exclaimed.

"Who?"

"You know, that skater bloke."

"Oh, yes, I remember. Who was that other one?"

"Torville and Dean," said the cook, over her shoulder.

"Which one was the man, Clint?"

184

"Neither of them, Mo. Poofters both of them! Not that your boy is going to be a poofter. Didn't mean that. Anyway, see you next Saturday, Mo. Have a good week."

"You too, Clint," replied Mo, although I sensed she may well have wished him to perhaps come off his bike in front of traffic at some stage during the next seven days, such was the vigour with which she began to wipe down the counter.

The door opened once more - it was nearly half past nine. The latest entrant to the scene was a woman who looked to be nearly a hundred years old. Her blue white hair stood out from her wrinkled visage as if she were being dragged up to heaven by it and the frown lines on her face were but a testament as to how desperate she was to stay upon this earth. She wore a dark blue dress with yellow flowers upon it and she walked with a dignity that all but made me melt.

"Hello, Mo," she said when she finally reached the counter. "Do you have any sausage rolls left?"

"Do you mean sausage in a bread roll or sausage in a pastry roll, Mary?"

"In a pastry roll, dear."

"You want the bakers just down the road, Mary. They do sausage rolls that will knock your socks off. We do just the bread ones here."

"Thank you, dear."

"See you again next Saturday, Mary?"

"Yes, dear."

And Mary sauntered out of Mo's café with the same dignified walk, out onto the street and more than likely off to the bakers to ask for a fry-up. This is indeed a marvellous place.

The two other men in the café got up, handed their plates and mugs to Mo and slowly left.

"Turn round the sign on the door, won't you, love," Mo called out to them. They did as they were bidden and I was left alone, save for Mo. Even the cook seemed to have gone. My coffee was going cold and the word OPEN was facing me, dangling on a piece of card secured with a drawing pin.

I sighed and made to get up.

185

"Stay where you are, darling," said Mo, standing behind me and securing me to my seat with a heavy hand.

"Another coffee?"

"Erm, yes please. If that's alright?"

"Course it is. Wouldn't have asked you otherwise."

She then bent down to whisper in my ear.

"She'll be here soon, sweet 'art. Probably still deciding whether to put on some lippy if I know Julia. You just relax, Simon."

And that was how it was. A tingle went through me like the first time I heard John Lennon sing Twist and Shout. That had been a moment when I had sensed a deeper side to human life soulness and this moment now compared. Mo's café and John Lennon both occupied the same place in my heart from that time to this. And I think John would've liked that.

So there I was in Mo's Café in Tiptree, waiting for Julia who, evidently was in cahoots with Mo - the latter having adjudged that I was not the maniac of legend but a lovelorn man anxiously anticipating the arrival of his wife. But so many years had passed since last I'd seen her, I wasn't sure she would even recognise me. Yet Mo had obviously picked me out and we hadn't even met before.

I'm sure that if I hadn't had that gorgeous sausage sandwich and that hot black coffee I may well have become just a little, shhh, whisper it, paranoid!

The door clicked, the green greened and my heart stopped. There she was, Julia, my wife. I hadn't seen her for nearly a quarter of a century yet she still nailed me to the floor with her beauty. Were I of porcelain, I would have shattered, were I of paper I would have crumpled - but I was just a man; so my mouth went dry and a heat came to me. And I knocked over my mug of coffee in the process of coolly scratching my head. Just a man.

Julia sat down in the chair opposite me. Her eyes were as blue as I ever remembered and she smelled just like the air that has ever kept me breathing. I swear she looked no different from that day in the car when Robbie first started school.

Except now she wasn't tutting at me. And I just could not take my eyes off her.

"Would you like a drink?" I asked.

"I think I have one on its way," she replied.

And indeed she had. Clonk.

"Thank you for coming. I didn't think you would."

"Well, Simon. I haven't seen you for a few weeks - and I still only live just around the corner so what else was a girl to do?"

She smiled and reached out to cover my hand.

My heart beat hard as the blood rushed around me like so many children in a playground on the final day of school. A few weeks? I hadn't seen her for more than twenty years yet she had spoken of our last meeting as being in terms of a few weeks ago.

She read my mind better than any Doctor could.

"Simon, my love. I am your wife, what the hospitals and the police refer to as your 'next of kin'. Each time over the past twenty years when you have been admitted to hospital, when you have been Sectioned, when the police have picked you up, when you have gone missing, when you have appealed against your Section, when you have tried to kill yourself - each time, they have contacted me.

I could probably tell you the names of every nurse who cared for you, every social worker that sought my permission to Section and every doctor who shook his head at me. And I have cried lots of tears.

I have tried to help people to understand you and I have visited you whilst you lay with tubes coming out of you. I have let them Section you and I have told them of places where you are likely to be found when you have run away. And I have done all these things out of love.

I couldn't see you when you were awake, Simon. I just couldn't. I just didn't want to cause you any harm. They always said you were so fragile and I was scared I would make things worse.

It is so good to see you outside of all those circumstances. Just me and you at Mo's on a Saturday morning is just so, well, normal."

"Buy why now? Why are you seeing me now?"

"I spoke to one of the nurses when I got your note, one that I trust. She said she had never seen you so well. And I just couldn't resist."

"But I thought I had lost you, Julia."

"Lost me?"

"Yes, lost you."

"But you could never have lost me, Simon."

"Why not?"

"Because you never owned me."

I looked at her for that was all I wanted to do.

"You can't lose what you don't own, Simon. Love is not about possessing another but about sharing them with the world for the time you are both fortunate enough to be around. People talk of loss as if it is a tragic and terrible thing. The fact that some people feel they own others is what is tragic and terrible. People pass through your life and then pass on.

But when someone loves you, truly loves you, they will be all around you all the time, whether you know it or not."

Julia put her red lips to her white mug and took a luscious sip.

"And now you see why I am here."

She took my hand in her hers and traced the lines on palm with the very tip of her fingers.

BLAM is love!

22. Give Love Wherever You Go

Clonk.

Clonk.

Another coffee for myself and a tea for my wife. Earl Grey. Posh.

So Julia had maintained a distant vigil over me throughout all these years. Just a step away but my wife still. And there I had been, oblivious, rudderless and entirely unaware of the anchor that held me fast when I was apt to wander.

"I just didn't realise," I said at last. "I thought you had wanted nothing to do with me. I just didn't realise."

"Simon, I married you because I loved you."

I sought refuge in the wavy stream of steam that wafted from the mug before me. Droplets formed on my forehead as I gazed into my mug. And tears were not far from my eyes.

"When I got your note, it came as quite a shock. I suppose I felt comfortable loving you from a distance, making sure, as far as I could, that you were ok. I have a friend, Penny, who is a nurse. She works at Blackwater. You must know her."

I nodded.

"Well Penny keeps me up to date with how things are going with you, whether you are in hospital or at home, that sort of thing. All the records are kept on their computer system. I'm not sure she is really supposed to tell me as much she does, but friends are friends."

And then Julia proceeded to tell me during the course of the morning just what she had been through since the day I stepped out of that car, feeling so sorry for myself.

And it humbled me indeed.

"Of course, it wasn't all wonderful. I despised you before you left and I hated you when you eventually did leave. It was the drinking that I could neither stand nor understand. Whenever you woke up, or came into the house, the first thing you did was go to the fridge for beer or cider or whatever it was you needed. Then after that, you may have said hello to me or stood limp whilst I hugged you. I lost you to alcohol, Simon, not to anything else."

After we separated Julia had continued to live in the house in Tiptree that we had shared together. She had been barely into her early twenties and was in the position of having a young child with a learning disability, bills to pay and a wayward husband forever oscillated between the psychiatric hospital, The King's Head and his mother's.

It was true. All of it was true.

"I'm sorry. I can see all that now. I have hardly had a drink since I left hospital this time round - well not what I would call a drink."

Julia smiled. God, I love it when she smiles.

"I know. It's ok. Carrie, the barmaid in The King's Head keeps me up to date. I have my little spies everywhere you know!"

Julia winked. God, I love it when she winks.

I sipped some more of my coffee.

"Carrie Caseby is my finest spy. Pretty, yet intelligent. I always say to her if she learned to cook I would probably marry her myself!"

"But, you're married to me."

"Yes, I am, Simon. Yes, I am."

And there followed one of those natural pauses for which sighs were made.

"I couldn't carry on using all my energy up hating you and despising you, so I made a conscious decision to let all that go. It was literally as simple as that. I was sitting at home one evening eating chocolate and thought to myself - 'I'm just going to be nice to everybody I meet'. And that was that. I did favours for people expecting nothing in return. I gave money to every charity that asked it of me. I volunteered at school fetes and I picked up other people's rubbish when they dropped it on the floor. I read a book on Buddhism and realised that what I was doing didn't need a title. It was just about being good to people. And I guess that was what kept me in love with you, Simon."

190

Mo was beginning to hover around a little and I sensed she wanted to shut up shop for the day. Julia caught her glance and nodded at her, held up her hand as if to indicate five minutes, and fixed her blue-eyed gaze back upon me.

"So, Simon. You said in your note that a change had come to you. I'm intrigued. Do tell."

Where was I to start? Not at the beginning, surely - for that would take ages.

"Well," I began, as the Mo Clock ticked, "I saw an old man called The Walrus and he introduced me to some children who read me stories and poems and sang me songs that taught me how I should be living my life. And since then, I have tried to live my life that way. I feel so much better for it and so much more makes sense to me. But then I realised that my life isn't just about me. It's about you, you and…"

"Now I need to interrupt you two lovebirds I'm afraid. Mo needs to close up and get home before the hubby wakes up to an empty plate. And that, my friends, is not a pretty sight, I can tell you!"

"Ok, Mo darling. We will leave you to it. Text me later if you want to pop round for something to eat."

"Will do, my dear. Now hoppit, both of you!"

And so there we were outside Mo's Café, my wife and I.

My wife and I.

The sky was blue with clouds drifting in. I could smell rain in the air and I welcomed it. At times of deep emotion, the distraction of a physical reminder that this earth is greater than anything that may be troubling me has always done me good. Rain not only cleanses, but refocuses. Well, it does me, anyway. And we all need a little cleansing and refocusing at times, don't we?

Julia stood beside me, shorter than me yet so much greater than I could ever be. There was a serenity about her that was absolutely golden. It would not have surprised me if a crowd had gathered to behold her. She was a part of all that was around me, as deep as the breeze, as upright as an old tree, as intangible as breath itself. I guess that is what they call love.

"So, Simon," said Julia, moving close to me now and linking an arm through mine. "I must go. I have good deeds to do, don't you know. I need to spread a little love. But I would very much like to see you again."

I flinched from the physical contact. I could feel a heat in my cheeks and lowered my head for refuge. I was seven years old again - Gaynor Parkinshaw had lent me a pencil and blew me a kiss. She had been a massive Cliff Richard fan. It would never have worked.

"Ok," was all I could manage.

I could see Julia smiling, looking at me with what I can only describe as passion and it almost melted me where I stood. If I was a Fab lolly, she was the sun. And had I stood there any longer, the only clue to my presence would have been a myriad of multi-coloured sprinkles and a little wooden stick.

"Not this Monday coming, but the Monday after, meet me outside the Tollesbury Scout Hut and we shall see what we shall see."

"Ok."

I was numb and would have been adjudged to be perhaps the worst actor ever had anyone been around to judge that sort of thing.

"About seven?"

"Ok."

"Oh, and one more thing," said Julia, coquettishly, as she departed.

"Yes?"

"You should know before our second date that I have a son. His name is Robbie. And he is wonderful."

And away she floated.

192

23. Anger Devours the Soul

Just across from Mo's Café is a large supermarket. I went there very infrequently but thought I needed, ironically for me, to be around people following my time with Julia. I needed to know that what had just happened with Julia was real. A crotchety old woman bumping into me with her trolley would at least save me from having to pinch myself.

So Robbie is wonderful. I never doubted it for a moment. And Monday week, Julia is going to take me to the topper-most of the popper-most, to the tippest toppest of the skyest sky - a sky of diamonds of which Robbie would surely be one, shining, shining, shining. And the sky would be my sky and it would be Robbie's sky and it would be Julia's sky - the only firmament that truly mattered. And the earth below would but behold us in all our lovingest majesty. A holey moley trinity.

I walked into the supermarket with a deep urge for a simple meal. I hankered for a hunk o' bread and a chunk o' cheese. It was the country life and I was of the country. There was a history in me now that not only bubbled within my veins but lent me a sense of pride in where I once began. I was of this land and there are some things that will always sustain. Bread and cheese - food for the poor that makes a man rich.

I didn't need a trolley and I didn't need a basket. One hand held the bread and the other held the cheese, as was surely intended. I struggle with queues and with crowds to the extent I have fled in many a similar situation. The unpredictability of people has always frightened me. The doctors call it paranoia and state that it is a symptom of the illness with which they adjudge me to suffer. I know what frightens me. It is the unpredictability of people. But I possessed a strength these days that had long deserted me. So I stood in the shortest queue at the head of which was a kindly looking lady wearing a blue uniform and a name badge with three stars upon it.

Beside my queue were some machines that I had never seen before. There were four screens which people touched and scanned their food through before putting money or a card in a slot and walking off with their wares. Every now and then, my three-starred checkout lady would look over forlornly as the machines did their work. Was she picturing the four colleagues whom they had replaced and with whom she used to have a fag outside? Or was she staring off into fine space, really seeing nothing at all, a perfect nothingness?

Strange days, mama - strange days indeed.

To my left, in front of one of the magical screens, there was anger. My time in hospital over the years had heightened my senses in so many ways but had truly dulled them in others. When the nurses would pull their alarms, I would shut my eyes and wait for the noise to stop. Or if I was in my room, I would snuggle under my cold covers and force myself into an absent state.

But now, in the unreal world, just a few feet from me, there was a man from whom anger seeped. He held a lemon in his left hand. His other hand was balled into a fist.

"Fucking machines," he muttered. "Fucking machines!"

Heads in my queue turned. I knew better and just looked down and listened. There are sometimes alarms that go off that only I can hear.

"Can I help you, sir?" came a voice more stern than compassionate.

I glanced up briefly in case I was being spoken to. It was not. The short, square woman that had spoken was looking up at the man with the lemon, her hands on her hips and her five-starred name badge gleaming.

"It's this fucking machine. I've put this lemon on the thing loads of times and it won't recognise it. These fucking things are supposed to make things easier aren't they?"

"There's no need to use that language, sir. I'm sure the other customers really don't want to hear it."

The man looked around, lowering people's heads with the power of his questioning gaze.

"Really? They don't seem too bothered to me."

194

The five-starred woman reddened.

"Put the lemon on the scanner, if you please," she began. "That's it. Now you see those letters down the side of the screen, press the one that says 'L-P.' L is for lemon."

"Oh!" said the man. "And are those stars on your badge for spelling?"

The woman reddened further. People were staring now, as people do.

"If you could please just press the L-P button on the screen, we can get this over with. That's it. Thank you. Now, you have one lemon, so you need to press the number one."

"I do have one lemon. Well counted," replied the man. "And would P stand for Patronising?"

"If you continue to be abusive, I will have you ejected from the store," the woman managed at last, her voice absolutely quaking.

"And the 'O'," continued the man, "does that stand for 'Oh fuck am I going to be doing this job for the rest of my life?"

A couple of young lads behind me giggled. Part of me wanted to also. It had been a while since I had laughed in any fashion and I stemmed the impulse, not at all sure as to what my giggle would have sounded like.

"That's it! Now put your money in the slot, take your change, take your lemon and please leave!"

"And 'T'," said the man, as he put his money in the slot, took his change and picked up his lemon, "I bet that stands for 'time of the month' - although on second thoughts, you look like you're past all that."

The woman stormed off, entirely enraged. Seconds later, a call came over the loud speaker system; it was her voice but amplified. She needn't have bothered with the microphone; she was clearly shouting.

"And 'S' stands for 'Security'! Security to the self-serve tills please."

The guard that had been standing at the entrance, appearing more in his own little world than I had ever been, sprung into action. He walked quickly over to the man with the

195

lemon and escorted him to the exit. And just before they disappeared from view, I heard the lemon man shout,

"And 'R' stands for 'aaargh that hurts, you bastard!'"

I kind of liked him.

I paid for my bread and cheese and left the store. I was beginning to realise that not all the weird stuff in this world revolved around me. There's plenty to see if you just get out a bit!

And as I walked across the car park I saw the man who had been thrown out, sitting on one of the benches by the bushes. He was leaning forward with his elbows upon his knees and his hands propping up his head. The lemon was beside him on the bench. Neither moved as I approached and sat down on the bench opposite.

The man didn't even look up. I put my bread and cheese beside me. It was as if his lemon and my bread and cheese were our errant children. I would not have been at all surprised if the lemon had rolled off the bench, to be followed by my bread and cheese before they all skipped off to the little playground hidden in the bushes reserved only for food; leaving us adults to it. I think they would have been alright. The bread looked to be a sensible kind of fellow.

Then, what do you know, the lemon rolled off the bench and landed at my feet. I put out a hand to stay my bread and cheese as I leaned down and picked up the lemon. You just can't be too careful with little 'uns. I let the lemon balance in my open palm. The man looked up with his eyes but his head remained lowered. He took the lemon and cupped it in both his hands.

"Cheers," he said.

"It's ok."

We sat for a while in silence as shoppers came and went, cars parked, empty trolleys were filled and cars left again - commerce in action before our very eyes. The wheels on the bus went round and round, round and round, round and round. All day long.

"Made a tit of myself in there, didn't I?" he said at last. "Don't reckon they'll let me back in for a while. Bugger really.

196

I only live round the corner. It's just things like that make me so angry."

I nodded and tried to look sympathetic, which wasn't too difficult, as I could imagine how he felt. Once you've been Sectioned a few times, you develop an affinity for people that are excluded.

"Came out for a bloody lemon and end up getting chucked out by security."

"At least you got your lemon."

"There is that." The man smiled and looked down upon his bitter fruit.

"You going to have a sandwich?" he asked, nodding towards my bread and cheese.

"Yes."

"Nice. Can't beat a good old fashioned cheese sandwich."

I felt good. He was absolutely right.

"What is your lemon for?"

"No idea. The wife says to me - 'I need a lemon. We haven't got any lemons. I need a lemon!' So just for a bit of peace and quiet and to shut the bitch up, I came out to get her a precious fucking lemon."

He shook his head ruefully before continuing.

"You married?" he asked.

I nodded.

"She alright?"

"Wonderful," I replied. "Wonderful."

God, it was all beginning to make sense to me now.

"Lot easier not to get angry when you've got a good 'un I reckon."

I nodded again.

"Do you believe," I began, faltering a little, but gaining the courage to continue. "Do you believe that anger devours the soul?"

"Where did you hear that shit? You're not one of those religious lunatics are you?"

I smiled.

"I suppose you're half right." I replied.

197

He smiled too.

"Well I guess it don't do me any good. It's not pleasant being angry all the time. No fucker wants to be around you. Where did you hear that devouring the soul stuff anyway?"

"A small boy pretending to be an angry barber told me."

He sat back and looked at me with some intent.

"Figures," he said. "Well, fuck it. I'd best be off. Bloody wife's gonna kill me when I get in."

"You got the lemon though. You got what you came for." I said, in as reassuring a tone as I could muster.

At that, he stood up and hurled the lemon towards the shop window.

"Fuck the lemon. It was her fat arsed sister got me thrown out - her and her bloody stars. She's always been the fucking same ever since my mate did her round the back of the Bookie's for a bet. See you mate. Have a good one."

Ah, life - I do believe I am falling in love with you at last…

24. Look Deep or Do Not Look At All

Tollesbury salt marshes are a land in their own right. As the earth doth appear from the sky so do the marshes appear from where I stand. It is all life - in large and in miniature. From on high we are but specks yet in truth we are gods. And beneath the salty water and the vegetation there are further worlds and greater universes of which we may never be aware; lands within lands; life within life.

The sky cleared and my musings were disturbed as a bouncy golden retriever barked a welcome. Its striding owner murmured 'hello' as he followed the line of the sea wall as if it were a railway track and he were the train. And I watched, enthralled, as man and dog merged into the indeterminate horizon, slipping over the edge of this world only ever to remain, like all things, in my consciousness.

It was Old Jed - the man with the lolloping golden retriever whom I had seen the day I had submerged myself in the water, that day when everything had changed for me. For there had followed Zachariah Leonard and the FRUGALITY children, The Walrus and W.G. Were Old Jed and his dog more of Julia's army of spies or was he just a Tollesbury man who forever walked his dog around the edges of the Blackwater? I couldn't be sure and I really didn't mind. I nodded as he passed and soon he and his dog were gone.

Sitting down on the grassy bank, I looked into the salty marshland water, with not death, but learning on my mind.

So I sat down on the bank of the marshes and tried to focus on all that had happened to me. The last time I had been here my only intention had been to end my life. Yet now I had but hope on my mind. Hope - is that not one of the most beautiful of feelings? It is a sadness of life that when we are born, hope is not even in our constitution - it is all about sleeping and feeding and safety and warmth. But as we grow, the concept of hope is understood by the innocent child only at the time when the adult world intervenes. Hope has no role when you are in the perfect childworld. It raises its head only when you are convinced by others that this world is not as wonderful as you first imagined. And thereafter disappointment is always lurking.

BUT THAT IS THE GREAT DECEPTION.

FOR THERE IS ALWAYS WONDER TO BE HAD!!!!!!

There is a wonder in each and every moment; it's just so often we miss it, intent as we are on bemoaning our misfortune, the cards we are dealt, the burden that is ours alone. Wake up people! Wake up as I have awoken! For what is around us now is majestic, marvellous, magnificent!

Of course, I am in the countryside of old England, but wherever you find yourself, whatever your deep eyes do fall upon - look deep, look deeper.

And behold.

Have you ever heard of the Hen Harrier? We get them in Tollesbury and they are incredible. They glide over the marshes silent like breath, their V-shaped wings just a little more refined than that of the Marsh Harrier - smaller and slimmer and maybe a little more elegant. The male Hen Harrier is a ghost of a bird, the spirit of the Marsh Harrier, for it is not brown but almost completely white. It shimmers like a wave and is cut from the cloth of the morning mist. The only sign that these birds are of this world is the coal black wing-tips that leave darkening embers smouldering along the wing as they fly. And the markings on their tail go round and round in rings and rings of roses.

But that is not all. Suddenly, they fall and go a-tumbling from the sky, rocketing to earth like a parachutist whose chute has failed to open - yet there is no distress! Even in such a descent there is a beauty. And then - wham - the chute opens and the birds roar back up into the heavens - but just for a moment! This tumbling and rising goes on and on until the little Hen Harrier finds its way and wafts into the very firmament upon the breath of angels.

I am a man yet I am a Hen Harrier also. I am a drunkard and a dreamer. I am a Beatles fan and a lover of cricket. I am a husband and I am a father. I am all these things and more. And I am a friend of yours. I am the world's best friend. Just think of me not as a schizophrenic but as a Hen Harrier only. A Hen Harrier.

For there is no schizophrenia and there is no depression; no bi-polar disorder, personality disorder or post-traumatic stress disorder. There is just life and trying to get through it. That is all. Look past the drugs and past the diagnosis, look deeper than the despair and higher than the highs - and what you have is a soul that needs embracing, a mind that needs cradling and a heart that needs to beat its beat without condemnation.

Some weeks ago, I was at the marshes with just darkness on my mind. I was rushing to the depths. Yet now I float and I rise. The earth is the same yet I see with new eyes. I have learned that the world does not change. All that alters is the way we choose to see it.

I am not a schizophrenic.

I am a Hen Harrier.

And I'll have no more of your injections if that's ok.

Thank you.

As I walked up Station Road to The King's Head, I strode in the footsteps of my heroes - the farmer, the wheelwright, the baker, the blacksmith, the watchmaker, the carrier, the shoemaker, the thatcher, the seawaller, the saddler, the miller and the labourer - all are heroes to me.

I tingled as I made my journey for it all began to come home to me. AS THE BIRD IS OF THE SKY, SO I AM OF THE EARTH. I have grown from it as a seedling and become part of this Tollesbury. The oak tree is my father as the yellow-horned poppy is my daughter. The little tern is my baby as the marsh is my soul. And there is but a vibrant greeny green green churning through my throbbing veins.

I am no more a man than I am a schizophrenic. I live only in Tollesbury Time. And I will live in Tollesbury Time forever.

But if you just repeat the cycle, you go round and round yet unmoving like the spinning wheel of an upturned bicycle. So I stopped short of the pub and went instead into the corner shop. And moments later, I was on my way back home with eight cans of Scrumpy Jack and a bottle of Jack Daniels. I had looked deep into the earth and now it was time to confront those demons within myself - the two Jacks.

After tonight, I vowed as I walked the last few steps up to my front door, no more a drunk will I be.

No more a drunk will I be.

So I sat at my old wooden table, the drink lined up before me and surveyed the scene like Napoleon looking upon the landscape of Waterloo. And I knew not whether I would win the battle. Eight cans of Scrumpy and a bottle of Tennessee Whisky is a devious opposition indeed. But I had courage within me and a wife and a son ahead of me. What man could not win a battle fought on those terms?

I wanted to feel every cut, examine every scar and experience each moment of my victory. This was my last big drink and I demanded of myself to know why I had fought such a battle almost every day of my adult life. But don't get me wrong. I am not physically dependant on the stuff. I have just needed it to survive. I won't need a detox programme. I won't even have a headache in the morning. For my mind will be full of angels.

I drank the first can. Nothing. It may as well have been water. I set it back from the rest, full now of nothing but stale air. A corpse only. The second followed soon after. I began to feel a stirring in the base of my neck and my breath was a little more audible. I was being attuned to my senses by the rotting apples in the cider. Sweetness rose innocent in my throat.

With the falling of the third can, a lightness entered my head, splashing open into my mind, illuminating the dark corners of my soul. If I could have awoken each morning of my life having consumed three cans of strong cider in my sleep, I swear my time on this earth would have been more tolerable. But that was the trick of the enemy. It sucks you in on the second and kisses you with the third. Thereafter you are only ever its victim.

Can four - that was the crest of the hill. In a pub, if you leave before the fourth, you can retain your dignity, your self-respect, your sanity even. There is something in the fourth that differs from those preceding it. It must be a chemical thing. There is no going back from the fourth. But there I sat at my own table in my own little house and drank down that fourth can. The effect of it was to make me stand and wander around for a moment, like a man who has placed a bet at the Bookie's, a bet he knows he cannot afford to lose.

I sat back down. The race was on, the horses were raging and the crowd was roaring. Simon Anthony and Scrumpy Jack were neck and neck coming up to the fifth.

Both were over safely and that bottle of Jack Daniels pawed at the floor of its stable like some sort of ancient beast of ancient times, disturbing the earth beneath it and the wanton air around it.

By the time I had drunk the fifth can, I needed to use the toilet. I tripped up the first step of my staircase (how grand!) but made it back down without further mishap. I thereafter eschewed the dining chair and just sat on the floor, my back resting against the wooden door of the kitchen. Now that felt more right - legs outstretched, wood behind me. This was my territory now.

Number six went down as if it were not even alcohol. I guess, over the years, that had been my downfall. Only every third or fourth drink ever affected me. Those in-between just seemed to set me up for the next milestone. Yet had I tried to speak, I know my words would have been slurrrred and my mind would have been almost blank.

It is drinking on my own that has led me to drink so much - whether it be here in my home or at The King's Head. I declare that I have never been drunk except when forced to engage with others. I hoisted that flag upon the battlefield and felt rather pleased.

Where are you now mine enemy? But I knew exactly where he was. I could see him shimmering like gold, gazing at me as I downed the eighth and final can of Scrumpy Jack. The infantry had fallen, but here came the boom-boom cannons - and I was to be its boom-boom fodder.

You see, cider is just a chemical added to all the other chemicals in your body. It enhances some parts of you and debilitates others - there is a certain balance to all that, a consideration for what is required and a gentlemanly salute to your predicament. Whisky however confronts you with the power of the alchemist. It corners you, does not allow you to leave until you have opened up to it your heart and your mind. It whips you and you take it. It pushes you over and it smacks you hard. It is a punishment, a punishment that I have not only endured during my life, but begged for. For it unbridles your thoughts and makes them seem tolerable.

I knew all that, but still, after my eight cans were gone, I unscrewed the top off my nemesis friend. We were to dance together one final time. No glass for me. Just straight from the bottle, intimate, just my cider mouth and Jack Daniel's burning, open neck. Wash over my tongue oh fire and let's just see what happens.

At first it blurs and blinds and the pain is all, a pain not of hurt but of shatter and bleakness, of the splash of a hard wave and the crack of a bat upon ball. You have to take it to make it and you have to shake it to break it. The smell alone has a colour and the taste a texture. You just have to let it become a part of you and welcome that transmutation of tations, that elaborate thronging of foreboding. Come and get me, swallow me whole and take me down to the nether parts of the deep dark land of my soul. More and more and more. This is not a drink, it is a rope that pulls upon my past, my present and my future. It tugs and guides and pulls and glides, dragging me ever further to the very root of my clid clad mountain.

Up for air and in once more. One width, two widths, red stripe, yellow stripe - I spit water out from my lungs and laugh at your tears young lady. Tis fun, fun, fun with the finest hot chocolate in the world at the end of it. The Dene of Hills and The Hill of Dene - come back and make me a child once more

- oh give me back that spark of youth that was not quelled in the wash of adult despair. Tears are just water and salt. The ocean is but of tears and the universe is nothing but a twink. The world is not real. There is glass beneath my feet and I am glad of it and I will stamp with all my might to prove it so.

Half way down. Proud and dirty and uncaring. Come on! My boy shines!

Yeaaaaah you burn no more, you sparkle not! You are but flat to me now for I am building up my walls and my defences, my wood and my armour - you control me not though you be as beautiful as ever you were. I am now a-gulping and you are but a-sulking.

I recall now being in the sandpit of my youth - a small boy looking much like me is there too, sporting (yes sporting!) a red and black checked shirt and he plays with such abandon that he makes me an adult in his presence. He has no care but in what he creates. He takes the shoddy spite of all and just adds it to the sand, creates the landscape with hands of pure silver - he has flags and sticks and magic tricks and beauty brilliant wild and crashing and I am instantly in love with him. Yet destined was I never to see him again. It had always been a sense of woe to me but now in this whisky bourbon shift I see I was blessed. I am blessed.

BLESSED AM I AND ALL THAT SAIL IN ME!

Oh God if you do exist, spare me now a wink of your murmur, a dinky donk of your wisdom. It's all a game, I know that now. A game where everybody wins who sees nothing for, I repeat - THIS WORLD IS NOT REAL!!

I sigh a sigh and wave goodbye to invisible ladies and choo chonk sailors who fall upon me with their wealth and but float away as they touch the tinge sodden breakings of my broken heart - a heart that reforms before me, clinging to the floor, supping and sapping the dust and the claw and the whisky and the cider and the beer and the schiz, schiz, schiz and I AM WHOLE!!

AND HOW GREAT AM I??

The bottle is empty.

I am floating.

I am above all.

I am you.

I am you.

And as the sun rose in the Tollesbury sky, the morning did indeed greet me with angels.

It was a new day.

It was a new time.

"Hello Carrie."

"Hello Simon."

"What do people drink in here if they don't drink?" I asked. My voice was barely audible.

"If they don't drink?"

"Yes."

"You mean if they don't drink alcohol?"

"Yes."

I looked furtively about me. Just Jim and Bill were in, as usual.

"Shall I just get you something, Simon?" asked Carrie.

She was smiling more than I felt she ought.

I nodded.

She poured me a pint of orange juice and lemonade. It was a beautiful colour.

"Aye, aye! Looks like old Simon's gone poofter on us!"

It was Bill, having spied my drink.

"Poofter, poofter, poofter. Well who'd have known it? You see that Jim? Girl's drink."

"Leave him alone Bill," said Jim, softly. "Hello Simon, lad. You okay?" he added.

"Yes, thanks." I replied.

"Good man."

"Good man?" spluttered Bill. "Good man?? Have you seen what he's drinking? Soon be me and you as the only real drinkers in here Jim. Fucking orange juice and lemonade! This used to be a proper pub!"

"Any more of that," said Carrie to Bill, "and you and your boyfriend there might find yourselves drinking down the Legion!"

At that, Carrie Caseby, the most beautiful barmaid in all the universes, leaned forward and whispered into my ear.

"Not long now, Simon. Not long. Your Robbie is delicious."

"What day is today, Carrie?" I asked at last.

"Thursday."

"My nurse is coming tomorrow. Then it's the weekend. And then, on Monday, I think I'll be seeing Robbie."

I spoke as a child.

I drank my orange juice and lemonade.

It was disgusting.

But from that moment on, I didn't care.

I was just counting down the minutes.

25. Imagination Is Life

Listen.

Do you want to know my secret?

Closer now.

And I don't mind if you tell…

Imagination is life and life is imagination. All my years, that truth had evaded me, yet looking back I had surely always known it. From so young, I had lived on the brink of reality, teeter tottering into the well of what the world would call 'madness'. It is a fact that my eyes have seen wonders and my mind has experienced great things.

Closer.

At five years old, my bedroom wallpaper depicted Cowboys and Indians in various poses, some on foot, others prostrate and yet more still resplendent upon fiery horses. The pattern repeated itself all around me, whirring and moving slowly until I felt the square bedroom become a circle. That was when the Cowboys and Indians moved; making war and peace, always searching and never finding. Hair flowed and sand drifted across my landscape. Now whether they became real or I became paper, I know not. But I did become one with them. I sat upon a cliff for a day and a half, warming myself in the cold American night with a fire of my own devising. I was an Indian scout watching out for the white man, the pale face, the foreigner in my land. And I was the lonesome cavalry officer who had been parted from his troops and taken in by a squaw, nursed back to health and set free upon the wide majestic plains.

And one fateful night, back when I was five years old, the Indian scout me met the cavalry officer me. I rose from my fire and stared at my enemy. And I walked towards the flames and closed my eyes. My mother found me in my bed in the morning and asked me why I had been crying. I had not the words back then to explain. And I barely have them now, forty-five years later.

At the age of thirteen, I was inducted into the dark world of counter-intelligence. The service had never before known anyone of my sharpness of eye and ability to hide in the shadows. I was known throughout Europe as 'The Shade'. Mission after mission was thrust upon me and I toiled for my country. I wandered the streets till my feet were beat and I recorded every car that passed, made a note of the description of each person who so much as glanced in my direction. And in my sketch book, I worked it all out - the cars that never moved, the people who exchanged scraps of paper and the windows whose curtains only ever opened when the moon was at its brightest. I connected all with dark arrows until it all made sense.

But the spy world just wore me down in the end. It was as my career was nearing its finality that I learned something fundamental about my character. I was nothing without approval. When you are 'The Shade', you go unnoticed for that is the very trick, the very lie upon which your reputation as a master spy is built. The spy must not want affection or approval. Great though I was, I had to turn my back on my country. I was sixteen when 'The Shade' handed in his badge and gun. It had been a tough time indeed.

Just when I thought the world had disowned me, I became a bass player in a rock and roll band. I was so cool you would not believe it. Even my own band members did not know my name. I never spoke you see, just stood on stage, unmoving, defiant. As the drummer crashed and the guitarist wailed and the singer roared, I kept them all together, drove them on and led them to blues heaven.

I was given the task of documenting our gigs and I did so religiously - from set lists, to information about the venues, crowd sizes and even little stick diagrams of how we were set up on stage. Playing bass in a blues band was the perfect antidote to the deception of my spying years. I was there for all to see yet I remained an enigma. I dressed all in black, wore dark glasses and a Stetson hat.

The band played on, the band you've known for all these years, but I became lonely and heart-broken. The fame satisfied me no more than did being 'The Shade'. I longed to go deeper, to go back into the history of the world, for I was at last seeing as I entered my thirties that time is entirely meaningless. As the world did not exist, so neither did time. And neither did I.

I spent the next ten years as a reclusive author smoking lots of dope and drinking lots of whisky. I had several best selling novels that you may very well have read. I used different names in order to reduce the impact of my fame on the village of Tollesbury. There were times when I saw someone in the pub or at the bus stop reading one of my novels, my pseudonym writ large upon the cover. I admit I was occasionally tempted to inform the reader that I was indeed the author. I resisted, however, retaining my anonymity to this day.

You may not be surprised to hear that I declined all requests to be interviewed.

So where was there left for me to go but back in time? The present appalled me and the future was just blank. I knew I was of the earth and of this land - the five year old Indian scout had been as close to my true self as ever I had been. And thus had I found myself in Tollesbury, the year being 1836. But you already know that, don't you?

Life is Imagination.

Imagination is life.

Such thoughts did I think as I sat in my old armchair, waiting for the nurse to come into my home and inject me.

26. Trust Everybody For At Heart People Are Good

Somebody passed my window and shortly after there was a knock upon my door, a gentle knock, a knock that reminded me of the tapping together of drumsticks that our drummer used to do to count us in on the slower numbers.

I got up to open the door and there stood a man I hadn't seen before. He looked as wayward as I as he delved in his trouser pocket. He glanced up at me apologetically as he retrieved a sad photograph of himself on a rather tatty name badge. Stuart Ayris - Community Psychiatric Nurse - Blackwater Mental Health Trust. My nurse for this week. Hey ho.

"Please come in," I said, almost feeling sorry for him.

Whether it was a newfound confidence in myself or a lack of confidence on his part, I had the feeling that we were on an equal footing. Maybe he was as mad and confused as I.

"I'm sorry the house is a bit of a mess," I ventured.

"Should I take my boots off?" he asked.

Boots! He wore cowboy boots!

"No, it's ok," I replied.

"I'm Stuart, by the way. Sorry, I didn't introduce myself."

"Hello Stuart."

"So how are you? Sorry, I meant to say that I'm here because Frank is on leave this week and he asked me to do your injection and see you and stuff. I hope that's ok."

"Of course."

He didn't seem to know where to look.

"So how have you been, Simon? What have you been up to since Frank last saw you?"

He spoke quickly and his accent reminded me of my dad.

To tell or not to tell, that is the question! Whatever I say, they write in their books and type into their computers and call that treatment. But what could I ever say that anyone would understand. Whenever I tell them what I really think, they increase my medication or drag me into hospital.

"I've not been up to much really. It's pretty quiet around here."

"It seems like a nice place. I've never been here before. My wife grew up in a village - it's the sort of place she would like."

I smiled and nodded. Already I maybe knew more about him than he knew about me. Funny how it all happens.

"So you work with Frank then do you, Stuart?"

"Yes. I've not been with the team long though."

"And what does your wife do?"

"She's a nurse as well."

"Oh. That's nice. Did you want a drink, tea or coffee or anything?"

"No thank you. I'll be fine thanks."

"So your wife is a nurse like you then?"

"Well she works on the wards. Has done for years. I've not been qualified that long."

"Then I'm sure I may well have met her. I was a patient not so long ago, earlier in the summer."

"It's Penny, my wife's name. Penny Shoraton. She kept her maiden name because she said pennyayris sounds like some sort of infection. She speaks about you a lot. It's actually really nice to finally meet you."

Penny Shoraton - the angel of all angels, the beauty of the beautiest, the absolute light of all that is perfect in this world. Penny Shoraton. I could not help but sigh at the very thought of her.

"She is a wonderful nurse."

"Thank you."

"My wife has spoken about her. I think they know each other."

"They are good friends. Mo, too, from the café. Proper little witches of Tiptree when they get together."

"And Carrie, the barmaid?"

"I've never met her, but Penny knows her."

212

It all began to make some sort of sense to me now - Julia's little network of informants, all letting her know how I am and what I'm up to. Seems I'm not the only spy in the village after all!

"And Old Jed, the man with the golden retriever. Do you know him?"

Stuart shook his head.

"Am I as mad as you thought I was?" I asked.

Stuart leaned back on the settee and looked at me properly for the first time. He smiled the sort of smile I had seen once when someone had given me the wrong medication.

"To be honest", he said, "I don't really believe in mental illness and madness and tablets and all that. We're all just people trying to get through life as far as I'm concerned. That's the only way I can see it. I think some people just make it too complicated, too big. I don't really understand anything at all. I guess I'm not too much help to you am I?"

The boots hadn't lied it seemed.

"I have come to the conclusion, Stuart, that it's just about not getting caught. Bob Dylan once said - 'if my thought-dreams could be seen, they'd probably put my head in a guillotine.' That's what it's all about really. I have wonderful thought-dreams yet people over the years have tried to take them away, make them disappear with tablets and injections."

"But you have tried to kill yourself before, haven't you? A few times from what Penny says."

He had a point. And it was a point upon which my theory of the nature of madness often came to a clumsy end. My thoughts, experiences, hallucinations, delusions, whatever you want to call them, had oftentimes ended up with me in a bad way.

"I'm sorry," said Stuart. "Not for me to say really. Sorry."

"No, no. It's fine. You are very easy to talk to."

"Thanks. Not what Penny says."

Without knowing it, he was patching up my heart.

"The times I have tried to kill myself have obviously never ended in me actually dying. And they have always been

213

for a reason - unless you have been interrogated in Berlin, been fired from a successful band or sacrificed your life for that of a child I guess that won't make any sense. Each of my suicide attempts have been a culmination of experiences that have in turn led to new understandings for which I am very grateful. And what is death but a new experience? And anyway, if I had not been hanged in July, would you be here talking to me now?"

"Not been hanged? I thought you had hanged yourself. That's what I read anyway."

"It's all the same," I replied.

A peaceful silence came to us both and we each studied the dusty wooden floor, searching for clues.

"Do you mind if I use your toilet?" he asked, eventually. "Lot of coffee today. Kind of comes with the job."

At that, he clomped up my stairs and out of view. The clomping stopped when he reached the top and well before he had reached the bathroom. I knew then that he had seen what I had been up to since the last time Frank was here. He was looking at the writing. Not having any interior doors had made it impossible for him to have missed my scribblings. I had covered my bedroom wall, worked my way along the landing and had extended my work to just at the level of the top stair. Well a man has to express himself. And if every time he opens his mouth he has a tablet shoved in, he has to find alternatives.

After some moments, the clomping recommenced, and Stuart returned to the settee. I did not mention the writing on the walls and neither did he. He did though begin to assemble my injection, doing so with the silence and concentration of a hunter in the dusk. I had seen it done a thousand times, but on each occasion, my heart sought refuge and my soul escape.

It always felt as if I had been found guilty of some crime for which now I had to be punished, to be filled with a drug that would contain me, survey me, control me until the next time when my system would be topped up - another needle, another face, another nurse doing society's bidding - saving the fine people of this nation from the mad ones such as I, the ones whose thoughts and behaviours are not what the good doctor ordered. Stab - you're cured mate - well not cured, obviously, but it's the best we can do for now.

And when your cowboy boots have clomped out of my house, my friend, I will lie on my bed and think of how best to write all this on the remaining walls.

"Do you trust me, Simon?" he asked, syringe in hand.

"I'm sorry?"

"Do you trust me?" he asked again.

I nodded.

"Well that's handy," he replied.

At that, he unsheathed the needle and revealed its sharp point which dripped with the oily fluid that would be soon injected into me. I waited for him to go through the pleasantries - which side do you want it? Standing up or lying down? Here or upstairs etc? But he said none of those things. In fact, he just let out a deep sigh and expelled the liquid back into its vial. Then he put all the pieces, including the syringe, into a little yellow container and snapped it shut.

"What are you doing?"

"Just giving you your injection," he replied.

I didn't know what to say. There was nothing I could say.

"Oh, just to let you know that your wife asked my wife to ask me to remind you about meeting her at the Scout Hut down the road at seven on Monday. There's some sort of thing going on for disabled people."

He stood as if to leave. And I shook the hand of my cavalry soldier allowing myself to linger there in his flesh for just a while longer than I ought.

27. You are Wonderful

On Saturday 6th Sep2008, I awoke; a free man. No alcohol sweated through my skin and no oily medication grasped at my thoughts. My emotions were my own and the puppeteer's strings dangled at my side like a spider's web sliced to pieces. I was neither a diagnosis nor a walking corpse. I was a man once more. I did not shudder. I did not shake. For the first time in as long as I could remember, there was not a blurring around the edges of my world.

The morning light shone upon me as I sat at my old wooden table, drinking my coffee and munching my toast. The White Album was on the CD player. The day was just beginning. I was Simon Anthony, a fifty year old man living in a small house in a beautiful English village. And I realised that wasn't at all a bad thing to be.

I spent the majority of that weekend writing on the walls of my front room and dining room. At times I had to stand on a chair, but then when I reached the bottom of a wall, I would lie down flat on the dusty floor, my old knees creaking a little as I made my way back to the surface. I did not read back over anything I wrote. The upstairs had been completed some days ago, but I couldn't even remember where I had started and where I had finished. It was of no concern. I was just passing the time, adorning my little home with the thoughts and remembrances of its only inhabitant.

Yet even then, with just the kitchen left to go, I had a feeling that once I had run out of space to write upon so perhaps my story would end.

Thus Saturday and Sunday wore on and I entered Monday aching and stiff. It's a strange thing, this writing lark, spending all your time working away at something no-one will ever read, or would ever want to read, just to get a few things off your mind in order to pass the time. Still, it has kept me out of the pub, I suppose.

The Scout Hut was about a fifteen minute walk from my home. I was never in the Scouts. I was in the Boys' Brigade for a while I think but things like that are vague to me these days. There was dodge ball I think and cold floors and dust and grey windows and a breeze and then there was the tuck shop with penny-chews and sherbet and high church ceilings. There was marching and blue hats and badges and saluting and a stage upon which nobody ever stood. That was the Boys' Brigade to me.

I had never before been to the Scout Hut, although I had of course passed it on my walks and my wanderings, seen it from the outside, guarded by recycling bins and a car park. For that to be the place where I would finally be reunited with my son, well, if it was in a novel, you would surely never believe it.

The minutes passed and the hours turned to flowers. The light was light and the day drifted into the evening as the sun did fall in grace beneath the gaze of its sibling stars. All was pale - there was neither darkness nor brightness. It was as if the world itself were awaiting further instruction. And so I did leave my home that Monday evening and walk slowly down East Street, turning left at the Butcher's and on towards the harbour.

God, this village is beautiful. The closer I get to finding the true meaning of my existence, so does the living universe around me just astound all the more. It is there for us all.

It is a sadness of our society that we are taught to open our eyes and see as opposed to being taught to close our eyes and feel. When, as we grow, we stumble upon this error, we can only hope it is not too late. I am truly one of the lucky ones.

So there I was in my English village, on the horizon of the world, a dot, a speck a blib blab blib, a triumph of our times; there I was, standing outside the door of a small hall on a summer's eve like a renegade about to enter the saloon of his ultimate falling. From within, the door was pulled open and Julia, my wife, filled the void as I ever believed she would.

"Hello Simon," she said, touching my arm gently. "How are you?"

"Not bad," I replied, trembling, quaking, shaking, rocking and rolling. "Not bad."

"I should have explained," added Julia, coming out now and closing the door behind her, during which time I briefly heard music and gabbling and people and hum. "Every month there is a get together of carers and families who know or have someone with a disability. We move around the area. We are in Tollesbury about twice a year."

"Oh, ok."

I thought of all the times my wife and my son had just been so close yet I had been nowhere near them.

"Does Robbie know I'm going to be here?" I asked. I had to ask.

"Yes. I told him."

"What did he say?"

"He just nodded."

"Oh right."

"He understands so much, Simon. He is so beautiful. He is twenty-six now, you know."

All I could do was look at her, for she was beautiful too. I felt a tear come to my eye. I had a beautiful son. And I was about to meet him.

"Do you think he will be okay with me?" I asked.

"He is okay with everyone," she replied. "Let's go in." Julia held my hand and led me inside.

To have a woman you love hold your hand is as wondrous a thing as a lonely man could want. Just that touch will amplify the beating of the heart, will set free the sparks and will ignite the very firmament. It's all in the recognition, the acceptance that the beauty of life is no more complicated than one hand held by another, fingers entwined like lovers and wrists a-pulsing. Anything is truly possible.

It was the darkness that hit me as ever it did. That's what comes from staring too much into the sun, I guess. I could see some tables around the edge of the hall about which stood and sat various people. I could make out only their forms, however,

218

so slowly did my ageing eyes adjust to the gloom. Some were in wheelchairs and others tottered a little. There was a life force that abounded.

If there was anybody in this hall that was truly disabled, it was I - if there was anybody here that was handicapped it was none other than me. For souls are perfect and all that was before me were souls of the purest, sweetest kind.

Bang, bang, bang - do you larve me? Dar de dar - do you larve me?

And there rolling out from a corner with a bowl and a stroll was a young man who began to fill the room with his dancing and his love. I could see he wore glasses and that his jeans came down almost to the floor. And he wore a denim jacket too. And indeed, everybody did love him. His body reeled as if upon the sea, he threw his head back and at times sank to his knees. He was absolutely fantastic and I couldn't help but grin.

Do you larve me, now that I can darnce??

Oh God I do!

When Julia whispered to me that it was Robbie, they were whispered words wasted; for Robbie danced not alone, but with my big old heart. Bam, bam, beauty, beauty - my son was making me whole.

The darkness hid my wonder and the music played on.

Julia squeezed my hand tight. I was quivering like a bubble. My wife rested her head upon my upper arm and I began to cry.

And silence.

Then darkness.

Not a sound.

Not a breath.

The moon appears in the window and gazes upon my son as he kneels upon the floor, his head bowed.

And then a song began that rooted me where I stood. It had been our wedding song. I didn't know the words then and I can barely remember them now to write on my kitchen wall, but I will try...

219

Oohh
There must-be-lightning burning brighter
Somewhere
Great-a-big birds
flying higher
In-a-sky so blue

I stand near Robbie now and see him clench a fist. His eyes are closed and he sways a little. Then he goes down on his knees, facing the darkness head-on.

There must-be-peaceful understanding
Sometime
Some kind of promise
That-will
Blow-away
The dubious fear

Robbie is still on his knees but his back is straight now and he stares straight ahead. My whole body tingles as I watch him.

Just wanna dream
Of-a brighter sun
Where love keeps raining on everyone

He raises his right arm in the air, his fist tight - all rigid and hard.

Tell me Dad
Oh Dad
Oh why won't that rain come down?

And suddenly he stands, his arms by his side - and he turns in one motion to face me, his father, the man that had abandoned him.

We're lost in the mist

With too-much pain
We're trapped in-a-dream
Again and again
But as long as I know
My dad is near
I can survive
And-I
Can
Fly

The air is his to command. There are drums and there are strings yet they are inconsequential against the throbbing of my son's entire being. Everybody hears it. Everybody feels it.

Deep-in-my soul
There's a wandering
Feeling
But-I-just know
That you will,
You will come back
Someday
Over the park
We'll play us some cricket
Yeah

He is back on his knees now, both arms raised high, palms open, head up, eyes looking into mine, bringing me down to where he is.

And while I can breathe, while I can walk
While I can smile, while I can talk
While I can think, please let my dad
Come back
Right now…

And there I am now, kneeling down before my son as he kneels before me. We lean into one another as the band plays

221

on and Elvis dreams and we all dream. The tears on both our faces are mine.

Robbie led me out into the blackness and we stood there beneath the white stars. We sat on the grass, looking off into the direction of the salt marshes, much like Zachariah Leonard and I had once done. I spoke to Robbie of FRUGALITY and of my hopes and my love for him - he spoke not a word in response. How much he could understand of what I said, I knew not. I just kept talking.

The music continued on inside, but Robbie and I preferred the cold of the evening. Time seemed to have stopped, or perhaps it no longer had any bearing or relevance. It was Tollesbury Time.

"Dad," said Robbie at last. He spoke in a deep, hollow kind of voice as if there were no restrictions between the boom of his heart and the opening of his mouth.

"Yes," I replied, turning to him.

"You are wonderful."

As the moon did reach into the sky and the stars did sparkle a greeting, so Julia re-emerged into the brightening night.

"So, Simon," said Julia, coming to sit down beside me. "Robbie says you and he have been talking?"

Robbie, seated cross legged on my other side put his hand in mine.

"Me and Dad are going to frugal up the frugals, Mum. It's going to be great!" reported Robbie, proudly.

I just had to smile.

"Now is that so, boys?"

Robbie and I both nodded.

"Well in that case, I believe it is my duty as a wife and mother to frugal up the frugals too."

Julia held my other hand and put her head upon my shoulder. She smelled of roses and of heaven and of sweet soul music.

222

"I love you, Simon Anthony," she whispered. I could feel her soft red lips resting gently upon my ear as she spoke. And all was well in the Tollesbury night.

Epilogue

I have not seen Simon since that day I didn't give him his injection. Every now and then Penny gets a letter from Julia, something vague and excitable, but never any mention of them all returning. We don't even know where they are.

Of course there was an investigation at work, a review of his care and treatment as there always is in such circumstances. I gave my evidence and then resigned before I was sacked. I still have my nursing registration so I can return if I want to; I can't imagine I ever will.

It took me three weeks to transcribe Simon Anthony's words from the walls to my laptop. Julia had given Mo Simon's spare key and Mo in turn had let me have it.

I slept in a sleeping bag on Simon's floor and got lunch from the Bakery every day. Penny knew me well enough to know this was something I had to do. Sometimes I would go to the King's Head or the marshes, to see what Simon would see, to feel what he would have felt.

And one night, as the bells of St Mary's church tolled, I rolled out of my sleeping bag, left the little house in East Street and went to the village square. I walked over to the village lock-up, pulled open the battered old wooden door and stepped inside. Closing the door behind me, I sat on the floor, shut my eyes and waited for something to happen…

Printed in Great Britain
by Amazon.co.uk, Ltd.,
Marston Gate.